About the Author

Vindicated was Leonard's first completed project since gaining a publisher, Pegasus Elliot Mackenzie, in 2018.

His first title to be released by them, *A Life's Work,* was in fact his third novel written. Since then, they have re-released his second novel, *Primus,* in 2019, and most recently, his tenth title, *Fallen Victim.*

Despite this significant progression in his writing career, Leonard still works full-time within the police, although at the time of writing *Vindicated,* he was not on the frontline, as his anxiety had temporarily forced him into a non-operational role. He has now returned to full operational duties.

However, it is still his ambition to one day retire from full-time employment and to commit himself to writing on a professional level.

As a result of Pegasus Elliot Mackenzie's efforts to publicise his releases, Leonard has been the focus of a local newspaper article, as well as being interviewed on BBC local radio.

VINDICATED

John T. Leonard

VINDICATED

Vanguard Press

A CIP catalogue record for this title is
available from the British Library.

ISBN 978 1 78465 789 5

Vanguard Press is an imprint of
Pegasus Elliot MacKenzie Publishers Ltd.
www.pegasuspublishers.com

First Published in 2020

Vanguard Press
Sheraton House Castle Park
Cambridge England

Printed & Bound in Great Britain

Dedication

To all those;
who fight the fight, without enemies,
and live in the prison without walls.

Also from John T. Leonard

• Denotes a publisher release.

"If an injury has to be done to a man,
it should be so severe that his vengeance
need not be feared."

Niccolo Machiavelli
(1469-1527)

1

"Would the defendant please stand?" the clerk of the court asked of the man sat on a chair within the enclosure that was the magistrate court's dock.

He sat across the courtroom from where the magistrate sat.

Once the defendant had obliged the request, the magistrate herself continued.

"Mister Foster," she began. "You have been found guilty of the charge of failing to provide a specimen of breath for preliminary analysis, having been requested to do so by a police officer following a road traffic collision to which you were involved... Is there anything you wish to say before I pass sentence on you?"

There was an air of silence in the scantily occupied courtroom, as the magistrate watched the defendant, waiting to see if he was intending to offer anything in way of a response.

But, instead of offering an immediate reply, the defendant, Albert Foster looked over towards his legal representation, who was sat at a table centrally situated within the courtroom.

Foster beckoned his solicitor to approach him so to allow a brief consultation to take place out of earshot of the wider court. Foster leant over the dock's railings to be closer to his solicitor.

After a few moments of them appearing to be engrossed in debate, Foster stepped back, pushing himself away from the railing on which he had been leaning, appearing to distance himself from his solicitor.

This suggested to the court that the discussion was at an end, and he appeared to be most displeased with the conclusions that had been reached.

Instead of returning to his seat, his solicitor turned to face the bench where the magistrate was sat. He cleared his throat as he prepared to address her.

The private discussion between solicitor and client had concluded with Foster's solicitor confirming that it would be best if it were he who addressed the court on his client's behalf.

"Your Honour," he began.

But before he could get any further into his prepared monologue, Foster interrupted him.

"Yeah, actually, I *do* wanna say something," Foster said, speaking over his solicitor.

The magistrate appeared to be somewhat shocked by the lack of decorum on the part of the defendant. But she had seen a lot worse during her time on the bench.

The magistrate then addressed the defence.

"It looks as though you'll have to wait your turn Mister Marshall," she said, specifically addressing the solicitor.

The solicitor for the defence, James Marshall, was somewhat shocked himself. But from his discussion with his client, and their meetings beforehand, he felt he knew exactly what Foster was planning to say.

He also knew that if Foster wanted to sabotage his own defence, then who was he to stop him? His role was a legal advisor, and nothing more.

Marshall retook his seat to allow Foster to address the courtroom as he had been invited, and was entitled to do.

"Your honour, the way I see it is this," Foster began. "There's absolutely no evidence to prove I was drinking that night... Absolutely nothing. So how on earth can I be charged with a drink-driving offence?"

Although the magistrate felt like allowing Foster to continue to gather enough rope in which to hang himself, she did have a full docket of cases to hear following Foster's, so an attempt had to be made on her part in order to expedite proceedings.

"Mister Foster, I feel I need to clarify... You have been found guilty of *failing to provide a breath specimen when required to do so*, as legalised under section seven of the road traffic act. *Not*, as you seem to believe, for driving whilst intoxicated," the magistrate emphatically clarified.

"So, let me get this straight," Foster continued after the bench yet again fell silent. "What you're saying to me is, the outcome is based on a decision I am supposed to have made when I'm pissed, not saying I *was* pissed mind you… But, let's say I get nicked for shoplifting or something, anything, you lot have to wait until I'm sober before you can interview me about it… Now why is that? Surely if you're not allowed to ask me questions when I'm drunk in case it prejudices my defence, then how come all this is being based on a question asked of me when I *am* drunk?"

Gleefully, the magistrate took advantage of the faux pas that Foster had left dangling there for all to hear.

"Are you admitting before this court, and whilst under oath, that you were in fact intoxicated when the question as to whether or not you were prepared to provide an evidential sample was put to you Mister Foster?" he asked.

"Of course, I ain't, I'm speaking hypothetically," Foster replied adamantly.

The magistrate decided that this back and forth debate had gone on long enough, and as a result, she felt compelled to bring matters to a conclusion.

"Mister Foster, I am not prepared to waste the court's time by discussing the intricacies of criminal law with you... You have been found guilty as charged. Now, is there anything relevant you wish to say before I pass sentence?"

To this, James Marshall again stood. He looked over towards Foster in the dock. The court could see Marshall slightly shake his head, and that he mouthed something towards Foster. Having been the only person in the court to understand the silent message, Foster sat down looking like a scolded child.

Marshall then took a brief moment to reconsider what he was going to say.

"Your honour, I feel what I was going to say earlier is no longer relevant, so I'll skip to the end… My client is by occupation a sales director. And as a result, he spends a great deal of his time at work behind the wheel. His being able to drive is crucial to his job, and his career. I feel I need to mention that he is the sole breadwinner for his family which includes two children of school age… With this in mind, I would like to ask the court to tip the balance of the sentence towards a fine, and points on his licence as opposed to issuing him with a driving ban."

At this, the crown prosecutor, who had remained silent since Foster's guilt had been determined, rose to his feet and addressed the bench.

"Your honour, the prosecution will leave sentencing to your discretion, but I must make you aware that this is not Mister Foster's first conviction for a prescribed limit offence," he said.

"Thank you for bringing that to the court's attention," the magistrate replied.

The magistrate then looked over at Foster who had retaken his seat.

"Mister Foster, would you please stand for sentence to be passed?" she asked of him.

Again, in a manner similar to that of a petulant, and slovenly child, Foster rose to his feet.

He stood defiantly, his arms now folded, and his gaze towards the coat of arms which was mounted on the wall above the magistrate's head.

"I have listened carefully to what has been said, and appealed to this court today," she began. "And it is the sentence of this court that your licence be suspended for a period of three months, and that its reinstatement is conditional on your completion of an alcohol referral program. You are also to be fined one thousand pounds plus court costs, and you are to have your licence endorsed with ten penalty points. This means that should you commit even the most minor traffic offence that puts points on your licence, then you will lose it again… The ball is now well and truly in your court, Mister Foster."

The magistrate struck the gavel on the block in front of her and the court session was concluded.

oOo

"Well, all I can say is, thank fuck that's over," Foster said having ventured outside of the courthouse, closely followed by Marshall.

"Y'know, Albert, if you're gonna keep asking me to defend you, you gonna have to do one small thing for me?" Marshall asked.

"Yeah, and what's that?" he replied, whilst in the process of lighting a cigarette.

"Learn when to shut the fuck up, okay?" Marshall replied. "I'll tell you one thing for free, I'm amazed you only got a three-month ban. Y'know, given your track record, *and* your little speech in there, you should've got two years… Minimum!"

"Yeah, I know," Foster replied. "I got lucky."

"It wasn't luck," Marshall continued.

"I know," Foster said. "Don't need luck when I've got you, now do I?"

Foster flicked his hand against Marshall's shoulder to emphasise his remark, showering them both in cigarette ash.

Marshall shook his head in disgust at the flippant remark and the gesture.

James Marshall had been a criminal defence solicitor for many years, and in all that time, he had never had a client who appeared to be so hellbent on alienating the court as sentence was about to be passed.

It was only when Foster came out with yet another grotesque comment that he brought Marshall back to the moment.

"Y'know, with this ban, you're gonna have to give me a lift home… Y'know, just for appearances sake," he said.

Marshall was quite frankly shocked that Foster had actually driven himself to court on the day of such a hearing. When he knew his chances of escaping a conviction and a driving ban were minute at best.

Marshall only agreed to giving him a lift home, as he didn't want to be complicit in Foster committing further offences by driving his car mere minutes after being given a ban.

Marshall walked back towards his car. He looked back at Foster who was a few steps behind him, still puffing away on his cigarette.

Marshall deliberately waited until Foster had finished the cigarette before unlocking the doors. He opened his door and got in. As Foster did the same, Marshall could feel the car filling with the putrid smell of cigarette smoke. In the confinement, he could tell that Foster's clothes reeked of it.

Marshall put his seatbelt on and started the engine. He looked over at Foster who had made no efforts to do the same.

"Seatbelt, please," Marshall felt compelled to ask, in order to highlight the reason for his delay in pulling away.

"Never usually bother," Foster replied.

"Well, you *will* today," Marshall reiterated. "Unless you want to walk?"

He could then see Foster appear to thread the seatbelt behind himself, before remembering his audience and the consequences, and finally fastening it correctly.

As Marshall pulled out of the courthouse car park, he saw Foster fumbling with his keys out of the corner of his eye.

Eventually, Foster managed to extricate the key for his own car from the split ring. He then dropped it into the coin tray in Marshall's centre console.

"Probably best you hold on to that for me for the time being," Foster said. "You know what I'm like… Temptation will probably get the better of me."

Marshall didn't reply. He just glanced down at the key and shook his head so minutely it was invisible to anyone looking on.

"How are you going to get your car home from the courts then?" Marshall asked upon the obvious having occurred to him.

Foster had been so cocksure as to the outcome of his hearing, and his influence over the court, that he had driven to the courthouse, with his car now sat redundant in the car park, inevitably due a ticket for an overstayed visit.

"Oh, I'll have the missus pick it up later," Foster replied.

"Won't *she* need the key then?" Marshall enquired.

"Nah, she has her own key," Foster added nonchalantly.

"And how is she going to get here to drive it home?" Marshall asked, expecting the answer that was imminent.

"She can get the bus or something," Foster replied.

By this time, Marshall had driven them away from the courts and they were passing through town on their way to Foster's home address.

"Tell you what," Foster said. "Drop me here. I've got some celebrating to do… Care to join me?"

Marshall saw that Foster was indicating that he should be dropped off at a pub they were approaching.

Although it was a Friday, it was barely midday. Marshall was thinking that Foster was most likely planning to spend the rest of his day in the pub *celebrating*.

"No thanks," said Marshall as he indicated to turn off the main road into the pub's car park.

Marshall pulled up in front of the main entrance to the pub. He knew he wasn't staying, so he held the car stationery on the foot brake.

"You sure I can't tempt you?" Foster said as he eased himself out of the car. "First round is on me."

Marshall couldn't believe the absurdity of the moment.

"No, I'm still on call... Are you sure you want me to hold onto this key?" Marshall replied, holding up the car key that he had retrieved from the coin tray.

Foster nodded. He appeared to be almost salivating at the thought of the range of beverages that awaited him beyond the front door. His mind was clearly elsewhere.

"You hold on to it," Foster said. "Thanks again Jimmy."

Marshall shook his head again as he watched Foster eagerly enter the pub. This familiarity was misplaced, even more so as Marshall's soon-to-be-ex-wife Nicky was the only person who used to refer to him as *Jimmy* with any regularity.

Now he was on his own, he was able to connect his mobile phone to the car's hands-free kit.

Once the Bluetooth had connected, Marshall called up his voicemail service.

"You have three new messages," the synthesised voice said over the in-car speaker.

As Marshall pulled out of the pub car park, he began to listen to his messages.

Although Foster had already begun celebrating, James Marshall's day was far from over.

2

One of the messages that Marshall picked up from his voicemail was a request for him to make a call to his office.

The same message also gave him brief details that he was also required in his role of the duty defence solicitor to attend the police force's local custody centre.

One of the rights of a person who has been arrested under the Police and Criminal Evidence Act (PACE) is that they have a right to seek free and independent legal advice. This can be in the form of a private and confidential telephone conversation. But, more often it is the case that a solicitor or legal advisor attends a custody centre in person to liaise with the detained person. Once there, they can advise the suspect both prior to and during any interviews.

As Marshall started to head in the direction of the custody centre mentioned in the message, he phoned his office in order to get more details as to the assignment.

oOo

It wasn't long before Marshall's Mercedes pulled through the security gates at the side of the custody centre.

They were kept open during the day, so not to impede the everyday goings on of the neighbouring industrial units. However, after dark, they were routinely kept closed, and entry was only permitted by use of an access card, or by using the intercom.

Following austerity and other financially motivated factors, many custody centres had changed from being departments located within police station premises to being established remotely on industrial estates, where pre-fabricated, self-contained units were put together, and were then wired and plumbed into the building's utilities.

A similar thing was also seen happening to fire stations, where crews and appliances were inhabiting retro-fitted industrial units as opposed to specifically designed buildings.

One such fire station was situated across from the custody centre. Its crew were in the process of maintaining their fire appliance as Marshall pulled up in his Mercedes, and parked in a designated bay in front of the custody centre.

Marshall then got out of his car, and collected his briefcase that he had placed behind his seat, in order to allow Foster to earlier ride shotgun.

Apart from the police force crest and a sign over the pedestrian entrance that read *Custody Centre,* there was no way of telling this unit's designated purpose. Although the dozen or so police vehicles that were parked in front were something of a giveaway.

There were other doors along the front of the unit. One was marked *Police Personnel Only,* and the other was a large roller shutter to a vehicle bay which was only used for prisoner transport.

Marshall approached the visitors' entrance to the custody centre and pressed the call button on the intercom next to the secured front door.

He was so well known to the staff at the custody centre, that they opened the door without even asking him to identify himself.

"Thank you," Marshall said out of courtesy as the front door automatically opened for him.

Once inside, Marshall was treated differently to members of the public that were already there and sat waiting in the public area.

They were most likely there either waiting for a voluntary attendance interview, where they were interviewed under caution without the necessity of having to be arrested. Or they were waiting for some who had been detained to be released.

The detention officer who was working the reception desk recognised Marshall, and after a brief moment of introductions and pleasantries, he pressed a button under the counter to release the electromagnetic lock on the pass door which segregated the detention area from the public area.

Only members of the public who were under arrest, or who were acting as an appropriate adult for a prisoner, were allowed into the secure detention area of the custody centre.

Beyond that, everyone else had a specific purpose for being there. That could be a medical or mental health role, or in Marshall's case, a legal representative, and of course there were numerous police officers and staff in various roles.

Once within the secure area, Marshall headed straight for the booking-in desks at the front of the administrative area, commonly known as *the bridge*.

In this facility, it consisted of a slightly raised area whereby the custody sergeants were able to have an elevated overview of the booking-in area.

It also had the added benefit that the booking-in desks were about chest height to most of the prisoners being brought in. This served as an adequate barrier, should they ever become unruly.

This area, as with the whole of the custody centre was heavily monitored by CCTV. But traditionally, the booking-in area was where there was a greater chance of having a prisoner become physically violent, or *kick-off*.

Marshall waited for one of the detention officers at a desk to become free. Although it wasn't by choice, he had come at a particularly busy time. He checked the digital clock behind the bridge. It read 13:03. Marshall checked that against his watch. It was spot on.

He was now regretting having missed lunch, and not at least grabbing a snack between the courthouse and custody. He was hoping he wouldn't be in custody for long, otherwise he would have a long wait until he would get a chance to get something to eat.

It was then, when his mind was on his stomach, that he heard his name called, and it wasn't by a member of the custody centre staff.

"You all right there, James?" an overly friendly voice called out to him.

Marshall turned to see a prisoner being brought out from the cells, and walking down a corridor behind him. He was being led to one of the desks where a police officer was waiting for him. It was as he got closer, that Marshall finally saw the prisoner that was addressing him.

Before Marshall even had a chance to recognise him, the prisoner continued.

"Could've fucking done with you in my corner this morning," he began. "Where the fuck were ya? Y'know, I asked for you by name when they booked me in… But they said you weren't available… Had some fucking numpty batting for me instead. Not sure his mum knows he's out this late, if you know what I mean?"

Marshall smiled at the remark although it wasn't as original as it was perhaps intended to be.

Then as he began to compose a suitable response, he had given himself time to recognise the prisoner, and more importantly how he should know him.

The prisoner, or detained person as they were sometimes known, was eventually recognised as Robert Fraser. He was a prolific burglar, and someone who was known well to Marshall, who had represented him on more than one occasion both in custody and in court.

Their relationship was purely professional, despite the overly familiar way that Fraser had chosen to speak to him.

Marshall didn't mind his clients referring to him as *James*, and when it was appropriate, he encouraged it in order to build rapport. But he did not consider this to be such an appropriate time, and following on from Foster's earlier abuse of this privilege by referring to him as *Jimmy*, Fraser instantly got under Marshall's skin.

"I was in court this morning," Marshall replied. "*That's* why I was unavailable."

Fraser didn't need to know any more than that, and Marshall was not inclined to indulge him beyond the imparting the bare minimum of information.

"A fuck lot of good that's done me," Fraser replied, as if somehow, he held Marshall responsible for his earlier non-availability.

Marshall looked Fraser up and down. He was a scrawny excuse for a man with drawn features and pronounced cheekbones, all signs that were synonymous with a certain adopted lifestyle that in turn lent itself to stealing as a means of funding it.

Fraser was dressed in custody-issued sweatpants and sweatshirt. Marshall knew from experience that these were only given out if the

23

prisoner's clothes were saturated, or, and this was most likely the case with Fraser, if his clothing had been seized for forensic examination as part of the reason that he had been arrested.

"How have you been keeping?" Marshall then asked in an attempt to change the subject, and avoid an uncomfortable silence.

Despite the fact that he knew it to be a redundant question; firstly, because as they were having this conversation in police custody, which meant that Fraser was still up to his old tricks, and secondly, Marshall didn't really give a hoot at how Fraser was keeping. So, regardless of how Fraser chose to respond to such a question, Marshall paid it little attention.

"Ah, you know me, peachy fuckin' creamy... Anyway, these fuckers ain't got nothing on me. If they did, they'd be charging me. As it is, I'm off up the pub after this," Fraser confidently bragged.

Marshall started to see a pattern forming. It appeared that when anyone left court or custody, they heading straight for the nearest boozer to celebrate their freedom.

If only they took into consideration that celebrating freedom in such a manner appeared to Marshall to only be the actions of a guilty person who had managed to beat the system.

With the conversation at an end, Fraser casually approached the plain-clothed police officer who was keeping Fraser's place at the front of the queue to one of the desks. Although he was out of uniform, this man was identifiable as a police officer as he was wearing his warrant card around his neck on a lanyard.

As he approached, Fraser pulled at his navy-blue sweatshirt, wanting to bring it to the officer's attention.

"So, when do I get my stuff back then?" he asked. "Don't wanna be wearing this shit when I get outta here."

As Marshall was not representing Fraser, he would not normally be privy to such a conversation, and as it stood, Marshall really couldn't care less. But as he was still waiting to be seen, he chose to occupy this time by paying attention to Fraser.

"Not for some time, I'm afraid. You know how this works," the plain-clothed police officer replied. "Now, I need you to listen to the custody sergeant."

From where Marshall stood, waiting at the next desk, he could clearly see a formation of officers lined up behind a partition that separated Fraser's desk from the one beyond it.

Although Marshall could see them, he doubted that Fraser could from where he was standing, having propped himself up against the chest-high barrier that separated prisoners from the bridge.

Again, from experience, Marshall knew exactly what was being prepared for, and knowing Fraser as he did, he could foresee the need that the officers were there for.

"Robert Fraser," the custody sergeant began. "You are being charged with three counts of burglary. And you are going to be reman…"

At hearing that news, Fraser instantly erupted into rage.

He pushed himself away from the desk, and tried to swing for the plain-clothed detective who was in charge of the investigation.

Upon seeing that the detective was now out of his striking range, having anticipated this reaction, Fraser then tried to lurch forward again, and over the top of the desk to strike at the custody sergeant.

By this time, the cavalry, consisting of the officers that until then were waiting silently in the wings, were well on their way.

Within seconds, Fraser was surrounded by four uniformed officers. Two of them had grabbed an arm each. One went around the front of Fraser, and the last stayed to the rear.

In a split second, Fraser had gone from being a man possessed to being restrained, and back under control.

Four onto one would often be considered as an unfair contest. As a result, it doesn't generally sit well with the public when witnessed or broadcast over the media. However, situations like that aren't meant to be a fair fight, and the objective isn't to win.

The objective is to subdue the aggressor as quickly and as safely as possible, giving him little opportunity to lash out, thus reducing the potential for injury to anyone, including the subject as much as possible. The only way to effectively achieve this is to rapidly overwhelm them.

Once pinioned, Fraser attempted to slam his face down against the front of the counter, but again his behaviour was anticipated, and the officer who had positioned himself in front of Fraser was there to prevent him from causing himself any harm until he could be further restrained.

Having realised the game was up as far as striking anyone, Fraser could only revert to verbally taunting the officers and staff.

"You motherfuckers, I'll fucking have you, you fucking bastards," he bellowed as loud as he could, despite the constricted position he now found himself in.

The four officers then secured Fraser in what was known as the *cell placement formation*. This was used when there was a violent or deranged prisoner who needed to be led to a cell and released from any restraints in a safe and efficient manner.

But all Marshall got to see was Fraser being led back in the direction that he had first come from, bent over at the waist, with both arms extended out and behind him, much like an abusive and demented albatross trying to take flight.

Then once they had all passed through a fire door that led to a corridor of cells, the tirade of abuse subsided. Then, in an instant, the booking-in area returned to some sense of normality.

Marshall could see the surplus officers exit the detention area through a side door, probably relived that they didn't need to get involved. They probably had too much paperwork to deal with without the need to add to it.

Once the officer in front of Marshall had been dealt with, it was then his turn.

"Good afternoon," Marshall said as he began to address a detention officer he didn't recognise. "James Marshall, duty solicitor for Brett Cable."

As the detention officer didn't recognise Marshall in return, he turned to seek approval from the sergeant before proceeding.

"Can you let the officer in the case know I'm here, and can I get a copy of the custody record?"

After a few moments the detention officer left, only to return with several printed sheets that he handed to Marshall. He then picked up the phone and dialled a telephone extension within the building.

"The solicitor for Cable is here," he said once the call had been answered.

"They'll be right down," the detention officer then said to Marshall having ended the call.

As there was no one behind Marshall waiting to be seen, he remained at the desk and began to read through Cable's custody record. This had all the details of his arrest, as well as a running log of the time he had been in custody.

Marshall could see that Cable had been arrested on suspicion of assault, with the injuries allegedly inflicted being consistent with the definition of grievous bodily harm. He could also see that Cable had been arrested at just after nine o'clock the previous evening. This immediately surprised him.

After a couple of minutes, the door that all the surplus officers had earlier disappeared through reopened, and a suited officer came into the booking-in area.

Immediately Marshall was able to determine that the officer in charge of the case was most likely a detective, as the other plain-clothed officer had been as opposed to a habitually uniformed police constable.

This didn't have any bearing on the situation, except the level of investigative training was likely to be higher.

As the officer approached where Marshall waited, he again had to again confess to himself as to not knowing them. As a result, it was back to basics with the introductions.

"Good afternoon," Marshall said, extending a hand to be shook. "James Marshall, of Reid, Salmon and Hounslow solicitors."

The detective took hold of the outstretched hand and shook it.

"Detective Heather Arnold," she replied. "Are you ready for disclosure?"

"If you are?" Marshall replied.

He then followed on behind Arnold as she led him towards a consultation room.

As Arnold walked ahead of Marshall, he couldn't help but allow himself a downward glance.

He hoped no one saw him enjoy a brief moment of indulgence. Although his approving smile was undoubtedly captured on CCTV somewhere.

Once inside a private consultation room, they both took a seat. Both on wooden and metal benches that had been secured to the floor. This was so that in the event of an outburst similar to that shown by Fraser, then the seats themselves couldn't be used as weapons.

Arnold handed over two identical sheets of printed paper, on which carefully considered facts had been bullet-pointed. Marshall read down the list.

"So, my client has been in custody for fourteen hours already," Marshall began having scrutinised Cable's custody record. "And what has been achieved in that time?"

"A lot of it has been waiting for your client to sober up, and to be seen by our medic," Arnold replied.

"Okay, so he was intoxicated, and he's sustained injuries… So, are we possibly looking at self-defence here?" Marshall asked.

"The other party is *still* in hospital. The injuries between the parties appears to be disproportionate, so I think not," Arnold again replied.

"Is this still being treated as a GBH? We're not going to end up with a common assault here, are we?" Marshall asked, enquiring deeper.

GBH, or grievous bodily harm refers to life changing injuries, whereas actual bodily harm, or ABH is a lesser offence of causing superficial injuries. With common assault being even lower on the same scale, being an assault where no physical injuries are sustained.

It was also procedure to arrest and investigate for the more serious suspected crime until such time it could be downgraded if appropriate. Going the other way would be problematic as certain investigative opportunities, such as forensics, would be missed.

"We'll need to await the result of the CT scan and MRI before we can make that call," Arnold answered. "At the moment, we're considering it to be GBH."

Since the time of the offence, both involved parties had been taken to the local hospital. However, Cable's injuries were insignificant compared to that of his alleged victim. As a result, he was then brought to custody, whilst the other party remained within A&E.

"Is the other party under arrest?" Marshall asked.

"No," came Arnold's reply.

"And why not?" Marshall asked.

"It's not deemed necessary at this time," Arnold explained. "There are officers with him, and all forensics have been secured... As I said, we are awaiting the test results before deciding on the next step."

"Fair enough," Marshall replied. "Are you looking for anyone else in connection with this incident?"

"Until we are able to get a full account from both parties, we just don't know," Arnold explained.

"So, you don't even have an allegation yet?" Marshall said, leaping on the admission that Arnold had just made, that the victim had yet to be spoken to. "How did you come to identify my client as even being involved then?"

"He was located near to the scene," Arnold began. "And he looked like he had been in a fight."

"That's it?" Marshall said, with more than a hint of sarcasm. "So, I'm guessing you're just looking to interview and bail him then... After all, you're not going to get an extension to his detention on these grounds, just to wait around for the CT and MRI results, are you?"

Arnold merely shrugged. She felt Marshall's last question was rhetorical, but even if it wasn't, she felt it was too presumptuous to deserve a response.

"There's no mention of a weapon here, do you have one?" Marshall asked. "Or are we looking at GBH with his bare hands?"

"That's a no, we don't have one, and I don't know," came Arnold's reply.

"Any witnesses?" Marshall asked.

"No," Arnold replied.

"It says here that you have CCTV," Marshall asked, seeking clarification. "Does it show the assault?"

Arnold inhaled deeply. She turned to face away from Marshall as she considered her reply. She knew she couldn't mislead the defence by saying it did if it didn't. Also, should she say something that was later proved to be misleading, it could place the whole case in jeopardy. She knew Marshall had her right where he wanted to.

"No, it doesn't," she replied.

"Does it show my client?" Marshall then asked.

"We believe so," Arnold replied. "We're waiting for it to be enhanced."

Marshall pondered the facts in front of him.

"So, you have *no* witnesses, *no* weapon, *no* CCTV *really*, and this is most likely an ABH at best, or worst I s'pose how you look at it," Marshall summed up. "Just to let you know now, I will be instructing my client to go *no comment*... Can you arrange for him to be sent in?"

Marshall then signed one copy of the disclosure document and slid it back across the table towards Arnold, keeping the unsigned one for himself.

Arnold then stood, retrieved her copy from the table, before she turned and headed back towards the door.

"I'll have him sent in," she said as she left the consultation room.

Marshall's attention then reverted to that of his stomach. He was relieved in the knowledge that based on his experience, this interview process shouldn't take long, and that he could finally get something to eat.

3

A detention officer led a man who was dressed similarly to the unruly prisoner Robert Fraser to the consultation room in which Marshall waited.

The detention officer held the door open for the prisoner to enter, but did not enter the room himself.

Upon seeing them, Marshall stood until the detention officer had left them alone, closing the door behind him.

"Brett Cable?" Marshall asked.

"Yeah, that's me," the man replied.

"Sit yourself down, Brett," Marshall said. "My name is James Marshall, I'm the duty solicitor. You can call me James, if you like... How are you feeling, are you ready to have a little chat with me?"

Cable took a seat across from him, and merely nodded in way of a response. Given that Marshall had asked two questions of him, as well as imparting information, he didn't know to what, if anything the nod was referring to. Regardless, as time was an issue, he continued.

"This is showing to be your first arrest in this county," Marshall began, indicating towards a copy of the custody record that he had open on the table between them. "No convictions... Have you *ever* been arrested anywhere before?"

"A couple of times up north," came a strained reply.

"And, what was that for?" Marshall asked.

"Drug possession," Cable replied.

"But nothing was ever charged?" Marshall asked, feeling the need to further clarify Cable's criminal past. "I mean, you never went to court for anything."

Cable just shook his head.

"Okay, so I take it you're aware that this, what we're doing now is a privileged conversation...? And by that, I mean, that nothing you say here is disclosable. Whatever you choose to tell me, or talk to me about,

31

stays between us, okay? But that said, what you do choose to tell me, can help me to best advise you as things move forward. Do you understand, Brett, I'm here to help *you*?"

Again, all Marshall got in way of a response was another nod.

"Look Brett, you're gonna have to do a lot better than that if you want me to be *able* to help you," Marshall explained. "Now, you were asked if you wanted my help, well, here I am... At this moment in time, all I know is what the police know, and I'll tell ya, that's not a great deal... So, how about just tell me where you were when you got arrested... It says here, you were found in Noakes Road, near to the alleyway that leads to the High Street, is that right?"

"Yeah," Cable replied.

"Okay, good, that's a start. I've been told that you looked like you'd just been in a fight, I can see you've had your clothes seized, and you've got some injuries, do you want to tell me how that happened?"

"There's not much to tell, really," Cable admitted.

"Well, indulge me, tell me anyway," Marshall replied

oOo

It was a little after ten o'clock the previous evening when Brett Cable entered the working men's club on the High Street.

From just inside the front door, he was able to see pretty much the entire public bar area. In one corner, next to the door to the toilets, he saw the reason that he was there.

Cable had gone to the club in the hope of meeting a man named Paul Greene, who was someone he had been recommended as being able to get hold of the drugs that Cable had become rather partial to during his time *up north.*

Cable didn't immediately rush over to introduce himself to Greene, instead he waited, biding his time. This he spent nursing a pint at the bar until the crowd that was around Greene had dissipated.

Having sized Greene up, he then further waited for Greene to go to into the toilets before deciding to approach him. When he eventually did, Cable followed on shortly behind him.

Inside of the men's toilet, Cable caught what must have been the tail-end of Greene being passed something through the open toilet window. All Cable saw was Greene retrieving his hand from the window, before tucking something inside his jacket.

"What the fuck are you looking at?" Greene said to Cable, when he realised, he was being watched.

"Nothing," Cable replied. "I was just hoping you could sort me out with some gear, I ain't been down this way long, but I've been told you're the guy to see?"

"Oh yeah, who told you that then? Who gave you my name?" Greene asked. "I'm clean, ask anybody."

Until he had been convinced otherwise, Greene knew it best to deny everything.

"Billy Whiz, he told me to come see you," Cable replied.

Greene nodded his approval, having known and served time with Billy.

Billy Whiz, although referring to a real person, wasn't the name his parents had given him.

Billy and Whiz were instead slang terms for amphetamines, illegal drugs which lent themselves rather appropriately to Billy's illicit pastime.

"You ain't the filth, are ya?" he then asked in order to avoid any risk of entrapment.

If an undercover police officer was to be asked such a question, they had to answer it truthfully. If not, then any following interaction could be considered as entrapment, and be prejudicial to the investigation, and any subsequent trial. Any court defence would likely to succeed in getting any evidence obtained by such means excluded if an agent working for the police was seen to be actively encouraging a suspect to commit or admit to a crime. Greene was well aware of this.

"Fuck no," Cable replied. He chuckled, having found the question amusing.

"Good enough," Greene replied. "So, what'll it be then?"

"Just some weed and some white," Cable asked, referring to wanting to buy some herbal cannabis and cocaine.

"How much do you want?" Greene asked.

33

Cable initially didn't reply, instead he just held up a fistful of bank notes.

"As much as I can get for this," he eventually asked.

Greene took the cash from him, and counted it to see how much was there. He opened his coat, and rummaged through his pockets.

He placed a couple of small envelopes on the side of a washbasin. He then added the counted cash to a large bundle of notes which he tucked back inside his coat.

Seeing what appeared to be a substantial amount of cash being stuffed into the coat caused Cable's eyes to bulge. For a moment, he didn't see Greene picking up the envelopes, and holding them out for Cable to take.

"Do you want these, or not?" Greene asked emphatically.

Cable, having come back to the moment, stepped forward and took the envelopes. He then gave a nod of gratitude to Greene, before turning around and leaving the toilets.

Having concluded the only reason for him being there, Cable headed straight for the front door of the club.

Once outside, Cable walked around to the back of the club. This he accessed having used the service road between the club and a neighbouring premises.

Behind the club was a service area that was shared with neighbouring businesses. The portion that was allocated to the club was marked out as parking bays. But it also had an area that was reserved for delivery vehicles.

Having found an empty beer keg upon which to sit down, Cable rolled himself a joint using his recent acquisition and cigarette papers that he already had. He then lit it using matches as opposed to a lighter.

It was as he smoked, that he had a casual look around the service area whilst he entertained thoughts that had only recently entered his head.

It was then, as he indulged these thoughts, that he found a couple of hand tools that had been left on a low wall by the back door to the club. They included an adjustable wrench and a claw hammer.

But it was only as he picked up the hammer, that the thoughts that had until that moment been the subject of some debate in his mind suddenly became the sole course of a decided action.

As Cable held the hammer in his hand, he tightened his grip around it, before he swung it in a downward stroke. A look of maniacal menace, one fuelled by greed, came across his face.

Cable remained sat there in the shadows of the service area, waiting for the club to close. He had, unbeknownst to him, chosen a good vantage point from which to view the car park.

Cable was playing the odds as he didn't know exactly how, or in what direction Greene would be leaving the club. But as he didn't appear to be drunk when they spoke, and as he was possibly there only to attend to business, it was a fair assumption to make that he had driven there.

As it turned out, Greene hadn't driven, not as far as the club car park anyway. This was confirmed, as from his vantage point, Cable saw Greene walk across the car park and into an alleyway that ran adjacent to the car park, separated only by a low wall.

This alleyway led from the High Street to residential streets behind it.

Allowing Greene to have something of a head start, Cable then followed on behind him into the alleyway.

The alleyway was quite a long one, as once behind the High Street businesses, it then ran along the back of a school.

There was a single streetlight about midway along the alleyway. This was where the path split into two. One path continued straight on, separating two houses on the road where it eventually emerged. The other ran perpendicular to the main path, away from the school, again coming out on a residential road.

Once Greene had walked beyond the streetlight, Cable rushed to catch up with him. He needed to know which path Greene had taken, and he was reliant on the glare of the streetlight to mask his movements should Greene feel the urge to turn around and look behind him.

Greene had stayed on the main path, and had walked clear of the beam of the streetlight by the time that Cable had closed the distance on him.

Unfortunately for them both, Cable's approach wasn't anywhere near as stealthy as he had intended it to be.

Having heard footsteps rushing up behind him, Greene instinctively turned to face them. This was just in time for him to see Cable bring the raised claw hammer down on him.

But, instead of striking the intended target of Greene's back, it came down to strike him on a forearm that he had instinctively raised to protect himself against his silhouetted assailant.

The impact of the blow caused Greene to cry out in pain. This was the last thing that Cable wanted, as it was sure to draw unwanted attention to his actions from anyone in the vicinity.

The only thing that was now playing to his advantage was that the streetlight was behind him. As a result, he was silhouetted against it, his face hidden in its shadows.

Yet the same light illuminated Greene as he lay on his back, having fallen to the ground. He was cradling his injured arm in agony. He was sure it was broken.

Greene was under no illusion that this was a robbery, and against such a ferocious attacker, and short of handing over everything he had to appease him, Greene knew his only chance of survival was to summon help. He again cried out in the hope that someone would hear him, and come to his aid.

But the more he screamed, the more Cable became panicked, and the more Cable panicked, the greater the urgency he felt to silence Greene.

Another hammer blow rained down on Greene. This time it was aimed at the stationary target that was his head.

Again, Greene had attempted to shield himself with his arms, but this time to little effect. The blow struck him hard, causing a significant wound to his right temple. This was enough to silence him.

With Greene incapacitated, Cable gave his downed victim the briefest glance of contempt. Greene had blood streaming down the side of his head. A pool was already collecting on the pavement beneath where he lay.

Cable then began to ransack the pockets of his coat. He knew exactly what he was looking for, and where to find it. But, despite a thorough search, what he was looking for was nowhere to found.

Despite his pain and injuries, Greene was still conscious., and with Cable still crouched over him, he tried to grab hold of Cable with his one good arm.

Cable pulled at his arm, and freed the weakened grip from him. All Greene had achieved was to partially rip the front pocket from Cable's shirt, and to spatter blood on them both.

In disappointed frustration, at having gone to all this effort without any payoff, Cable set the hammer down beside them both. He then grabbed Greene by the collar of his ransacked coat, and hoisted him to a seated position.

He punched Greene once to the face, before letting him go, and allowing him to fall back again to the ground.

Cable stood up, he then reclaimed the hammer, before running off along the alleyway. As he ran, he threw the hammer over a fence, and into the school playing field.

Cable continued along the alleyway, eventually emerging onto Noakes Road.

oOo

"Well, the police have not mentioned anything about a hammer. So, I'm guessing they haven't found it," Marshall said, having absorbed Cable's account. "What injuries do you have?"

"Nothing much, a few cuts and bruises," Cable replied, showing Marshall the backs of his hands.

Marshall could see that the injuries were consistent with having punched something.

"But you said your clothes got ripped?" Marshall questioned.

"Yeah," Cable answered.

Marshall paused in order to weigh up the evidence presented against the account provided by Cable.

"Okay, the way I see this is… They may very well have forensic evidence against you, but as you didn't steal anything from this other guy, then they can't use robbery as a contributing factor," Marshall began to explain. "For all they know, this was either a fight that got out of hand, or, that *you* may well have been the intended victim of a robbery yourself, and you just got the upper hand at some point... Given what we have here, and what the police actually know, and more importantly, what they can actually prove, it's my recommendation that you go *no comment* during your interview, or at the very least go down the lines of defending yourself when *you* were attacked. How does that sound to you?"

"Sounds good to me," Cable replied, as a broad smile appeared on his face.

4

In the interview room, and once the audio recording had been started but before any questioning could commence, Detective Constable Arnold had firstly to go through a structured introduction where she had to have everyone introduce themselves, as well as giving their reason for being there for the benefit of the recording.

In addition to this, Arnold had to reiterate the caution that Cable was placed under at the time of his arrest, as well as reminding him of his rights. This included that he was not required to answer any questions put to him, but also to be aware that an inference might be drawn by his refusal to provide an answer.

Only once all that had been completed, was Arnold able to actually begin questioning Cable regarding the offence to which he had been arrested on suspicion of committing.

Unfortunately for everyone concerned, it wasn't merely an option to assume that Cable was going to respond with *no comment* to every question as Marshall had alluded to in the disclosure briefing. As a consequence, each question still had to be asked individually, in order for him to be given the opportunity to give a response.

Although this was a laborious and time-consuming process it had to be undertaken for legal reasons. Cable had to be given the opportunity to respond to each question in turn, in order for individual inferences to be able to be drawn should he fail to reply to a specific question during the interview, only to reply to the same question at a later time.

"Mister Cable, you were arrested in the early hours of this morning following reports that an assault had taken place in the alleyway that runs between the High Street and Noakes Road… You were subsequently found in Noakes Road, near to where the alleyway comes out. And as you were seen to have apparent injuries and wearing bloodied and torn clothing, consistent with having been involved in a physical altercation, you were stopped by officers and subsequently arrested… Please can you tell me what you know about this incident?" Arnold asked as her opening question.

Unfortunately for Detective Constable Arnold, as soon as she had left an opportunity for Cable to provide his response, he merely looked to his left in order to gain approval from Marshall, who was sat next to him.

Then when Marshall nodded to confirm they were to proceed with the previously agreed course of action, Cable looked forward again.

"No comment," he replied, with a wry smile on his face.

Although Arnold had been told to expect this, she was nevertheless frustrated by it. She openly sighed, which couldn't fail to be picked up by the microphone mounted on the table between them.

However, police officers are taught to prepare for this eventuality, and have the questions to be asked listed, or at the very least, have the interview mapped out, so that all relevant topics and aspects were covered during questioning.

Resorting to her alternative strategy, Arnold continued.

"Can you then tell me how you came to be in Noakes Road where officers found and arrested you?" she asked.

"No comment," Cable replied in a monotonous voice.

"Can you tell me how you came to be wearing torn and bloodied clothing at the time you were arrested?"

"No comment," Cable replied.

"Where had you been earlier last night, *before* entering Noakes Road?" continued Arnold.

"No comment," again came Cable's reply.

Before continuing, Arnold felt the need to address the stance that Cable had adopted regarding the questions being put to him.

"Mister Cable, I want to interrupt the questions at this point just to clarify something for you," Arnold began to explain. "It would appear that you have been advised to respond to every question I will ask of you with a 'no comment' answer... But just because you have been advised so, doesn't mean you have to take that advice... After all, it won't be your solicitor having to explain as to why you declined to answer these questions should this matter go to court... Do you understand?"

"Uh huh," Cable replied.

Taking this as a positive response of understanding, Arnold continued.

Each and every question that Arnold had to ask of Cable was then responded to in exactly the same way as before, despite the warning.

But, again regardless of this, Arnold still had to allow sufficient time between each question in order to give Cable every opportunity to offer a response.

Had she just rushed from one question to the next, Marshall could argue against any inference by saying that his client was not given adequate time to consider a response, before the next question was asked of him.

Both Arnold and Marshall knew it was all a game. A game which they both had played many times, but on opposite teams, and like any game, there were rules they both had to abide by.

After a lengthy period of questioning, Arnold offered one last question.

"Before I end this interview, is there anything you wish to add or clarify?" she asked.

Cable merely shook his head.

"Please can you verbalise a response for the benefit of the tape?"

The audio recording was in fact a digitised file on a hard drive, so no tapes, or even DVDs were used anymore. It was just a habitual response, given Arnold's length of service from when they did use actually use cassette tapes to record the interviews on.

Regardless of the antiquated remark, Cable's reply remained the same.

"No comment," he said with an impatient sigh.

"Is there anything you wish to add?" Arnold said looking towards Marshall.

"No, thank you," he replied.

"Okay, that being the case, the time by the interview room clock is two twenty-seven; this interview is finished."

Once Marshall had seen Arnold use the touchscreen computer to end the audio recording, he felt it an appropriate time to make an enquiry.

"So, what are you looking to do now?" he asked. "Are you looking to *RUI* him, or is he being bailed?"

41

Marshall knew that Arnold didn't presently have enough evidence on Cable to charge him with the assault. The only reason he was arrested was because he was found in the locality of the incident looking the way he did. With that in mind, the police didn't even have enough evidence to impose any restrictions or conditions on him upon his release.

Arnold then addressed Cable knowing her response would appease Marshall at the same time.

"Okay, so at this time you're gonna be *released under investigation*," Arnold began. "Your clothing will be sent away for forensic analysis, and when we have the results, we may be looking to speak to you further… But, before we release you, we'd like to ask you to take part in an identity procedure… This will show an image of you amongst a number of images of similar looking people, to see if you are identifiable to being involved by any other persons involved in the incident."

Cable again looked over at Marshall, who gave another approving nod in response. Cable then nodded agreement himself.

"Good," Arnold continued. "It's designed to eliminate you as a suspect as much as anything else."

With that, Arnold collected up her papers.

She stood up and walked over to the interview room door where she held it open for Cable and Marshall to exit the room ahead of her.

One tip Arnold had learned early on in her career was to never allow a suspect to follow you. Luckily, she hadn't learned this lesson the hard way, although, a number of her colleagues had, when they were attacked from behind even whilst in custody.

Back at the bridge, Arnold explained the requirement for the identification procedure to the custody sergeant. As she did, Marshall had the opportunity to speak to Cable.

"Here's my card," he said. "If you're called back in for this, then give me a call. You can then request me to attend any interviews you have, okay?"

Marshall then shook Cable's hand. He then left Cable at the bridge, before exiting the custody centre as he had entered it.

Once outside by his car, Marshall looked at his watch. It was nearly three o'clock. He was still on call, but he was hopeful that he wouldn't be called upon to again attend custody.

He had a magistrate court plea hearing on the Monday morning, and he was keen to make a start on his preparation for it that evening, so as to keep his weekend free.

5

"It's only me," Marshall said having turned the key and opened the front door to his parent's house.

He had the key, with which gave him the freedom to come and go as he pleased. But he always afforded them the courtesy of announcing his arrival so as not to startle them or cause them any distress, should they suddenly see someone in their house prior to recognising it to be their son, James.

His parents were both in their late seventies, and their health was reflected in their years. The way Marshall saw it, the last thing they needed was an easily avoidable scare.

Marshall stood in the hallway awaiting a response before advancing. As he waited, he slipped off his suit jacket and draped it over the bottom of the bannister.

It was then he heard the response he was waiting for.

"James? Is that you?" his mother called from the kitchen.

This was then followed by a familiar face popping around the side of the door that led to the kitchen,

"What a lovely surprise," she continued. "Come on through. Your father's in the garden."

Marshall walked through to the kitchen. His mother beamed as she saw him. She quickly dried her hands on a tea towel hung over a base unit cupboard door. Then when she was saw that they were dry enough, she beckoned her son to come closer to her so she could give him a hug.

"Oh, it's lovely to see you," she said. "To what do we owe this visit?"

"Nothing," Marshall replied. "I was just passing by, and I thought I'd drop in."

"Well, it's good that you did. There's something your father and I want to talk to you about when he comes back inside," his mother said. "Can I get you a cup of tea?"

"That'd be lovely," Marshall replied. "What's it about?"

His mother paused and sighed.

"It's probably best I leave it to your father to tell you… As you've been so busy lately, we weren't expecting to see you until the weekend itself," she continued. "Are you going to be able to see the children this weekend at all?"

Marshall took a long inhalation, followed by an equally long sigh before he gave his response with something of a smirk on his face.

"Funny you say that… I got a text message from Nicky on the way here, seems she's got plans with the kids this weekend, so no… Oh, well, guess we'll try again next week, I s'pose," Marshall replied. "On the plus side, I get the whole weekend prepping for my hearing on Monday now."

Despite the upbeat way in which he spoke, Marshall was despondent, given the efforts he had made in order to keep his weekend free.

"Oh dear… Apart from that, how are things with Nicky?" his mother asked with concern.

"Could be better," Marshall began. "She's already served the divorce petition, and I've already returned it. I told you that right…? Well, we're onto sorting out the finances now, and so far, that has involved a lot of back and forth, bickering over the little things. I have to admit, I'm just as bad as she is… I'm lucky, though. I've got a guy in my office doing my end of it for mate's rates."

Marshall offered his mother a smile, hoping she would reciprocate.

"Is this the reason that you're not getting to see your children this weekend then?" his mother asked.

"She hasn't said as much, but I'm just getting excuse after excuse at the mo… Added to which, she's shacked up with her new fella too, means my two see more of him than they do me. He's got his own kids there too. It's just like the bloody *Brady Bunch*."

His mother shook her head in disappointment.

"Well, I do hope that two of you can work things out," his mother continued. "I still don't understand why all of this had to happen in the first place?"

"You said it yourself, mum," Marshall said. "I've been working way too much… I'm the first one to admit that my caseload is overwhelming.

But if I want to make partner in my firm, then I need to be seen to put in the effort now."

"At what cost?" she replied. "Your children need their father."

It was then that Marshall's father came in from being outside in the garden.

By this time, three mugs of tea sat steaming away on the kitchen counter.

Marshall considered his father's entrance a salvation, so he used the intervention to quickly change the subject.

"What was it you guys wanted to talk to me about?" he asked.

For a moment, a puzzled look fell over both of his parent's faces; his mother because she had forgotten that she had introduced the topic of discussion to him, and his father being blissfully unaware that she had.

Once the penny had dropped, it was his mother that suggested they all take a seat in the living room.

"We had this man come to the door in the middle of the week, Wednesday evening I think it was," his mother began. "He was very well dressed and spoke politely enough... He wanted us to sign up for something, I can't remember exactly what it was now, he just wouldn't take *no* for an answer, oh he got me so flustered."

Seeing the account given by his wife becoming ever more sporadic, Marshall's father decided to take up the reins and continued to fill in the gaps that his wife had left during her rendition.

"He was selling something to do with digital television," his father continued. "Oh, he had all of the brochures. He said he needed to check our aerial... If we had a certain type of aerial, he said he could upgrade our service there and then... I told him we weren't interested. You know, I only watch the news, and your mother has her soaps, that's about it for us... We just don't need however many channels he was going on about... But he *wouldn't* listen. We kept saying *no* to him. But he was so pushy... He tried to get in the front door past me, but we managed to keep him on the doorstep... In the end, I told him that this was a rented house, and that we were only tenants. It was then either that, or the neighbours coming home next-door that compelled him to leave... He did leave saying something about popping back another time though."

"Oh, I hope he doesn't," Marshall's mother added. "He was truly awful towards the end."

Being of the older generation, neither of his parents wanted to blow what had happened out of proportion. But they wanted their learned son's opinion on the incident, and more importantly what, if anything they should do next.

"Well, you certainly did the right thing by not letting him come into the house," Marshall began to explain. "Chances are that he was not on his own either. So, whenever you took him anywhere, upstairs to look at the aerial, his mate would come in and grab anything of value that he could lay his hands on... I must say, I've not heard of a TV aerial scam before. It's usually a gas or water leak. But I guess people are becoming too aware of that one now."

"But what should we do if he does come back?" his mother added.

"To be honest, I don't believe that he will come back," Marshall replied. "But *if* he does, certainly don't let him in the house, don't even open the front door to him, and if he refuses to leave, then call the police... What did he look like?"

Marshall could see him mother trying to recall the events. She finally relented.

"Oh, I can't remember," his mother answered. "I couldn't even tell you what he was wearing, except that he was dressed smartly. Your father is better at that sort of thing than I am."

Having taken a mouthful of his tea, Marshall felt the need to prompt his father as his mind appeared elsewhere.

"Dad?" Marshall said, redirecting the same question to his father.

"Um, I would say he was about my height, but he would be a lot younger than you," his father said.

"What about hair colour?" Marshall asked, in the hope of prompting the focus of their memories.

"Oh, I don't know," his father replied, beginning to echo his wife's sentiments.

"Well, fingers crossed that he doesn't come back," Marshall reaffirmed. "But if he does, whatever you do, don't let him in, keep the door shut and phone the police straight away, *then* call me, okay?"

6

The following Monday had Marshall again scheduled to attend the local magistrates court.

This time he was representing a client who was once again standing before the judge facing charges of arson.

Charlie Maclean was a habitual arsonist, and like so many other arsonists was fascinated not by the destruction caused, but by the fire itself. It was this fascination that had led Maclean to be arrested on this occasion.

But what separated Maclean from so many other arsonists and pyromaniacs was that Maclean was, in fact, a thirty-five-year-old woman, with Charlie being short for Charlotte.

Statistics had proven that male arsonists outweighed their female counterparts by a ratio of 2:1. This was not a sexist or derogatory remark. It was just a proven fact that fewer females found an attraction in the inflammatory arts.

Maclean's psychosis, fascination and potentially her motivation for her crimes appeared to have been borne out of tragedy. As it had become apparent from a previous case against her, and through Marshall's research in preparing for this hearing, she had lost a sibling in a house fire when they were both children.

This however, wasn't enough to absolve her from her responsibility for her crimes, and hence didn't relinquish her of any guilt.

This did, however, lend itself to whether or not there was any *mens rea,* or guilty mind involved in the commission of the offences, and this had heavily lent itself to form the basis of Marshall's preparation for this case.

However, on this occasion, Maclean was arrested solely based on the fact that she remained at the crime scene in order to watch the conflagration she had caused engulf the building.

It was for these reasons that Marshall was once again meeting with Maclean prior to the court hearing in order to consult with her regarding her intended plea.

"Are you still happy to go forward as we've discussed?" Marshall asked of Charlie Maclean as they sat in a consultation room, waiting for their hearing to be called.

As Maclean hadn't been remanded after being charged for this most recent offence, she didn't have to wait in the holding cells beneath the courthouse. She merely had a scheduled appointment to keep in order to attend her hearing, but should she have chosen not to keep that appointment, it would have resulted in a warrant being issued by the court for her arrest.

"I'll do whatever *you* think is best," Charlie replied.

"It's not a case of what I think, Charlie," Marshall began to explain. "I can only explain the options available to you, and explain the perils and pitfalls of each... But ultimately the choice has to be yours, I'm afraid. I'm sorry. Now, whatever you do, I'll be on hand to help and support you, and get you through this as easily as possible... But, all that said, when you're giving your plea, and when you're in the dock, you *will* be on your own."

Charlie took a moment to contemplate the options that she had previously discussed with Marshall.

She could plead guilty to the charges at this hearing, and take whatever sentence was imposed.

Or, she could plead not guilty, and then she would have to face the rigours of a trial, whereby at its conclusion, a verdict would be reached by a jury.

Arson with intent/reckless as to whether life was endangered, the offence to which Charlie had been charged, had been deemed under UK law as an indictable offence, and carried with it the possibility of a life sentence. This meant that even if Charlie were to plead guilty at this first hearing, then the case would be automatically commuted to a crown court for sentencing.

That would mean, regardless of her plea at this hearing, it would not be the end of it for Charlie.

"Do you have *any* opinion on this?" Charlie asked, desperately looking for some guidance.

"Okay, personally, I don't think you should even *be* here," Marshall replied. "Your fire setting, in my opinion, isn't an act of criminality. You lost your sister in a fire, and now it's almost as if watching the fire itself now brings you peace... And should this go to trial, then that'll be the basis of your defence."

With that confirmation from her legal representative, Charlie felt confident in her decision.

oOo

They didn't have to wait much longer until Charlie's case was called.

As before, when Marshall was presiding over Albert Foster on drink driving charges, the magistrates' court was sparsely populated.

On this occasion, as before, only a single district magistrate presided, as opposed to the alternative of having three lay-magistrates presiding.

Marshall preferred to stand before a district magistrate as they had a legal education. Lay magistrates were members of the community who relied on the court clerk for the legal aspects of the case.

He found that, as a result, the district magistrate tended to be more flexible in their application of the law as they were not having to interpret someone else's explanation of the legal aspects and ramifications to them.

After the crown prosecutor had laid down the details of the offence to which Charlie had been charged, Charlie was given the opportunity to enter her plea into the court record.

She stood when instructed to do so. But before verbalising her response, a moment of doubt descended upon her.

Sensing this doubt, Marshall looked towards Charlie who was stood alone in the dock.

"Are you okay?" he asked. "Just do what we discussed."

"I'm not sure I can," she replied, but in a volume audible only to Marshall and not to the rest of the court.

Marshall then again broke with protocol. He stood from his desk in the middle of the courtroom, and approached the dock where Charlie stood all alone.

"I don't think I can go through with this, not if it goes to trial," she continued.

"You're *not* a criminal, Charlie," Marshall whispered to her. "You shouldn't even be here. But I can't tell you what to do."

Seeing this breach of protocol, the magistrate felt compelled to address the issue.

"Do you wish to request an adjournment before entering a plea?" the magistrate asked having seen Charlie's hesitation.

Marshall who had momentarily turned to face the magistrate again turned to face Charlie.

"Do you want more time to decide?" he asked.

Charlie took a moment to weigh up her options, before shaking her head. She then whispered something back to Marshall. He smiled at hearing this.

He then stepped back, away from the dock, intentionally creating distance between them, indicating to the court and to Charlie that the impromptu consultation was at an end.

"Your worship, we would like to enter a plea of *not guilty*," he said vehemently on Charlie's behalf.

"Very well," the magistrate replied.

The magistrate then looked over at the clerk of the court who was already in the process of selecting a date for the trial. Marshall and Charlie both retook their seats.

Once a suitable date had been chosen, this information was passed to the magistrate who reviewed the details.

"This case will now be heard at the crown court, commencing on Monday the fourth of August at ten o'clock in the morning," he said. "This session is adjourned."

The magistrate then struck his gavel, signifying the same.

"All rise," the court usher then announced.

Once the magistrate and clerk had left the courtroom, Marshall and Charlie found themselves alone, albeit for the usher who was waiting for them to leave so he could prepare the room for the next hearing.

"Are we doing the right thing?" Charlie asked nervously.

"Absolutely," Marshall replied. "This is a court for criminals, and you are most certainly not one."

7

As Charlie's trial had been deferred to the county's crown court following her *not guilty* plea, Marshall didn't have any immediate or urgent obligations to the case. Charlie herself was again bailed to attend the crown court on the 4th of August, and she was under no restrictions or conditions until then.

The only warning she had been given was that, whilst released on court bail, any further offenses committed would be dealt with more harshly. But apart from that, she was free to come and go as she pleased.

oOo

The next day had Marshall back on the roster as duty solicitor, and lo and behold, it wasn't long before he found himself back in custody.

Though this occasion was not nearly as dramatic as his visit the previous week. This time, there were no outbursts that had to be subdued, and nothing on the part of the person being represented to involve Marshall even having to take an active role in the interview.

Unlike the previous interview with Cable, this prisoner, who had been arrested for a domestic-related assault on her partner, was more than happy to provide the interviewing police officer with a comprehensive account of what had happened that had ultimately led to her arrest.

Marshall considered that the way this interview was progressing it would lead to an immediate charging decision being sought, with there being the possibility of a caution being administered as the young lady in question was a first-time offender.

This would hopefully mean he could make an early departure, and more importantly, being able to heed his father's advice, as such a disposal would hopefully not cause this incident to add to his already overwhelming case load.

It was in this brief moment of contemplation, as the suspect was in the middle of giving a response to a question, that there was suddenly a knock at the interview room door.

This was very unusual as a recorded interview was well underway, and the *Room in Use* sign had been illuminated on the outside of the interview room, indicating to anyone outside that the room was in use, and that entry was prohibited.

Given the irregularity of this, and the apparent urgency of the knocking, the interviewing officer chose to pause the interview on the audio recording in order to answer the door. He had to announce this for the benefit of the recording.

"Pausing interview to answer to knocking at interview room door," he said.

The interviewing officer then paused the recording as he stood. Having gone over to the door, he opened it slightly, so that no one in the room could see anything outside in the corridor, or vice versa.

At the door was a detention officer.

"Is it possible to have a quick word with Mister Marshall, please?" he asked.

Having heard this request from where he was sat, Marshall tilted in his seat. He was trying to see through the door despite the restriction caused by the interviewing officer.

He was as surprised as much as anyone else by the detention officer's request.

The interviewing officer then turned to face Marshall. He nodded towards Marshall, realising he had also heard the request, and then tilted his head towards the door, suggesting he leave the room to be spoken to.

As Marshall walked past the interviewing officer, he apologised for the interruption.

"Sorry about this," he said. "I won't be a minute."

Marshall then stepped out of the interview room to speak to the detention officer in the relative privacy of the corridor.

Once the interview room door was closed, the detention officer made the reason for the interruption known.

"We've just had a phone call from your office, Mister Marshall. They've been trying to get hold of you," he said. "Your mother has phoned them, she can't reach you either… It's your father, he's been taken to hospital."

A look of shock came over Marshall's face. He was momentarily dumbstruck, causing an enforced moment of silence.

"Did they say why?" Marshall eventually asked.

"I don't know," replied the detention officer. "That's all the details I have, I'm afraid."

Marshall took a moment to consider his options. He could either return to the interview for the remainder of its duration, not knowing exactly how much longer it would take. But he had to consider that he would no longer be best placed to represent his client as his mind would clearly be elsewhere.

Or, he could break with decorum and ask for the interview to be suspended until his services could be replaced by a colleague.

He decided that the latter was the best option for all concerned, especially him.

"Can you ask the officer to pop out for a moment?" Marshall asked of the detention officer.

Given the shocking news and the unexpected reaction it had on him, he didn't want to go back into the interview room himself.

"Of course," the detention officer replied.

He then disappeared into the interview room.

Moments later the interviewing officer emerged. He had left the detention officer in the interview room to supervise the prisoner in his absence, as the prisoner was not meant to be left unsupervised in an interview room.

Marshall then explained the necessity behind the interruption.

"I'm sorry, I've got to go," Marshall said.

Understanding Marshall's predicament, the interviewing officer wholeheartedly agreed.

"It's okay," the officer replied. "We're pretty much done here anyway. I'm sure I can wrap things up in your absence."

Marshall then thanked him for his understanding before leaving.

On his way out, Marshall briefly explained the situation to the custody sergeant, who reiterated the interviewing officer's sentiments.

Once outside, Marshall tried to call his mother to get an update. But her mobile phone went straight to its voicemail facility.

Both of Marshall's parents were technophobes. They had only got broadband the previous year, and that was only for his mother to be able to use the Kindle that Marshall had himself bought for her. Even then, it was he himself who had to set everything up for her, which included her very first email address, which has remained dormant ever since.

So, for the call to go to voicemail was not an indication of anything in itself. It was highly likely that his mother had turned it off, "to save the battery," she would say.

Once Marshall had got into his car, and had connected his mobile phone to the in-car set, he tried to phone his parents at home.

Once that call had rung out for their answer machine to pick up the call, Marshall deduced that they were most likely still at the hospital. He then started to drive towards their local hospital.

Along the way, he phoned his office. But unfortunately, they weren't able to provide him with any more information than the detention officer had already given him.

The next logical step was to phone the hospital itself. But as it turned out, Marshall was on hold to the accident and emergency department reception so long that he had managed to park at the hospital before the call was even answered.

oOo

Once inside the hospital, Marshall didn't need to stop at the reception desk for directions. He was familiar with the layout of the hospital's accident and emergency department, having had to make numerous visits to see clients there over the years.

He would, however, have to attend the nurses' station in order to find out which treatment cubicle his father was in.

However, when he arrived at the nurses' station, there was a lengthy queue of people already ahead of him.

Instead of waiting, and given the urgency of his visit as well as his renowned lack of patience, Marshall took it upon himself to wander the department in the hope of locating his father on his own.

This task did not prove to be too difficult, as one cubicle could be seen from a distance to have a uniformed police officer standing in front of it.

Although the nature of his father's admission had so far eluded him, Marshall was drawn to this cubicle to confirm any relevance before moving on.

As he approached, he felt his heart start to race with anticipation. He was hoping with every cell in his body that the reason police were in the hospital had absolutely nothing to do with his father's admission.

But with every step, the voices within the cubicle became louder and clearer, and it wasn't long before he began to recognise one of them. It was his mother, she was speaking to one of the police officers.

Marshall's heart fell. But as he emerged beyond the closed curtains of the preceding cubicle, his mother saw him. He could see the joy of his arrival had in her eyes.

Upon seeing him, his mother immediately ceased her conversation and stood up, she then rushed over and hugged him.

She remained clinging to his arm at his side as she gave a brief explanation as to why they were all there.

The police officers present remained silent until an appropriate time came for them to continue.

One of them recognised Marshall as being a frequent visitor in his legal representative capacity at their custody centre. But due to the severity of the situation, he withheld any familiarities.

"I was about to begin asking your father about what happened," the officer said.

Marshall knew the urgency by which the police had to acquire as much detail as they could about any incident as quickly as possible. This was with the intent of improving their chances of locating a suspect in a timely fashion in order to secure evidence to support any charges, to ultimately lead to a conviction. As a result, he didn't want to delay the officers in their task.

"Go right ahead," Marshall replied.

The officer then reverted his attention to Marshall's father.

"Do you feel up to speaking to me?" the officer asked.

Marshall looked down at his father. He was struggling to reposition himself on the trolley bed. Marshall could see the pain in his face caused by every movement and breath he took.

His father appeared to be very protective of his left side. He cradled his left forearm, with his right hand across his abdomen, and he was listing slightly to his right.

From this, Marshall deduced that the injuries he had sustained involved either his ribs, his left arm or shoulder.

Marshall's mother could also see the pain and distress her husband was in.

"Can this not wait?" she asked.

Unlike her son, she was unaware of the police processes, or their rationale behind the urgency in which this information was required.

"It's fine," Marshall's father replied. "Let's just get this done."

His wife remained unconvinced, given the grimace on her husband's face as he spoke.

"Okay," the officer began. "First things first. What's your name and your date of birth please?"

Marshall's father then shifted and grimaced once more before replying.

"Leonard John Marshall, the twentieth of June nineteen forty-two," Leonard replied.

"Okay, thank you... So, from the beginning, tell me what happened then?" the officer asked.

Leonard Marshall took a deep breath, which in itself caused him pain.

"Well, I was at home, when there was a knock at the door," he began.

"Do you know approximately what time this was?"

"I would say it was just after six o'clock."

"What makes you say that?"

"The evening news had not long started."

"Okay... So, there was a knock at the door, what happened next?"

"Well, neither of us were expecting anybody. So, I told my wife that it was likely to be the same guy who called on us last week. We had told James about this, and we all agreed not to answer the door to him."

58

"Were there lights on in the house suggesting that someone was home?"

"Unfortunately, yes, that's probably the reason he kept knocking."

"How many times did they knock?"

"I can't say for sure. But then when it stopped, I waited for a moment, then I went to the front window to see if I could see him walking away at all."

"And did you...? See him walking away, I mean?"

"No, he was staring right at me through the living room window."

"Then what did he do?"

"Well, he then disappeared from sight, and I thought that he had now gone... But then I heard my wife scream out. He had gone around the back of the house, to the back door."

"Was the back door locked?"

"No... Seeing him at the back door, my wife then went to lock it, but he burst in before she could get to the door."

"What did you do then?"

"Well, upon hearing her scream, I rushed through to the kitchen as quickly as I could, I saw him standing there. My wife looked terrified."

"What did he do then?"

"On seeing me, he pushed past my wife, knocking her sideways. He then came for me in the hallway."

"Is that where he attacked you?"

"Yes... I was expecting him to make demands, y'know, tell him where we kept the jewellery, or if we had any cash in the house. But he didn't say anything like that."

"How did he assault you?"

"First of all, he pushed me backwards, further down the hallway, away from the kitchen... Then he punched me in the stomach. Then when I was bent over, he hit me to the back of my neck."

"Did you fall to the ground at all?"

"Yes. And when I was on the floor, he kicked me a few times."

"Where did he kick you?"

"It was mainly to the back of my legs, but one caught me higher, in the kidneys."

"Then what did he do?"

"He went upstairs."

"How long would you say he was up there?"

"Not long. Long enough for Pam, my wife to come from the kitchen to help me."

"When he came back down, did he say, or did he do anything more to *either* of you?"

"Not that I recall… When he came back downstairs, he just stared at me, like he was going to hit me again… He then left out of the front door."

"Can you tell me what he looked like?"

"He was a young lad."

"How young would you say?"

"I don't know, maybe in his twenties, maybe a bit older. It's so difficult to tell these days."

"Okay. How tall? And what sort of build did he have?"

"I would say he was about my height."

"And how tall are you?"

"Five foot nine. I don't know, just average build, not skinny at all."

"What colour hair did he have, and any facial hair?"

"He had light brown hair. No facial hair, just hadn't shaved for a few days though."

"How long was his hair?"

"Short, like yours."

"Okay, good. What was he wearing?"

"I didn't really see. It was all over so quickly that I really didn't get a chance to pay much attention to it… I'm sorry."

"Oh, please, don't be sorry, you're doing great. Do you recall if he had gloves on at all?"

"I really couldn't say for sure."

"How long would you say it all lasted from when there was the first knock at the door to when he finally left?"

"Oh, I don't know. The news was still on if that helps."

"Big help. And had you ever seen this man before?"

"Only when he came one evening last week trying to sell us something."

60

"So, it was definitely the same person who came last week then? Can you add anything to your account or description of him based on what happened last week?"

"Not really, I'm afraid. I wasn't really paying him any attention beyond trying to make him leave."

"Why was he there last week?"

"He was trying to sell us something."

"What was he trying to sell you?"

"Oh, it was something to do with a television aerial upgrade or something."

"Okay, that's a new one on me."

The officer then reviewed the account that he had just written down. It wasn't an official police statement. It was what was known as a first account. A statement could be taken at a later time when the victim, Leonard Marshall was out of hospital and in less discomfort.

This account would be used to kickstart the investigation and to act as a memory jogger at a later date.

"Is there anything else that you can add to this, Missus Marshall?" the officer then asked.

"Well, I did hear him say something as he was coming back downstairs," she replied. "It was the only time I heard him speak today."

"And what exactly did he say?" replied the officer with intrigue.

"Oh, it was something along the lines of 'payback's a bitch,' then he left," she said.

"Payback's a bitch," the officer muttered to himself as he jotted down what Mrs Marshall had just told him.

"And you've never seen him *before* last week?" the officer said, addressing his question to them both.

They both shook their heads.

"Well, thank you very much for your time, that's all we need from you at the moment," the officer concluded. "We'll be in touch with you very shortly."

The officer then left with his colleague. They also took with them the clothing they had earlier seized from Marshall's father, which had been placed in brown paper evidence bags.

"What on earth am I going to wear home?" Leonard asked.

Despite everything that had taken place, this was the first question that occurred to him to ask.

"I'll bring you something from home when I come back," his wife replied. "He's not likely to be allowed home tonight, is he?"

This question, which was meant for her son, but was lost on him.

Marshall, having said goodbye and given thanks to the officers, had more compelling issues to contemplate.

"James?" she asked, hoping to regain his attention.

"Yeah?" he eventually replied.

"Is your father likely to have to stay here?" she went on ask.

"I would've thought so," Marshall replied. "He'll probably be kept in overnight, so they can keep an eye on him."

8

Marshall stayed at the hospital until late into the evening. He remained there until his father had been x-rayed, and the full extent of his injuries had been determined.

The only time he left his father's bedside, apart from the scans, was to go outside and update his office, so they could clear his schedule. He went outside not to ensure privacy, but because the cellular reception within the depth of the accident and emergency department was appalling, and outside was the only place that he had the assurance of a strong signal.

The diagnosis was that Leonard Marshall had sustained a mild concussion. But what concerned the medical staff was that he had also sustained a fracture to the left clavicle, or collarbone, and had extensive bruising around the shoulder. This was evidently as a result of him being knocked to the ground and kicked whilst he was down.

Had he been a younger fellow, Leonard would probably have been allowed home that same evening. But given his age, it was decided as purely a precautionary measure to keep him in to allow for continued observations.

It took a lot of persuasion from both Marshall and his father to have his mother leave her husband's bedside. But eventually, she relented and allowed her son to drive her home.

By the time Marshall got home himself, it was nearly midnight. He, in turn, didn't want to leave his mother until he was sure that she was going to be okay at home on her own.

But once he was home, sleep was the last thing on his mind. He couldn't get the comment made by the attacker that his mother added to the police report out of his head: "payback's a bitch."

Just the words used in such circumstances conjured up a variety of possible motives behind them.

Primarily, Marshall considered that the motive was because his parents had suggested that the attacker come back after his failed first visit. Then when he did, they refused to open the door to him, and his motive was nothing more than they had intentionally wasted his time.

But as his thoughts then focused as to why there was such a rapid escalation in the assailant's behaviour and the ferocity of the attack. Marshall began to explore other options before finally settling on the last remaining plausible, yet most disturbing explanation.

Were his parents targeted solely because they were *his* parents? Was the payback motivated by *him*, and *not* his parents?

Marshall started to wrack his brain. He tried to recollect any previous clients that he had represented where things hadn't gone to plan. Or where things were left with some animosity being felt towards him.

Off the top of his head, Marshall was unable to draw any immediate conclusions. But he felt there was only one way in which to explore this as an option.

oOo

Marshall spent the rest of the night going through his case file history. Over the course of his career as a criminal solicitor he had amassed a significant number of clients, and as a result there was a gargantuan amount of associated paperwork. His intention was to attempt to identify a suspect which he could then pass details of to the police to in order to assist them in their investigation into his father's attack.

When the full extent of his client history was apparent to him, he wasn't surprised to discover that he had no recollection as to any grudge or hostility felt towards him, or even the method, or *modus operandi*, being used in the way the attacker had approached his parents.

As Marshall had progressed through his case history, he first gave scrutiny to those where the verdict didn't go the client's way. Where they had been found guilty despite all efforts and given a custodial sentence.

Those cases which qualified under this criterion were then set aside and were given even greater scrutiny. But, given the guilty verdict, and subsequent sentencing, Marshall concluded that a number of these clients were still incarcerated.

This wouldn't necessarily rule them out completely, as a determined individual could always get someone on the outside to do their dirty work for them. But in order to cover as much ground as possible, Marshall moved on, at least for the time being.

During his career, he had dealt with defendants who had been charged with a vast array of offences. They ranged from summary-only offences dealt with solely at magistrates' court, all the way up to those charged with rape and murder, resulting in crown court trials.

But they all had at least two things in common. Firstly, the presumption of innocence until proven otherwise. Added to which, Marshall had to represent each client to the best of his ability without passion or prejudice.

Due to being engrossed in his research, Marshall lost all track of time. He only realised how long he had been up when his morning alarm on his mobile phone went off. It was set to go off at 05:30hrs.

Having realised that he had been up all night, he knew he couldn't face a day in custody.

He didn't have any court hearings, so he knew that he would be top of the list should his firm of solicitors have to provide one on the duty rotation.

He sent his secretary a text message, which read;

> I ended up spending most of the night at the hospital. I won't be in today. I'll work from home. Will call later...

Marshall got up from where he had left his files strewn across the living room floor to stretch his legs. But as he got up, he kicked his coffee cup over. The dregs left in the bottom splashed across a few of the files.

"Fucking hell," he said, cursing himself out loud.

Then having returned from the kitchen with a tea towel, he proceeded to clear the untarnished files to one side. After that he began dabbing the liquid from the spoilt files, before finally patting the carpet dry.

Lastly, Marshall laid out the damp files across his dining table for them to dry out completely, with the collected stack of unaffected files beside them.

He then chucked the coffee-stained tea towel down on the kitchen floor in front of the washing machine, before finally retreating upstairs for some sleep.

9

It had gone midday by the time Marshall awoke from his impromptu sleep, and given the events of the previous day, the last thing that he wanted to focus on was work.

Instead, the first thing he did, whilst making himself a coffee, was to call his mother.

"Did you sleep okay?" he asked.

"Hardly a wink," she replied. "The house felt so big, and so lonely."

Marshall could feel his mother's pain. The house where his parents lived was the same house that Marshall and his sister were brought home to from the hospital after their births.

His parents had never felt any compulsion to move for the sake of it. They were financially stable, so they did not have to consider the need for downsizing either.

It had been his parents' home for over fifty years, and his mother could count the times she had been there overnight on her own on the fingers of one hand.

"If you want," Marshall began to suggest. "I could come and stay over, or you could always come stay at mine."

"No, I'll be fine," she stubbornly replied. "I'm sure tonight will be a lot easier."

Marshall had expected that response. But he felt better having at least made the offer. It gave his mother options should that night not turn out to be any better.

"Are you planning on going to see dad today?" Marshall asked.

"Well, I would like to," she replied. "It's just that getting there is so tricky. I was planning to go tomorrow."

"Okay, well how's about I pick you up in an hour or so, and we go together?" Marshall suggested.

Once again, his mother replied on instinct as opposed to having taken time to contemplate the question.

"Oh, I don't want to put you out," she replied, again dismissing the offer.

"Well, I was going anyway," Marshall said, although this wasn't the truth. "And you're not that far outta my way to pick you up."

"Oh, all right then," his mother replied, eventually relenting. "I'll be ready in an hour."

oOo

It was fifty-four minutes later when Marshall pulled up in front of his parents' house. But instead of having the time to park up and approach the front door, he found his mother was already waiting at the end of the driveway for him.

"How did I know you'd be there waiting for me?" he joked as she got into the car beside him.

Once they got to the hospital, but before going to visit Leonard on the ward that he had been transferred to, both Marshall and his mother stopped at the nurses' station to enquire as to an update of his condition.

Following the decision to keep him in for observations, he was moved onto a ward. This was a preferential environment for him to recuperate as it was quieter and calmer, compared to the bustle and stress that was A&E.

"As you know he was diagnosed with a concussion," the nurse began. "Well, this appears to be slightly more serious than we previously gauged it to be."

Fearing that further bad news was coming, Marshall felt his mother take hold of his hand with both of hers.

"When we checked on him last night, he was complaining of a chronic headache," the nurse continued. "We administered pain relief, but this didn't appear to appease it in any way... We then did some basic cognitive function tests to determine his memory recall, and this *did* appear to be somewhat impaired... We then scheduled him for a CT scan, but that appears to be all clear... We're gonna be keeping him in for a few more days, just to keep an eye on him."

Marshall felt his mother's grip on his hand loosen. His first instinct was that his mother was about to faint. Instead, much to his relief, it was just the opposite, she was relieved by the update. It was likely that everything that was said was better than her own prognosis.

Marshall and his mother then went in to visit Leonard. They stayed on the ward for the entire duration of the visiting period.

However, Marshall, made an excuse of having to make a couple of phone calls in order to allow his parents to have some time alone together. As once again, he knew that any direct offer to give them some privacy would be dismissed by either or both of them.

Again, at the end of visiting hours, Marshall stepped away to allow his parents to again have some privacy. Even at his age, he felt awkward watching them kiss. As far as he was concerned, the stork had delivered him to the cabbage patch.

Once his mother had stepped away, Marshall moved in and planted a kiss on the top of his father's head.

"I'll try to get back before the weekend if I can," Marshall said. "But I've got to get some time in at the office... See you soon."

10

The following day, a Wednesday, Marshall felt he no longer had any excuses to avoid going to work.

He knew his father was on the mend, and as a result his mother was also feeling better.

But, once again, he knew he didn't have anything pressing to do in the office, so consequently he would be nominated to attend custody if a duty solicitor was required from his firm.

However, this was fortuitous, as Marshall was hoping he would have the opportunity to speak to an officer involved in his father's case, to see if there had been any developments.

Unfortunately, there had been a large public order incident the previous evening, which had resulted in a significant number of people getting arrested.

So, on this occasion, Marshall's time in custody was taken up by literally going from representing one prisoner to the next.

This meant that during his time there, he was kept busy, but it also meant that it went relatively quickly.

He was also potentially able to secure future representation for the prisoners, when they would most likely have to return having been released under investigation. This was a necessity, as in this case, the investigating officers needed to obtain statements from witnesses, as well as scrutinise the CCTV footage they had to still obtain of the incident. But, still receiving an update on his father's investigation eluded him.

It was a convenience that those he had represented were RUI, because that meant that there weren't any immediate preparations required for any imminent court hearings. This effectively gave Marshall the rare event of having a weekday evening to himself.

Given that eventuality, Marshall decided to try and get the update for himself by other means.

He knew that phoning the police station would be pointless because he was not an involved party. He was not a victim or a witness to the incident, or even a next of kin. As a result, there was no need for the investigating officer to pass any information of the active investigation to him.

But Marshall was hoping the personal touch, and being a familiar face, as being known to the officers as being a relative of the victim, would be more productive if he attended a police station in person. With that in mind, he decided to take a detour via the police station on his way home.

By the time Marshall had finally left the custody centre, it was late into the evening, it was now dark, made even more so by heavy clouds. Even the dense foliage of the trees was combating the yellowish glow provided by streetlights.

As he pulled up in front of the police station, he saw that none of the visitors' parking bays by the front office were free.

Given the parking restrictions on the roads immediately around the police station, Marshall found he had to park a short distance away, in a residential road, and walk back to the police station to make his enquiries.

As he walked to the station, he saw a figure walking in the opposite direction. They appeared to have come from the police station themselves, but they crossed over the road only to be lost in the shadows before they ever got close enough to be recognisable.

Having attended the front office, and made his request, it turned out there was no one available at the police station at that time to speak to him.

However, the member of staff who was working the front office gave Marshall the name and extension number for the officer in charge of the investigation, and suggested that he leave him a message to have return contact made. With that, Marshall left.

As Marshall walked back to his car, he did take a moment to notice how eerily quiet it had become.

But it was only when he got back to his car that the deathly silence was broken.

Just as he unlocked his car, and took hold of the handle to pull open the door, he heard a voice speak from somewhere behind him.

"Hey Marshall," a voice said. "That's a pretty fucking flash car you got there… You pay for that with the money you got for selling me out?"

Marshall instinctively turned in the direction of the voice. It was then that he saw a man step out from the shadows. He was only then given vague illumination from the sole streetlight in the road.

Still not knowing who was addressing him, Marshall gave a generalistic response.

"I don't know what you mean?" Marshall replied.

As the figure got closer, Marshall could finally identify the man before him.

He recognised him to be Robert Fraser, as he kept walking towards Marshall until he was standing menacingly close to him.

"You fucking solicitors are all the same. You're scum, *fucking* leaches," Fraser continued. "You're only in it for the fucking money. You don't give a shit about your clients… You could leave us there to rot in prison for all you fucking care… You weren't there for me when I needed you. I got fucking remanded for that, was in *all fucking weekend* until court on the Monday. Got bailed from there though. Got me signing on now too, that's the only fucking reason I'm here."

Despite Fraser's rant, Marshall knew his current predicament had nothing to do with him. But in order to appease the situation, he knew he had to offer a response.

"I don't know what you're talking about," he replied.

Uncertain as to what was about to happen, Marshall again locked his car using the remote.

The flash of the indicators lit up Fraser's face in a fiery orange, which made him look even more menacing.

"You fucking owe me," Fraser said. "A whole weekend by my reckoning."

"Wait a minute," Marshall replied, questioning Fraser's motivation. "Owe you for what…? Why?"

Fraser then squared up to Marshall, effectively forming a blockade preventing Marshall from escaping from beside his car without having to squeeze through the minimal space that Fraser had afforded him.

Suddenly the idea of locking himself out of his car no longer seemed like a good idea. It seemed to be a character flaw of his, putting material objects before people.

"What is it you want?" Marshall resigned himself to ask. "Is it money you want?"

"No, I don't want your *blood* money," Fraser replied. "Y'know, there's more than one way to pay a debt... I'll take terror in trade."

With that, Fraser smiled, showing what left he had in the way of decaying teeth, before he turned and disappeared back into the same shadows from whence he came.

Marshall fumbled with his keys in his haste to unlock the car and get inside. This had affected him more than he had thought.

Once inside, he immediately locked the doors before doing anything else. Eventually, having once composed himself, he started the engine, and left the area as quickly as possible.

It was only once he had returned to the safety and sanctuary of his home, did Marshall allow himself to relive what had just happened.

It was only then did it occur to him what Fraser had actually said to him, the exact phraseology that he had used.

"Pay a debt," Marshall repeated for his own benefit. "There's more than one way to *pay a debt.*"

He then struggled to recall the comment that his mother had made previously to the police officer whilst at the hospital. The comment his father's attacker had said before leaving their house. Then the words came to him.

"Payback's a bitch," he whispered when the words had finally occurred to him.

Payback... Pay a debt... Payback... Pay a debt," he repeated over and over, as if the mere mention of the words would eventually unveil a subliminal connection.

With that, Marshall went through to the dining room, where he had left the files on the table two nights earlier.

He found Fraser's to be amongst those that had been left out to dry due to coffee saturation. It had dried, and was now being subjected to even closer scrutiny.

However, Marshall couldn't make a valid connection between the recent events in custody and Fraser's need to make threats towards him.

The timeline of events certainly allowed for Fraser's involvement. Had he been remanded on the Friday when Marshall saw him in custody, and kept in all weekend until the first available court hearing on the following Monday, he could well have been released in time to attend his parents' address later that same day. But this would have meant that Fraser had first attended their address mid-week, being *before* the events in custody.

He was sure there must be something more to this. It was too much of a coincidence to just dismiss it.

This also raised another dilemma, should Marshall report what had just happened to the police? If he chose to, it would mean that Fraser would be arrested, and if charged, it would probably result in him remanded, having offended whilst on bail issued by the court.

For what had started out to be a fairly straightforward day, it had turned into something of a nightmare

11

"How are you feeling?" Marshall asked, as he sat down beside his father bed.

He was still in hospital, and still being kept in for observations on the same ward where Marshall and his mother had last visited him.

Although this was preferable to him being in A&E in many respects. There were still downsides. The main one was now having to abide by stipulated visiting hours.

In his ward bed, Leonard Marshall struggled to reposition himself further up the bed, so to be able to raise the head of the bed mechanically. He wanted to be in a more upright and seated position, which was more comfortable and practical for which to talk to his son.

"I've been better," his father replied. "It still hurts to move."

Marshall didn't need his father to explain such his symptoms. He saw how his manoeuvring on the bed had caused him to yet again grimace in pain.

"Well, the staff here are certainly happy with the progress you've been making," Marshall said. "All going well, they said you should be able to go home tomorrow."

"That's good," his father replied. "Because I'll put money on it that your mother is already making a list of things that she needs me to do when I get home... Y'know, when I saw you coming in, I was half expecting her to be with you?"

This was the first time that Marshall had attended the hospital without his mother being there.

"No, it's Thursday, she has bingo this evening," Marshall began to explain. "Besides that, I was hoping we could have a chat about something. Y'know, just you and me?"

Seeing a look of concern on his father's face, Marshall felt the need to clarify the situation somewhat in order to immediately put his father's mind at ease.

"Don't worry, it's got nothing to do with Nicky or the kids," Marshall said. "It's kinda to do with what happened to you, *and* a few other things too."

The explanation had done nothing to quell his father's concern. But, nonetheless, his son had his full attention.

"I just don't know if I'm cut out for this job anymore," Marshall declared. "Once upon a time it was exhilarating, getting the buzz from winning in court, and all that. But, now, dealing with these shitbags day in and day out... It gets to you."

At hearing this, his father took, much to his surprise, a pain-free deep breath before replying.

"James, we've been here before," his father began. "Remember when things first started going bad for you and Nicky, we had a similar conversation? And I'm sure we would reach similar conclusions now as we did back then, nothing has changed... You just dug deep before, and carried on, and..."

"And I lost my family because of it," Marshall said, cutting his father off in mid-sentence. "I don't feel I can leave my work at the office anymore. I feel that it's beginning to infest my entire life now."

"How do you mean?" his father asked.

"Like I said, when I first started out, the victories in court felt great... But over time, you just end up defending the same people over and over again, and these aren't good people... You hear them blaming everybody for what they've done, the courts, the police, society, even me... Never once taking responsibility for themselves. They make promises to the courts that you know they won't keep. So, then they're freed to once again commit further crimes and ruin yet more lives," Marshall said despairingly. "And you know what...? *I* do feel responsible. *I* feel that if I hadn't helped in getting them off, having challenged and discredited witnesses, having evidence dismissed, then they could've been found guilty and taken off the streets."

"Could've," his father interjected. "That's the operative word... Could've, there would never be any guarantee that of any of them would be found guilty. *You* were *not* responsible for anything these people chose to do. They made their own choices, *not* you!"

Marshall took a moment to ponder his next response. He repositioned himself in the chair beside the bed, before continuing.

"One lesson we had at law school explained that there are necessary elements required for a crime to take place," Marshall began. "*Every crime requires three elements: a victim, an offender and the opportunity. Take away just one of those elements and the crime can't take place...* I gave society the offender back, and I also gave the offender their opportunity."

His father could see the logic in his son's remark. Although he could see the flaws in his son's attempt in using this theory to bolster the shame he felt.

"Now, let's get something straight, just because you helped them to be put back on the streets, doesn't make you responsible for what happened next," his father said. "You merely gave them another chance to make something good of their lives... And if they then chose to again squander that chance, well, that's not down to you to shoulder any responsibility, or guilt."

Leonard then remained intentionally silent for a moment, in order to allow his son to absorb his wisdom.

"So, what are you going to do then?" he said when he was ready to continue. "What do you think your options are?"

Marshall always respected the way his father would never just come out with a solution to any problem, unless it was his own.

He would always make Marshall and his sister come up with their own options, and then decide the perils and pitfalls of each, before eventually deciding on an appropriate course of action.

His philosophy was that if anyone else provided a solution, they were also effectively making themselves a scapegoat should things not pan out as desired, with the person who took the advice blaming the person who gave the solution to them.

But, by coming up with one's own solutions, should it go awry, then one only has themselves to blame. It was a sound philosophy, and had always sat right with Marshall. That was why he wanted to speak to his father alone, as his mother, despite best intentions would serve only to cloud the issue.

"The way I see it is this, I have two options," Marshall began, showing that he had already given this matter significant thought prior to this conversation. "In its most basic form, I can either stay working in criminal law, or I can requalify to take on another aspect in my office."

His father remained silent. He was expecting a more engineered response, rather than just *take it or leave it*.

"Or... I could apply to the CPS, and train to become a prosecutor. But that would mean a significant pay-cut..."

"This is all well and good, James," his father replied. "But you're forgetting one glaring omission"

"What's that then?" Marshall replied insolently.

"Starting afresh is only part of your troubles... Everything that you've described that is eating you up is in your past, in the decisions you've already made... Sure, you can avoid being in a position where similar decisions are made in your future, but what's to stop your past continuing to haunt you?"

Marshall took a moment to contemplate his father's truthful remark.

"There's absolutely nothing I can do about that," Marshall replied. "What's done is done."

"Are you absolutely sure about that?" his father asked.

"I don't know what you mean?" Marshall replied.

"Oh, I'm sure you do," his father exclaimed. "Give it time, I'm sure the penny *will* drop for you... Anyway, what happened to me isn't what brought you to these conclusions... Now don't bullshit me son, what's the *real* reason you're here?"

Marshall knew that when his father used profanities, it was not the time to fool around, or *bullshit* him, as he so eloquently chose to phrase it.

"Fair enough... It's two things," Marshall began. He took a deep breath before continuing. "It was the other night I went to the police station to try and get an update on your investigation... Then afterwards, as I was walking back to my car, I was threatened by a past client of mine... I didn't think all that much of it at the time, I mean, similar things have kinda happened before... But, given the timing of it, and precisely what he said... I dunno, I'm feeling it may in some way be connected to what happened to you and mum."

His father now looked concerned, confused, and angered over this possible revelation. Not at his son for being the possible cause of him being in hospital. But that his son was now himself being threatened.

"This guy said I *owed* him, and that *there was more than one way to pay a debt*," Marshall began to explain in order to clarify his point. "Mum said your guy said *payback's a bitch* or something… And for these two things to happen only days apart, I'm starting to feel that this is more than just a coincidence."

Once again there was a moment of silence, as responses were being considered before being shared.

"And what did the police say about this?" his father asked.

"Nothing, I haven't told them anything about this, not *yet* anyway," Marshall said. "I need to get my facts straight first. I mean, if these things aren't connected, the last thing I want to do is cause any unnecessary escalation."

"So, what *are* you going to do then?" he father then asked.

"At the moment, I just don't know," Marshall replied. "Just take it one day at a time, I guess… Do some digging, and see what I can find out, but generally, see what pans out."

"That sounds fair enough," his father replied. "But, if I were you, I'd have some contingencies planned too… Y'know, just in case."

Marshall nodded in agreement. His father knew him too well, he was never one to leave things to chance, and tended to have taken contingencies into consideration, and have planned accordingly.

With the topic at hand at a conclusion, the conversation rapidly started to wane.

Marshall's visit was concluded by having his father promise to call him when he was being discharged, so that he could attend the hospital and take him home, and not be the cantankerous old sod he expected him to be and insist on getting a taxi.

After that was agreed, Marshall leant over and again kissed his father's forehead before leaving.

oOo

On the way home, a glint from reflected streetlight onto something metallic in the centre console of the Mercedes caught Marshall's eye.

Without slowing, he fumbled in the area of the console to find the object that was attracting his attention. Once located, he held it up in front of his forward-facing vision.

It was a single car key. It was Foster's car key. Albert Foster, habitual drink driver. A man who had played a subliminal part in the conversation that Marshall had just had with his father. A man who had bullshitted a court on many an occasion to avoid harsh sentencing.

Most recently, having acquired Marshall's assistance, Foster had managed to convince a court to keep his driving licence, and receiving only the inconvenience of a three-month ban.

He was a habitual offender with numerous convictions against him. A man with such a compulsion that he didn't even have the self-control to not drive during his ban. To such an extent, that he felt he had to give the key to his own car to his solicitor to prevent this from happening.

Foster was a typical example of the sort of man that Marshall had facilitated the opportunity to reoffend, time and time again, and Marshall felt that it was only a matter of time before Foster's offending ruined lives.

Marshall closed his fist around the key. An idea that he shouldn't be entertaining was beginning to play out for its own amusement.

It was then that it occurred to him that maybe this was what his father was alluding to when he spoke about righting decisions already made?

12

Having got home, all Marshall could do was sit at his dining table staring at the array of case files still strewn across it.

Although they had long since dried out from having coffee accidentally spilt on them, he had still not collected them up, or sorted them in any way. Instead, he just reviewed the names, dates, and offence types on the front cover of each file.

The dates covered his entire defence career with his current firm, and the offences covered everything from public order, through all the levels of assaults and burglaries, all the way up to stranger rapes. His case load even consisted of a murder charge. This case had been his crowning achievement.

That case had involved a man by the name of Victor Bergstrom. He had been charged with causing the intentional death of another man. The other man being Bergstrom's father.

The methodology of the killing was by means of an intentionally large dose of Warfarin being administered.

Warfarin is an anticoagulant, a blood thinner, which is used to treat or prevent blood clots in veins or arteries, in an attempt reduce the risk of strokes, heart attacks, or other serious conditions.

However, in the case against Bergstrom, he was accused of having administered a hugely excessive dose to his father.

This had resulted in exsanguination, massive blood loss, when his father haemorrhaged internally and bled out whilst sat on the toilet.

The crowning achievement was that Marshall had been able to have the case against Victor Bergstrom dismissed. He knew the crown's case against Bergstrom was ambitious, as soon as they had chosen to charge him with murder.

That being the case, all Marshall had to do was to establish reasonable doubt as far as any premeditation went. After that, securing a dismissal was easy.

Had the prosecution chosen to charge Bergstrom with the lesser offence of manslaughter, then the ambiguity over premeditation would no longer have been irrelevant, making Marshall task of securing a not guilty verdict or even an acquittal all the more difficult.

It was Marshall's sole role and responsibility to represent his clients to the best of his ability. For him to do that, he knew from day one as a defence solicitor that he would have to check his sense of morality at the door.

The Bergstrom case was like so many others that he had fought in court. A case where he knew the defendant, his client, was guilty as charged before they even stepped foot inside the courtroom.

But the evidence wasn't there to prove the crown's case. Had it been, then Marshall's job would have been a lot more difficult, and his success rate would be far less than what it was. With the Bergstrom case, as with so many others, Marshall had received an admission of guilt from the accused themselves at some point during the proceedings.

The confidential relationship between a lawyer and their client, sometimes called privilege, is an assurance of confidentiality which forms the basis of the profession.

It doesn't matter what the client admits to his or her lawyer: they are not guilty of an offence under the eyes of the law until they are convicted.

As per the adage "innocent until proven guilty," the defendant remains not guilty until the verdict has been ruled under law.

For so long, Marshall had enjoyed the spoils his success had earned him. But it was the knowledge accrued from this success that was now tearing him apart inside.

He had gained a formidable reputation as a defender from an early stage in his career, and as a result he found that his skills were called upon more than most.

However, this had the consequence that entered him into a vicious cycle, being assigned case after case after case, with little in the way of respite in between.

It was when his ambition became an obsession that his wife made the decision to leave him. But instead of being a wake-up call, and regardless of the earlier talk with his father, it merely fuelled his desire to lose himself in his work even more, though now the distinction was clouded between his career aspirations, and his work merely being a distraction to the painful experience of his divorce and losing his children.

Despite all this, his own morality never factored in any of his decisions whether or not to accept a case. To Marshall, every case was winnable, and as a result, he accepted every case that was offered to him.

But those days were now well and truly behind him. Although he was still surrounded by the fruits of his labours, none of it was any consolation to how he was feeling.

Marshall looked down at the filed representation of his career, something of which he was once proud. But instead, he now hung his head in shame.

He took Foster's car key from his pocket and placed it down on the table next to the files.

For a moment he again contemplated the idea which he had nurtured following his father's conception of it.

Marshall went through to the sideboard and poured himself a whisky. He stood sipping from the glass as he viewed the array of case files that had been left on the dining table. Next to them also lay Foster's key, just waiting to be involved somehow.

For a moment, Marshall considered the options he had suggested to his father; to becoming a prosecutor, or to consider another legal role within his office. Then his father's response came to him, "but what's to stop your past continuing to haunt you?"

It was then that the penny did drop. Marshall took another sip from his glass before setting it down on the dining table. He went back over to the sideboard, where he picked up a framed picture of himself with his children. It was a picture that been taken in a local pizza restaurant on the first fathers' day following his separation from their mother.

It was the only framed picture he had of himself and his children. It was also one that Nicky herself had taken, as it was during the time that she had concerns about leaving the children alone with him.

This was a measure that she had chosen to put in place, as although she didn't want to deny him access to the children, or them to their father, she believed him to be irrational and unpredictable. Which not only contributed to her decision to end their marriage, but also felt was compounded in the fallout of the same decision.

As he held the picture, he contemplated all the thoughts of the past, bringing them into the present, and believed how they could lead into his future, and these thoughts terrified him.

He then gave further consideration that maybe the attack on his parents was merely the beginning of something greater and far more vindictive. Given how loquacious he had been with clients, in order to set them at ease and to build the all-important rapport, he had talked openly about his personal life and his family. He wondered if such a predator who would target an elderly couple in order to get back at him, would go on to also target his children.

He remembered snippets of conversations he'd had with a past clients, where he had discussed his children's successes in the classroom and at sports, and the failure of his marriage, and how disparaging he had been about his wife. He then recalled on one occasion, his client said that he "could have someone pull out her fingernails for fifty quid." Although this was probably intended to be a joke, it obviously came with very sinister undertones.

As this notion began to consume him, so did his emotions begin to have a subconscious physical effect on him, and unbeknown to him, his muscles began to tighten. This tension through his arms contorted the photo frame, until it flexed to such an extent that the glass cracked beneath where his thumbs rested on it.

The cracked glass caused a laceration across Marshall's right thumb. Blood immediately flowed from the wound and penetrated the crack in the glass. The forces applied to the frame had caused a void to emerge between the glass and the photograph, this allowed the blood to spread across the photograph, and across the face of one of his children, covering it entirely. Marshall looked at this image as if it showed them as a prophesied victim of some dastardly deed yet to befall them. This fantasised image had a startling effect on Marshall.

He fell to his knees, dropping the frame, allowing it to fall to the floor in front of him. This caused the glass to shatter completely. He stared at the gruesome image of himself and his family behind shattered glass.

To Marshall, the broken and bloodied image before him was eerily reminiscent of images of road traffic collisions, such as those he had seen during the trials of past clients that he had defended on charges of drink or dangerous driving. However, he saw this as not being as the result of any past accident, but as a prophecy.

Supporting his upper body weight on his left arm, Marshall raised his injured right hand above his head. Then as he looked down at the image of himself with his children, he pinched his injured thumb against his fist, then watched as droplets of blood rained down upon the faces of himself and his children.

Marshall laid himself down besides the photo frame. Then after a few moments, he fumbled with a hand in the space next to him until he located it. Having found it, he pushed it against his side until he had raised it from the carpet sufficiently to pick it up. As he lifted it, shattered glass fell from the frame. Then holding the frame with both hands, Marshall held it aloft in front of him to again look upon the image.

As the blood had yet to clot, puddles formed into droplets, and a few fell from the photograph onto his face. One landed on his cheek, just below his eye, and Marshall felt the cold as it ran down his face like a tear.

He then held the picture frame close to his chest, and felt his heartbeat resonate against it.

Having seen the bloody image of all those he held dearest was the trigger that allowed the irrational to suddenly become rational. Maybe this was what Nicky had foreseen, and maybe this was the reason she had concerns about his mental stability.

It was then that a thought occurred to him, and that thought required immediate action.

He was up from his floor like a bullet, having cast aside his precious possession.

Marshall grabbed his coat, and was out of the front door.

13

Marshall had left his home in the dead of night to drive to Noakes Road. Once there, he parked up, and got out of his car.

The first thing he then did, before even taking a single step away from his car, was to listen. Noakes Road itself at that time of night, was blissfully quiet.

Marshall looked at his watch, it was just after midnight. Even being a weekday, there was no reason why it should be anything other than peacefully quiet.

In fact, the only noise to be heard was a dull hum of activity which was emanating from behind a row of houses, where beyond their gardens laid the properties of the High Street.

But Marshall wasn't interested in what Noakes Road had to offer, and he certainly wasn't interested in venturing as far as the High Street. What interested him, and his reason for being here at that time of night lay somewhere in between.

Unfortunately for Marshall, somewhere was the operative word. He knew what he was looking for, but he only had a very rough idea as to where he might find it.

From his file regarding the interview he had attended following Brett Cable's arrest on suspicion of the GBH attack on Paul Greene, Marshall had jotted down what Cable had told him regarding the whereabouts of the only outstanding piece of physical evidence in the case. This was the claw hammer that Cable found and used to inflict Greene's injuries.

The note that Marshall had scribbled down simply read;

Threw hammer over fence into School playing field.

Marshall was somewhat familiar with the area. But with that knowledge also came the extent of the dilemma that faced him. The reality of which became abundantly clear as he walked along the alleyway towards the High Street.

The alleyway was a good two hundred metres from one end to the other. On one side, the majority of the length of the alleyway backed onto the playground for a junior school that was normally accessible from a road that linked Noakes Road to the High Street. The opposite side of the alleyway ran across the back of the service yard to a garage.

The only saving grace that Marshall had from the police investigation was that no weapon had been found. He knew from the police that a search dog had been deployed into the school grounds. But, despite that, nothing had been located.

Marshall therefore concluded that if Cable was telling the truth, and Marshall had no reason to believe that he wasn't, that if the hammer had been thrown into the school grounds, then it hadn't fallen to ground level.

Without any firm evidence to suggest that the weapon was in the school grounds, the police dog would have conducted a cursory search of the school and the garage, and it would have been left at that.

This led Marshall to conclude that the hammer must have been caught on something above ground level, in a tree perhaps. So that would form the basis of his search.

There was also no doubt in Marshall's mind that the police would make contact with the school, requesting that should such an item be found, to then retrieve it and inform them. However, he would not be privy to this update until he returned to further represent Cable.

So, in the absence of anything to the contrary, he would proceed as planned.

From the alleyway, Marshall scrutinised the six-foot tall chicken wire fence that ran along the back of the school for areas of weakness. He was looking for any points that could gain him easier access to the school grounds without doing too much in the way of damage to the fence, and compromising the security of the school.

Marshall knew that what he was doing was both illegal and unethical.

Although he was contemplating trespassing into the school grounds, this was only a civil offence as opposed to criminal one. That is, unless the intrusion had an unlawful mitigating factor as stated under the historical legislation of the Vagrancy Act 1824, which made use of such terms as "rogue and vagabond."

Despite the legality of the trespass, Marshall's intentions were, however, criminal and unethical. As he was intending to locate and remove evidence of a crime, for which he could face charges of perverting the course of justice, and also face disbarment under the Bar Council, the governing body which represents solicitors and barristers in England and Wales.

Without causing any damage, Marshall found a way to negotiate the fence. In the corner, where the school boundary met with that of residential gardens, the corner post was reinforced with a diagonal support. This allowed Marshall to scale the fence without causing any damage to the fence, or injury to himself.

Once in the grounds, it was a case of narrowing the search parameters. Marshall knew the police had stated that they had deployed a police dog unit to search the grounds. But they didn't know what they were looking for, if anything.

They simply based their search on the assumption that a weapon had been used to inflict the injuries to Greene. They then had to be seen to make sufficient efforts to locate such a weapon for the sake of the investigation, and it was most likely deemed that searching school grounds was less intrusive at that time of night to searching residential gardens and waking the occupants.

With that in mind, Marshall felt he could initially rule out any searching at ground level. If anything had fallen to the ground, he was fairly sure that the police dog would have located it on the night, or the school since.

He began by walking the tree line that hid the houses from the school, and insulated them from the noise of the playground.

He stayed on the house side of the trees so that that any light from his torch would be shone away from the houses, in the hopes that it would be less likely to alert anyone within them to the activity in the school grounds.

Marshall followed the line of trees until it ceased. It was only then that he realised just how far he had walked from the alleyway. He looked back in the direction he had come from. He had covered a distance of at least one-hundred metres.

"There's no way he could've thrown the hammer this far," Marshall muttered to himself. "Prick!"

This insult was directed at himself as opposed to Cable. He was disappointed that he had wasted time in searching outside of the prophesised search area.

This was wasting valuable time, and given his location and the task at hand, every second he was there longer than he absolutely had to be, just increased his chances of being caught.

Marshall then retraced his steps back towards the fence. He knew that this would be his last chance of finding the hammer. He wouldn't be able to waste any more time on this, not on this occasion anyway.

As Marshall made his way back towards the alleyway, the lights from the street in front of the school were now behind him. With that changed perspective, it was as he glanced up at the trees that he saw a glint of light reflecting off of something metallic. But as he got closer to the supporting tree, he completely lost sight of his goal.

Marshall had to take a few steps backwards in order to reclaim his line of sight on the object. He then had to hypothesise as to which tree was attached to the branch on which this object rested.

The trees were fairly young Poplars, which meant that once Marshall had found the tree in question, he should be able to push on the trunk and cause the whole tree to sway, hopefully releasing the item.

He repeated this until the hammer was eventually dislodged and fell to the ground. As it fell, it narrowly missed Marshall before landing on the grass with a dull thud.

Marshall was now back on track. The variables of actually locating the hammer were now behind him.

He picked up the hammer from the ground, having first put his hand into an inside out zip-lock bag. Then once he had picked up the hammer, he turned the bag right-side out before sealing it up for transportation.

With his objective achieved, Marshall immediately headed back to the corner of the fence. Having checked that the coast was clear, he again used the corner support to help him back get up and over the fence.

Once back in the alleyway, he allowed himself a brief moment to catch his breath before walking back along the alleyway towards Noakes Road.

Although his actions would now appear to be wholly innocent, he paused before emerging from the alleyway, having seen a milk float approaching.

Marshall maintained his position, keeping his eyes on the milkman until he was out of sight.

Marshall then casually walked back to his car. From there, he headed home.

oOo

Once home, he placed the hammer, still in its bag down on the dining table next to Foster's car key.

Without anything more to be considered or achieved that night, Marshall went to bed, only to lay awake for some time, further contemplating the uncontemplatable.

14

"Mister Garmin, you stand before this court having previously pleaded *not guilty* to the charges of accumulating and distributing indecent images of children categorised as being extreme in nature," the judge read out the charges against the defendant. "Before this trial commences, do you wish to change your plea?"

Garmin stood in the crown court dock dressed immaculately in a bespoke suit. This somewhat diminished the efforts of his legal representation, James Marshall, who sat between him and the judge addressing him.

At this stage of the trial, the court itself consisted of only the defendant, his representation, the crown prosecutor, clerk of the court, usher and the judge himself. No jury wasn't present, as they were not needed at this stage, and should a guilty plea be entered into the record, then their need could be averted.

However, Garmin remained mute. He declined to offer a reply, he made no indication to even hear the judge's question.

Marshall turned to face his client. The look of urgency on Marshall's face gave some indication that Garmin needed to show the court some respect and vocalise a response.

From the bench, the judge could see what he could only deduce to be a non-verbal disagreement between the two men.

In the interest of not wasting the court's time, he felt compelled to expedite the conversation in order to address the question at hand.

It was then that Marshall stood in order to show respect whilst addressing the court.

"Your honour," Marshall began. "the defendant wishes to change his plea."

This plea change had been based on numerous discussions between Marshall and Garmin, and Marshall had felt they had reached an accord in deciding to mitigate the damage caused by sentencing by entering a *guilty* plea.

"Very well, let it be noted that the defendant wishes to plead no contest to the charges against him," the judge reiterated.

"Like fuck, do I," erupted Garmin. "No *way* am I admitting to that horseshit. You told me we had a chance to fight this shit, so fight it we will."

Disappointed at the outburst, Marshall had to recomposed himself before once again turning to face the bench.

"Your honour," he sighed. "We would like to reaffirm our plea of *not* guilty."

"Not guilty it is," replied the judge. "In that case, court will be adjourned until ten o'clock on Wednesday morning."

The judge then struck his gavel signifying that the hearing was at and end.

The court usher then addressed the court.

"All rise," she said.

Once the judge had left the courtroom, shortly followed by the court officials and the crown prosecutor, Marshall soon found himself alone in the courtroom with Garmin.

"Now you had better be every *fucking* bit as good as you say you are," Garmin began to rant. "I stand to lose a great deal if all this goes tits up."

Garmin then continued to rant, but Marshall had tuned out.

Shouldn't have downloaded kiddie porn then, you fucking nonce, was all he could think.

The case against Garmin had yet to be proven, so under the eyes of the law he wasn't guilty, *innocent until proven guilty.*

During the pre-trial preparations, Garmin had sat down with Marshall and discussed how best to deal with the charges against him. It was during these discussions that Garmin had admitted his guilt. As it turned out, the charges for which he was to appear in court to answer were only the tip of the proverbial iceberg.

The extent of Garmin's involvement in such disgusting and depraved enterprises went much further than what the police were aware of. But given the privilege that existed between the client and his solicitor, it was not down to Marshall to impart this information to the police.

Allan Garmin had a family, or at least he did until the day he was charged with a number of offences of having indecent images of children on his computer.

His wife had remained steadfast, showing loyalty to her husband following his arrest. This loyalty continued right up until the moment that he was charged.

Since he was charged, he had bail conditions imposed upon him, that he couldn't be left alone with any person under the age of eighteen, and that should a child be present, then another adult had to be there, and that they had to be aware of the charges against him and had to be prepared to take responsibility for the child.

As a result, since being charged, Garmin had been staying in a local hotel, and had been commuting to work from there.

Unlike his wife, who had the luxury of seeing everything in black and white, his employer on the other hand, who was a large multinational petroleum company found themselves in a rather awkward position. One that they had never had to deal with, or even contemplate before.

Garmin's arrest had taken place at his office on their premises, and the subsequent investigation involved regular liaison between the police and the company in order to provide documentation and a timeline as to his computer usage.

But, once again, *innocent until proven guilty* had to be the stance the company took, and as a result Garmin was allowed to continue to work there.

The only restriction was that he was no longer allowed to work remotely, which had involved working from the home or another location using a company-provided laptop computer.

The company had to somehow walk the fine line of remaining impartial, yet vigilant and responsible, and compassionate towards its customers, as the company's actions and reputation were also under public scrutiny.

Marshall had remained oblivious to Garmin's tirade of abuse that had ensued since the court hearing was adjourned. To such an extent, that he wasn't even aware that the he had accompanied Garmin outside of the courthouse.

"Don't worry about a thing," Marshall said in an attempt to appease Garmin. "It's a strong case against us, but it's circumstantial at best... Now, it's jury selection tomorrow, you don't need to be here for that. So, try to enjoy your day off, and I'll see you back here on Wednesday, okay?"

"Sorry about earlier," Garmin said, as he extended a hand for Marshall to shake. "I'm under a lot of pressure, y'know."

Only what you've made for yourself, Marshall thought, as he took the hand and shook it.

With that, Garmin turned and walked off towards his car. Marshall watched him disappear off into the court car park.

From the outside, Garmin appeared to be a normal hard-working man. He had been successful in every aspect of his life, both business and family. He was a father: he had two children under ten, a boy and a younger daughter.

Marshall was also a father. But being a father or not, he couldn't understand the psychology behind such abhorrent behaviour. Marshall realised that there seemed to be no limit to human depravity.

It was then that Marshall saw Garmin drive past him, and out of the car park. He drove a top-of-the-range Audi, probably another company perk, again giving an indication to his success and influence within the company.

What brings a man to do this? Marshall thought. *If only the police knew what I know, you wouldn't be going anywhere.*

Marshall was referring to his knowledge of the full extent of Garmin's admission into his depravity.

Had the police known it too, not only would the list of charges be much longer and more severe, but Garmin would most likely have been remanded, imprisoned awaiting trial.

Marshall looked at his watch. It was just after eleven o'clock in the morning. He had no more responsibilities to Garmin's case that day.

He needed to be on hand for jury selection the following morning. But until then his time was his own.

15

Having seen Garmin leave, Marshall then got into his own car. Once his mobile phone had connected to the car's Bluetooth capability, he scrolled through his phone's directory before dialling a number.

As he pulled out of the car park, the phone rang.

"Hi Charlie, it's James Marshall," he said when the call was answered. "Have you got a minute?"

Marshall was being presumptuous in Maclean's availability, as he was already driving towards her home address before even having confirmation that she was available, or even at home. Once he got the confirmation that she was free to talk on the phone he continued.

"Listen, I'm in the area, and I really need to talk to you about something that has come up with your case," he continued. "Are you free for me to pop round to see you now?"

Maclean had been bailed from her magistrates' court hearing, so she was free to come and go as she pleased in lieu of her trial beginning at crown court.

She already had a busy day ahead of her, but given Marshall's apparent urgency to speak to her, she readily agreed to have him visit.

"Fabulous," Marshall replied. "I'll be there in ten."

Just outside of the predicted arrival time, Marshall's Mercedes pulled up in front of Charlie Maclean's home address.

"So, what is it that you just *had* to tell me?" Charlie said with more than a hint of sarcasm in her voice.

At that, Marshall instantly knew that she probably did have things to do, and that she had cancelled or delayed them in order to be free for him to talk to her about urgent matters.

"Okay, I'll cut to the chase," Marshall began. "Now, this is going to sound really bizarre, but I need you to hear me out, okay?"

"I'm listening," Charlie replied.

"Okay, I don't know how to say this, so I'm just gonna say it…" he paused to take a breath.

He knew that what he was about to say was a rock on top of a very steep slope, and once it had been pushed over the edge, it couldn't be taken back.

"I need you to take a holiday?" he said.

"You need me to do what?" Charlie replied in somewhat disbelief.

"I need you to take a holiday," Marshall reiterated.

"What on *Earth* for?" Charlie replied.

"It's best you don't know, but please just trust me on this… I need you to be away for a couple of weeks," Marshall stressed.

"Well, I guess I could go and visit my aunt," Charlie answered, hoping this would appease Marshall's bizarre request.

"Where does she live?" Marshall replied with a sense of hope in his voice.

"Cornwall," Charlie replied.

"No good," Marshall abruptly replied. "It needs to be somewhere abroad… Somewhere you can have proof that you're there."

"James, I know you've never done me a bad turn, and please excuse my language… But what the *fuck* are you getting at with all this?" Charlie asked, being evidently on the verge of losing her patience with Marshall at the continued vagueness of his request.

"I'm being truthful, I really can't tell you," Marshall said, his tone now screaming with an agonising desperation.

Charlie looked at Marshall. She realised he wasn't going to give in lightly, and she knew he was adamant when he said that he wasn't going to impart any further information to her.

She hadn't known him all that long, and their relationship had only ever existed on a professional level, but nonetheless, she trusted him, and she knew that he had been looking out for her all the time that she had known him. She concluded that this request, however bizarre, had to be similarly motivated.

"Well, Lord knows I could do with some time away, y'know to clear my head and all that," she replied. "But, there's no way in hell I could afford it."

Leaping upon the presented opportunity, Marshall responded having anticipated this eventuality.

"If money's the only issue, I'll trump up the cash for you," he replied. "It *will* have to be cash though."

Now even more sceptical than before, Charlie gave the offer further consideration.

"Where though?" she asked.

"Anywhere," Marshall replied. "Two weeks anywhere, it just has to be abroad."

He waited with bated breath as she considered his offer. The offer that was effectively giving her a blank cheque.

He knew what he needed to achieve, and what he was prepared to do to achieve it. But had Charlie taken full advantage of his generosity and demand an all-inclusive Caribbean cruise, he didn't know what he would have done. All he knew was that he didn't want to have rescind the offer.

He could see that Charlie was giving the offer serious consideration. Eventually, she voiced a reply.

"Would Greece be okay?" she asked. "Or one of the islands?"

"Greece sounds perfect," Marshall replied. "I could even recommend Kefalonia to you... I went there once before the whole divorce thing started. We stayed at a lovely villa just up the coast from Skala. You should do that."

Marshall could see Charlie's approval as she started nodding along to his recollection of this holiday.

"Am I *allowed* to leave the country?" she asked.

"No travel restrictions have been imposed on you, and there's not been any request for you to relinquish your passport... So, you're free to come and go as you please... The only thing is, ideally you need to be going away within the week, so you may have your options limited by what the travel agent has available."

"Okay, I'll see what deals they have," Charlie said.

"Fab," Marshall replied. "What I'll do is, I'll drop a thousand in cash around tomorrow, I'll put an envelope through your door... That'll hopefully be enough. If it's less then you have some spending money whilst you're away, if it's not, then let me know and I'll top you up, okay?"

Despite the absurdity of the request, Charlie trusted Marshall. His understanding of her condition behind her offending had forged a trusting bond between them.

As a result, any doubts she might normally have had regarding the motive behind such a request were instantly dismissible.

She felt that Marshall was somehow protecting her by asking her to leave the country, and further protecting her by not stating why. She was sure when the time was right for her to know, he would tell her.

With that agreement in place, their conversation was over.

"Thank for that," Marshall said as he excused himself. "I'll let you get back to your day."

As Charlie walked Marshall to the front door, she could see the concern and desperation in his eyes. In an instant she knew the importance of the request he had just made of her.

But despite everything that was going on, he had her unquestionable faith and trust.

16

By day, Marshall attended crown court to further the campaign of representing Allan Garmin now that jury selection had taken place, and the trial itself had begun. By evening, he spent his time giving further analysis to his case file history, to further his own campaign, formed out of his father's inception, and his own delusional prophecy.

His own campaign had evolved from merely identifying and seeking retribution against his father's attacker, to righting the wrongs he had been complicit to.

Every so often, he would look up from his files, and cast a glance across the dining room table to the claw hammer that had now been taken from the zip-lock freezer bag and placed into a transparent airtight lunch box, and to the car key that had been entrusted to him by Albert Foster who was still serving his driving ban.

Through his research he had drawn up a list of names from all of his files. The names on this list stood apart from all the other clients that he had represented over his distinguished career.

The list only contained the names of those people who had made a full and frank admission to him whilst protected by legal privilege. This was information that he could not disclose to anyone.

Of all of the cases he had tried, only a small percentage had made such an admission to him. He knew he could quite easily add to this list with the names of those where the evidence against them was overwhelming. But, for whatever reason, be it skill on his part, or ineptitude on the part of the prosecution, the defendant ended up with a vastly reduced sentence, or in some cases, they walked free from court altogether.

Marshall was content to focus solely on those who had confessed their crimes to him. To him, that was a surer proof of guilt than any amount of evidence.

The name that found itself at the top of this list was that of Robert Fraser, the man who had followed him from the police station that evening and had made cryptic threats towards him.

It was these threats and the specific wording used that compelled Marshall to believe that Fraser had something to do with his father's wounding.

He had made the list not so much by any admission as to his involvement with Marshall's father's attack, or of his confessed involvement in any other crime in which Marshall had represented him.

The way Marshall saw it, an attack on his family was enough to earn Fraser an entry to the list.

The next name to make the list was Allan Garmin. Although he was currently on trial, and Marshall had every reason to believe that the eventual verdict would effectively remove his name from the list.

However, until such a time, he would remain on the list, chosen under his prior selection criteria until any verdict determined otherwise.

Again, for having fulfilled the entry criteria, Charlie Maclean was next to make it to the list. Marshall didn't plan on exercising any discretion at this stage to filter anyone off.

Albert Foster came next, the habitual drink driver. Again, the offences committed weren't relevant at this stage, merely that they had admitted their crimes to Marshall.

In Foster's case, he had already given a propensity to reoffend at any available opportunity, and to such an extent that he couldn't even trust himself to retain his own keys, so he wouldn't be able to drive whilst serving his ban.

Beyond that, the list next featured Bradley Simons, who was a habitual shoplifter and burglar. He was also an intravenous drug user, who admitted to stealing in order to fund his escalating habit.

Then, there was fraudster Akbar Jumal, who repeatedly targeted the elderly and vulnerable in society. He once bragged about the simplicity of his cons and the gullibility of those he targeted.

These admitted crimes had appalled Marshall. He used to imagine his parents being amongst those targeted, and that disgusted him, despite having to provide his client with his best efforts of a defence.

Lastly, and most unique amongst his compatriots, was Patrick McNeil. McNeil was a frequent guest of the police and a visitor to the custody centre.

But what separated McNeil from all the others on the list, and what had compelled his inclusion was not anything to do with any admissions regarding his previously investigated crimes. McNeil was on the list because of what he had stated to Marshall was his desire and ambition to accomplish.

McNeil was a down-and-out. He lived anywhere he could, which usually comprised of any derelict or abandoned structure that could provide shelter for him.

Like so many of a similar ilk, he turned to petty crime to prolong his existence. This could take the form of shoplifting, or street robbery, or even stealing gadgets and handbags from unattended cars. Basically, anything with a value to someone who would buy it for a pittance of its true value.

From there, he would adopt the triangle trade, having turned stolen goods into cash, and from there into drugs, and anything he had left went on food. But even this wasn't his reason for his inclusion.

McNeil was on the list because of what he stated he wanted to do, and what McNeil wanted to do was to abduct, molest, torture and kill children, "the younger the better," were the words he used to when describing his fantasy to Marshall.

He had originally confessed this during a psychiatric evaluation, whilst he was detained under the Mental Health Act. But a desire to commit a crime doesn't necessary lend himself to a propensity to commit that crime itself.

As a result, there was nothing to lend itself to detaining McNeil purely for having these thoughts as nothing he admitted to suggested any preparation, or manifestation to carry them out.

As McNeil had never been convicted or even arrested for a sexual offence, he was not to be bound under the law, or even placed on a sexual offenders' register.

The police were restricted in what they could actually do, even though they were abundantly aware of McNeil's fantasies.

Whenever there was a missing person in the area within the desired age group, his last known addresses were always checked as a matter of priority. But because none of these enquiries ever turned up anything, they ended up with nothing to substantiate the risk.

But it was this repeated desire that had been documented on virtually every occasion that McNeil had come into custody which led to his inclusion on Marshall's list. The most recent of which being the occasion that it had been elaborated to him directly.

Marshall believed McNeil to be a genuine risk to the public, a ticking time-bomb. He felt it was only a matter of time before detonation.

Marshall looked at his completed list. Although the names were added for individual reasons, they all had something in common.

The only thing that distinguished some from others was time. Some had committed their crimes, whilst for others there was still an ambition as yet unrealised.

17

The following evening, after a rather predictable day in court with Allan Garmin's trial, Marshall felt compelled to do some research into the habits of those on the list.

On this occasion, he chose to revisit the revelation in which Robert Fraser stated that had to sign on at the police station, in order to try and establish the frequency that this was required.

Signing on would be a condition of his bail when he was released following his court hearing. The frequency and in some cases the time frame would only be known to the suspect and his lawyer outside of the police force.

As Marshall didn't represent Fraser for this case, he would have to obtain this information by other means.

oOo

At just after seven o'clock in the evening, Marshall parked his car in a side road opposite the pedestrian entrance to the police station's front office.

He knew that the front office closed at ten o'clock, and that Fraser had accosted him at around eight o'clock on the previous occasion.

He knew this could potentially be a long and fruitless wait, as there was no guarantee that Fraser even needed to sign on that evening, or even if he were restricted to signing on in the evenings only.

Unfortunately for Marshall, ten o'clock slowly came and rapidly went. All this meant that was that Marshall would have to repeat the process the following evening.

This was something that he was planning to do anyway in order to form a pattern of behaviour, and to give himself options.

For Marshall, however, he was still in the planning and preparation stage, and had yet to commit himself to any defined course of action.

He recorded the evening's result in the form of a memo on his mobile phone. It took the form of something relevant only to him.

Beyond the pre-populated date and time, the message simply read:

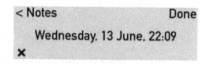

Marshall was still in a position to be able to indulge his fantasies and desires without having to cross the line into criminality.

As things stood, no one needed to ever know about him locating the hammer in the school grounds, and should he choose to go no further with his fledgling plans, then no one ever would.

oOo

The following day started off as a carbon copy of the last: a day in court with Garmin that was as predictable as it was uneventful.

The prosecution had continued to lay their evidence, so apart from the occasional challenge, the focus was away from Garmin and Marshall.

It was the evening, however, that turned out to be far more productive.

Once again, Marshall took up the same vantage point. He wasn't able to park in exactly the same spot as he had the previous evening as another car, possibly one belonging to a local resident had beaten him to it. As a result, he had to park a little further back along the same road.

Not only was he now further away, but he also had obstructions in his way, that of the cars parked between him and the police station.

Marshall was also conscious not to do anything that could draw any attention to himself, so using anything like binoculars was out of the question.

The last thing he wanted was for a concerned resident, thinking he was a pervert or a burglar, to phone the police and have them send an officer to investigate.

At least if he was just sat in a parked car, he could conjure up a plausible excuse of waiting for someone to leave the police station.

Marshall hadn't been there for very long when a figure emerged from the shadows to his right. At first sighting Marshall wasn't even able to distinguish an age or even a gender of the person in question.

But as they approached the front of the police station, and entered the cone of light as laid down by a solitary streetlight, Marshall was able to determine the person to be not only vastly older than Fraser, but that it was in fact a woman, and that she had a small dog in tow on an extendable lead. She carried on her way and soon disappeared to where thespians would describe as *stage right*.

The reason he had been initially unable to distinguish a gender for the dog walker, beyond the poor lighting, which was due to the local council's policy to reduce energy costs by only illuminating every other streetlight, was because she was wearing a long, shapeless, high-collared coat, and a hat. It was only her posture and gait that eventually gave her gender away.

But it was the coat that Marshall was focusing on. It had grown decidedly chillier than the previous evening, and he had not come out prepared for it. He had come out wearing the same suit that he had worn to court, with no consideration, or provision having been made for the cold weather.

He knew he must endure it, as any attempts to warm himself by running the engine to power the car's heaters would only risk drawing unwanted attention to him.

Knowing his preparations would most likely lead to a third evening spent in the same spot, he would be better prepared for the climate.

Marshall was never one to leave anything to chance. He was never much of a gambler. He liked to have a well-versed plan, and contingencies at every stage. That's how he played things out in life and in court, and this enterprise would be no different.

It was as Marshall was feverishly rubbing his hands along the length of his thighs in a vain attempt to stave off the cold that he saw another figure come into view from the direction the lady walking her dog was last seen.

This person was immediately distinguishable to be a male. A young male who evidently put fashion ahead of function.

He was dressed wearing only active wear; tracksuit trousers, which were dark colour with distinctive orange or red stripes down the side. It was impossible to determine the colour with any certainly due to the orange hue from the streetlight.

He also wore a hooded top, with the hood up. It was evident that he was feeling the effects of the cold as his head was bowed, his shoulders were hunched up, and his arms were tightly folded across his body.

As he got mid-way across Marshall's path of vision, he turned to his left and walked up the short path that led to the automatic sliding door of the police station's front office.

Once the male had entered the office, he pulled his hood down. Then once under white light of the office lobby, despite the office being further away than the footpath, Marshall could make out the faintest of facial features.

But from what he could see, Marshall was confident that this was Robert Fraser.

Marshall noted the time and result in a non-descript memo on his mobile phone.

As before, the memo already included a date and time for the entry, the memo itself read:

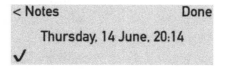

Marshall watched Fraser within the office. He was only in there for a few minutes.

Having completed all he was required to do, Fraser then left the front office.

Once back on the street, Fraser didn't go back the way he had come from. Instead, he continued to walk in the same direction as he had done to get there.

Marshall waited where he was parked for a few moments. He wanted to give Fraser a head-start along the road.

Marshall knew the road ahead, and that there were numerous ways off it. He was hoping that Fraser would give further indication to his ongoing route by committing himself to one of these routes.

As Marshall pulled out of the road opposite the police station, he looked right in the direction that Fraser had gone. He was now nowhere in sight.

Marshall then drove off in the same direction. As he passed a road that led off the main route, he slowed enough to be able to see into it. He repeated this for the road on the left, still nothing could be seen.

Then as he drove further along down the main road, he saw Fraser ahead of him.

Marshall slowed to stay behind him as along as possible. Marshall knew there was another road coming up, and he was hoping that Fraser would beat him to it.

However, Marshall found himself gaining on the pedestrian, and he knew that he couldn't afford to go any slower, as it would be too obvious. He had no choice but to pass Fraser.

But looking in his rear-view mirror, Marshall saw Fraser turn into the side road.

"Gotcha, you bastard," Marshall said.

With nothing more to achieve, Marshall turned at the next junction, and headed home.

He didn't want to document anything he had learned that evening; it would instead be something that he would commit to memory.

He was content with what he had accomplished, and glad that he didn't have to wait until ten o'clock for a no-show again.

He knew that with his next court appearance, he would most likely have to begin his defence of Allan Garmin, and as a result, he wanted to get a good night's sleep.

18

At court, everything went as Marshall had expected. It had been another unremarkable day. The only significant progression made that day was that Marshall had begun on his defence of Garmin.

This meant that the focus of the court's attention was now on him, and not on the prosecution as it had been until the conclusion of the crown's case against Garmin.

As a result, this meant that Marshall had to keep his thoughts within the walls of the courtroom, and more specifically on the case at hand.

Until that point, by his own admission, he would readily confess that his mind had wandered on more than one occasion, and even when it was fixated on a certain someone within the courtroom, it wasn't with the ambition to keep his unblemished winning streak intact.

Given the change of mindset brought on by recent events, Marshall was more interested in seeing justice served than his reputation.

The adjournment of the case at the end of the day, and at the end of its first week gave Marshall the opportunity he sorely desired in order to be able to address more pressing matters.

oOo

As he hadn't heard from Charlie Maclean since coming to an agreement for her to take a holiday at his expense, he felt there was no better time than the present to get an update from her.

As he drove away from the courthouse, he phoned her.

"Hi Charlie, it's James Marshall," he said when the call was answered.

"Have you been able to find anything you like, holiday-wise?" he continued.

There was a long pause at Marshall's end as Charlie elaborately responded to his question.

"That's fantastic," he replied. "Given all that's going on here, y'know, I wish I was going with you."

There was another silence as Charlie again responded.

"Ah, that's lovely of you to ask," Marshall replied. "But, I'm up to my neck in it at the moment... You enjoy yourself, and do me one favour, just promise me you'll send me a postcard, okay?"

After ending the call, Marshall then contemplated another list he had created for himself. Though this list didn't have any names on it, and it only existed in his head, but it was based on that other physical list.

There was a number of errands he had to run. His contemplation of it was just in deciding which to do first.

As it was still light, Marshall decided the most logical thing to do first was to try and locate Patrick McNeil.

19

Patrick McNeil had made the other list given his wanton ambition to be counted amongst the likes of Rose and Fred West, and Myra Hindley and Ian Brady.

Marshall was sure that someone with such ambition and role models gave him just cause to include him on his list.

It was a well-established fact that members of the criminal fraternity tended to be loyal to their legal representative, especially if they were previously responsible for securing a lenient sentence, or even an acquittal.

This was the case on a couple of occasions with McNeil. Had he a Christmas card list, then Marshall was sure he'd be on it.

It hadn't been all that long since Marshall had been last called upon to represent McNeil. From his file, Marshall had a last known whereabouts for McNeil. It wasn't so much a home address, as he was considered to be NFA, or of *no fixed abode*.

This was one of two identical acronyms used within Marshall's circles, the other referring to *no further action*, which was used when the police had decided not to pursue a matter against an individual any further. But in this case, NFA referred to McNeil being either a squatter, or sleeping rough.

Not that it could be used for sending any correspondence to, but the last address that Marshall had for McNeil was in fact a long-disused and now derelict public house, the Iron Horse.

It had been marked for demolition and development for several years, but due to the developer going out of business, the pub had just sat there, being allowed to slowly fall apart. The windows had been covered up with metal grates designed to prevent unauthorised access, and a hoarding had been erected around the entire site.

But the squatters had their ways of getting in, as much as they supposedly knew their rights under the ever-evolving law.

All the time the demolition and development of the site was imminent, the police had made regular patrols of the site to ensure that no one was sleeping rough when there was the likelihood of a wrecking ball to come smashing through a wall.

But since all plans had been put on hold whilst attempts were being made to find a new development company to take on the project, it was as if no one could be bothered to move anyone on anymore. This eventuality played well in Marshall's favour.

oOo

Marshall parked up a short distance away from the derelict pub. This was because he didn't want his vehicle being in any way associated with the site, or its mere presence being considered in any way suspicious.

He then made the final approach on foot. As this wasn't to be Marshall's first time visiting this site, he knew exactly how to get into the site, using the frequently used insecurity that had been created.

Previously, he had reason to attend so he could deliver court papers to McNeil for a previous case.

Despite knowing where he was going, the utilities to the building had long since been cut-off. It was for this reason alone that Marshall had chosen to put this visit at the top of his list. He needed a source of light by which to navigate the site.

Having slipped into the site by way of a hoarding board that had become detached on one side, effectively hinging it, Marshall then approached the rear of the building itself.

Since becoming derelict, it was evident that some local residents, and maybe even some from further afield were using the site as one large rubbish tip.

Some had taken to dumping household waste, and in some cases even kitchen whites, as there were a couple of fridge-freezers and even a washing machine that had been dumped over the fence. This had probably taken place in the dead of night, in order to avoid having to dispose of them responsibly, and incurring a fee at a council run facility.

Having negotiated a budget version of the *Krypton Factor* assault course, Marshall eventually reached the back of the building.

The padlock that had once secured the back door had long since been smashed off, and following that occasion, no effort had been made to re-secure the premises.

Marshall pushed against the door. It ended up taking much more exertion than he thought it would to open it.

Before entering, he briefly looked back, across the area that had once been a beer garden and car park, towards the hoarding that had allowed him entry. He was looking back to see if anyone was watching what he was doing. When he was confident that no one had been watching him, he stepped inside.

Despite the fact that all windows and external doors were covered and secured with metal grates, there was still sufficient light penetrating through the grates to allow Marshall to negotiate the interior with relative ease and safety.

He knew McNeil to have previously taken up lodgings upstairs. As Marshall wasn't there for the grand tour, he quickly located the stairs, and ascended them.

Once upstairs, Marshall momentarily waited. He listened. In that time his nostrils were filled with the smell of damp, rotting wood and urea, from whoever had lived there who had been using the toilet without any running water to flush their business away.

As he was confident that he was now out of earshot of the outside world, Marshall softly called out.

"Pat, are you in here?" he called.

The reason for this was so his presence didn't startle anyone, even McNeil, causing them to feel the need to defend themselves. There was nothing by way of a response.

Marshall then moved forwards from the head of the stairs and proceeded to the room where he remembered having last seen McNeil occupy.

As Marshall entered this room, he found it to be abandoned, and no longer appearing to serve any purpose.

But, before giving up hope, he realised that the floorboards of this room were sodden, and that there was a sizeable hole in the ceiling above where the plasterboards had collapsed, through which daylight was able to point a finger down into the room.

Marshall deduced that this room might have been abandoned because it was no longer weatherproof. Therefore, he knew he needed to check the rest of the upstairs before giving up.

It was in the second room that he checked that he had his conclusions confirmed. Collected in this room was most likely all of the furniture that had been left behind when the pub had closed down.

There were beer kegs now being used as seats and tables, and a pair of single metal-sprung bed frames, along with a chest of drawers.

There was also a double-sized bedspread that hung from one side of the room's only window that appeared to have found a second life as blackout curtains.

Given the amount of bedding, and the number of sleeping bags strewn around the room, it was difficult for Marshall to determine just how many people might be sleeping there, or if it *was* just the one person that he was looking for.

The last time he was there, Marshall had it confirmed by McNeil himself that he was there alone, that being the way he liked it. Marshall had no reason to believe that any of that had changed at all since their last encounter.

As he gave further scrutiny to the accommodation, he felt that whoever was living there did so on their own, at least currently.

There appeared to be a localised area around a single sleeping bag that was cleaner than the rest of the room.

Also, there was a collection of pornographic material strewn around the same sleeping bag. Nothing had been left in any concernable manner as to prevent it from being interfered with, suggesting that there was no one else staying there *to* interfere with it.

With that, there was nothing more to see, and no more conclusions to reach. Marshall resigned himself to not being able to achieve what he wanted to on this visit. Ideally, he wanted to have been able to confirm that McNeil was still squatting there.

But, unlike the police station, he wasn't prepared to sit around and wait for someone to return. He was confident that someone still bedded down here, and with that, this visit was over.

Marshall left the site quickly. He did however take a sneaky peek through the gap in the hoarding boards before stepping out into the world again.

Although he had an explanation ready should anyone want to challenge him as to what he was doing in the site, he would rather avoid having to use it.

Once back in his car, he sat there with the engine running, warming himself as he decided his next move.

It was then that he noticed the time. If he were to get across town to the police station in time to be there to see if Fraser had to attend again, he would need to set off sooner rather than later.

It was as Marshall turned onto the road that the Iron Horse had originally looked out on, that he drove past a man who he believed to be McNeil walking towards him, and back in the direction of the derelict pub.

He was wearing the same three-quarter length technicoloured patchwork woollen coat, one that would put Joseph's to shame, that he had worn when Marshall had last had dealings with him.

It was then that a dilemma fell upon him: should he go back and confirm that it was in fact McNeil? But if he did, he might very well miss seeing Fraser later at the police station.

Marshall decided to split the difference. He turned in a side road, and then headed back towards the derelict pub as quickly as he could. He then pulled into the side road that would've originally led to the pub car park.

Marshall was there in time to see the man he believed to be McNeil disappear through the same insecurity in the hoarding that Marshall had himself come out of only minutes earlier.

Marshall then turned his car around further up the road, and finally again headed in the direction of the police station. He had now achieved exactly what he had set out to do. After all, he wasn't intending to speak to McNeil. He had only ever sought confirmation that he was still squatting in the pub.

oOo

That same evening had proved fruitless as far as determining if Robert Fraser had to sign on at the police station on a Friday evening.

However, this was far from a wasted experience. As there was something else that needed to be done, regardless of the outcome.

As things stood, it was to be the following Thursday that Marshall was now aiming for all of his planned aspects to come together.

With Fraser's nightly obligations confirmed, Marshall now needed to confirm the regular plans and habits of Allan Garmin.

Obviously, he knew where Garmin would be Monday to Friday during the day, as he would be accompanying Marshall in court. But what Marshall needed to determine was where he would be of an evening.

For this, Marshall had an idea, but he would have to wait until the next hearing, on the Monday morning after the weekend, in order to start the ball rolling on it.

20

Marshall sat in his car in front of the law courts. He was prepared for what was the second, and most likely the final week of the trial.

He was waiting for Garmin to arrive as he needed to discuss his participation in the coming week's events. He also wanted to be able to soften the impact should things not go in their favour when the time came for the jury delivered their verdict.

As he waited, it occurred to Marshall that he still needed confirmation about Charlie's travel plans. In their last conversation on the subject, she confirmed having found a package deal that she liked and that suited their respective requirements. But since that conversation, nothing had been booked, and no departure date confirmed. So, in order to get the required information in a way that wouldn't interfere with his day in court, Marshall sent Charlie a text message.

> Do you know when
> you're going to be away
> yet?

There was no reply in the time that Marshall continued to wait for Garmin. He decided that if he hadn't heard back from Charlie by the end of court for that day, then he would chase it up again that evening.

He was, however, prevented from concerning himself any further on that subject, as he saw Garmin drive into the court car park.

They alighted from their cars in unison and met midway between them. They shook hands, appearing outwardly to be on convivial terms, before they both turned towards the court building, and started walking towards it to begin the second week of the trial.

As they walked, Marshall started to sow the seeds of what he wanted to achieve, to *soften the impact* as he saw it. He chose to format what he needed to say in the time-honoured tradition of the *shit sandwich*, by *sandwiching* bad news on either side with something pleasant, in order to reduce the impact.

"How was your weekend?" Marshall asked, though not having any genuine interest in any response that Garmin might have to offer as a reply.

"So, so," Garmin replied. "I wanted to see my children. But my wife refused me again, fucking bitch. Seems she's already found me guilty."

Can't really blame her, Marshall thought. *So much for the shit sandwich.*

"You got any kids?" Garmin asked. "We've never discussed it."

With someone like you, why would I? He thought.

But in an attempt to appease the situation, he offered a more diplomatic reply.

"Yeah, I've got two, one of each," Marshall replied.

"You're divorced though, right...? Do you get to see them much?" Garmin went on to ask.

"Meant to be every other weekend... Not this weekend just gone though, as it wasn't scheduled, and not the weekend before because she had plans," Marshall replied. "So, it'll be next weekend before I get to see them again."

As the first *slice* of conversation had already fallen on stony ground, the second element, that of the foul-smelling sandwich filling, would probably just make things go from bad to even worse.

"Allan, I need to ask you to consider something ahead of this week... Something we can keep in reserve should the need arise," Marshall began to explain. "Now, should things not go our way with the verdict, ideally, I would like to have a contingency already planned, discussed and agreed with you, in order to mitigate the damage."

This unexpected revelation brought Garmin to an immediate halt. He turned to face Marshall, and grabbed the sleeve of his suit jacket, spinning him on the spot to face him.

"What the fuck do you mean *not* go our way?" Garmin said in a voice loud enough to attract the attention of anyone who happened to be standing around them. "You told me we had an air-tight case here, and that you could get me off... I mean, what the *fuck* am I paying you for?"

Marshall then took hold of Garmin's hand that still had hold of his sleeve. He forcefully pulled it away, showing obvious disapproval of such an action.

"Look Allan," Marshall said, hoping to pacify his client and reduce the volume of the conversation to between just the two of them. "I just like to cover my bases, okay? Look, I'm going to do my part to the absolute *best* of my abilities for you… But I want you to consider the possibility, however remote it may be, that we may not win here. And, it is with *that* in mind, that I would like to have something in reserve."

Seeing reason, and the logic of having such a contingency, Garmin nodded, which in turn indicated to Marshall that he may elaborate on his suggestion.

"Now, what I propose is this… I want to be able to say to the court that you've accepted that what you're suffering from, and the motive behind your actions is that you have an illness…" Marshall said, deliberately pausing to allow Garmin to offer acknowledgement to what had been said thus far. "What I need from you is, *before* a verdict is reached, is for you to be registered at a clinic or therapy centre, and seeking treatment for your addiction."

"Whoa, whoa, whoa, I ain't fucking admitting to anything," Garmin bellowed, once again including the outside populous of the courthouse in their conversation.

"Allan, c'mon, *listen* to me. You won't be admitting anything to the court… That is, unless, things have already gone against us, and then, and *only* then, will we use this in our favour to mitigate any sentence. Do you understand?"

Garmin nodded, once again appearing to show understanding and restraint.

"Good, I just wanted to suggest this to you now, we can work out the details later," Marshall continued. He then nodded his head in the direction of the courthouse. "Come on, let's go get 'em."

Both men then again turned to face the courthouse, as they headed in for the second week of the trial.

oOo

During the morning session, Marshall heard his phone vibrate. This wasn't an unusual occurrence, but given the anticipation of receiving a reply from Charlie Maclean, he was anxious to reach the lunch break so he could check this message.

When the lunchtime recess was called, he excused himself from Garmin's company, and left the courtroom. When he was alone, he checked his phone.

He had received a reply from Maclean.

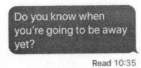

This brought a smile to Marshall's face. Everything was coming together nicely.

21

When Thursday arrived, Marshall had already conducted what was essentially a dummy run for the evening.

Two days earlier, on the Tuesday, Marshall had been sat in his car waiting for Fraser to sign on at the police station.

At what appeared to habitually be approximately the same time, Fraser entered the police station's front office. Having witnessed this, Marshall left his car and went ahead on foot along his predetermined ongoing route, in order to lay in wait for him to come back out.

Fraser had approached from the same direction, and as a result, Marshall had every reason to believe that he would also leave in the same direction as he had done so previously.

It was in this direction that Marshall had chosen to inconspicuously lay in wait from Fraser. He was hoping to be able to determine his ongoing route, presumably towards home, having stopped at the police station on his way home from work, or whatever it was he got up to during his days.

The route Fraser initially took led him along the road on which the police station was situated. Then after crossing a couple of residential side roads, Fraser left the main road to go into a road which serviced the local grammar school.

But little did he know that he was being watched, as he took every step nearer the grammar school service entrance.

Marshall had chosen to wait opposite the service road that he had previously seen Fraser to turn into, because he knew entering the service road would give Fraser further options, and he wanted to have a good vantage point by which to see which option was taken.

There was an alleyway which led along the side of the school that led towards the residential streets behind it. There was also a second route which extended diagonally from the service road through the churchyard of Saint Mary's church which was next to the school.

The route across the churchyard was a popular cut-through for pedestrians as it had the benefit of cutting their route into town practically in half.

Once Fraser had committed himself to the service road, Marshall then crossed the main road. He then waited on the corner of the service road to see which route Fraser had taken.

For what he already had in mind, Marshall had no preference; hoping that Fraser might take one route over the other was pointless, as each of them posed similar pros and cons.

As it turned out, Fraser took the diagonal path through the churchyard.

Tuesday was a clear but cold evening, and yet again, Fraser had declined to dress appropriately for the conditions.

As before, he wore a dark-coloured, hooded top and similarly coloured tracksuit trousers, with a contrasting logo and stripes. As he observed him, Marshall began to think that this was all Fraser's wardrobe consisted of.

As this was only a dummy run, not even a rehearsal of the real thing, Marshall was able to keep his distance behind Fraser. What he had already assimilated was all he really needed to know, ahead of what was to happen next.

Marshall followed Fraser across the churchyard. Then once he was able to determine which of the numerous exits Fraser had committed himself to taking, Marshall diverted his own course and took a different path, this was so, should Fraser inadvertently glance behind himself, he wouldn't deduce that he was in fact being followed.

Only when Marshall was certain that Fraser had left the churchyard, did he backtrack in order to find a suitable location along the route that Fraser had led him along.

This he found beneath a large yew tree which stood prominently near the centre of the churchyard. It had a bench erected beneath its canopy. Marshall felt that this would be an ideal place for what he had in mind.

As Marshall sat himself down on the bench, he deduced that even on the clearest night he would be entirely consumed by shadows, whilst still being able to see any foot traffic on the path coming towards him.

oOo

The following evening, the Wednesday, Marshall returned to the churchyard.

On this occasion it had no consequence as to what time he chose to attend, as this visit was only to leave something in readiness for the following evening.

He strategically placed a hammer underneath the bench, using a couple of thin cable ties to hold it in place. But this wasn't just any hammer, this was the claw hammer that he had retrieved from the school grounds following Brett Cable's attack on Paul Greene.

Once again, with nothing more to be achieved on this occasion, Marshall left the churchyard in order to continue to play the waiting game.

oOo

Thursday was the evening when everything that had been meticulously planned was to come to fruition.

Marshall sat waiting on the bench in the churchyard. He had arrived in good time, in order to be there ahead of the slightly varied times by which Fraser had attended the police station to sign on.

As he waited, sipped from a paper coffee cup with a plastic lid. The steam from the coffee caused a mist to form, which danced like a Chinese dragon in front of him.

He imagined if anyone looked upon him at that moment, and in that setting that he must look like something out of a *Hammer House of Horror* movie.

Marshall normally would have bought himself a cappuccino, but to ensure that the coffee to stay hot for longer, on this occasion he had chosen a black *Americano*.

Unlike the frequently observed Robert Fraser, Marshall was more than appropriately dressed for the weather conditions. Although it wasn't as clear or as chilly as the previous evenings, there was still a damp chill in the still air.

Marshall had chosen to wear a compression base layer, then a fleece layer to insulate against the cold, and finally a waterproof layer on top. He also wore gloves and a beanie-type hat. On this occasion, he had also resorted to tracksuit trousers himself, as well as training shoes which were double knotted in order to avoid any unfortunate mishaps.

As it turned out, the restlessness of having to wait affected Marshall more than the cold.

He had readied himself, having already taken the hammer from beneath the bench, and had also retrieved the broken ends of the cable ties that had been used to secure it. These were then put into a pocket in the waterproof jacket, which was then zipped shut.

Marshall had also taken the provision not to come out carrying anything in the way of personal items. He had left his phone and wallet at home. All he had brought with him was a single nondescript car remote key which was zipped away in an under layer.

He had walked to the churchyard having parked several streets away, utilising alleyways as much as possible. He had also left his house key in the car.

The first figure Marshall saw using the churchyard as a cut-through entered the same way that he had. It was a dog walker. Marshall knew that this was one of the variables that he had no control over, and anyone else within the confines of the churchyard at the opportune moment would be the only reason that Marshall could think for aborting his plan.

It was also whilst he waited that Marshall contemplated if what he was planning to do was too drastic. When balanced against what he was avenging and preventing, was he overreacting?

But his conclusion was that, as Fraser had already targeted his parents, and he was now threatening him directly, what would be his next step be?

Marshall felt that anything less than an absolute solution would only lead to further reprisals, and imminent escalation, and only with Fraser completely out of the way could he hope to bring this awful rigmarole to an end.

Marshall then justified his proposed actions basing it on his interpretation of the law. As far as he was concerned, this was a pre-emptive strike, striking at Fraser *before* he was struck at himself.

Therefore, in his mind, this made what he was planning nothing more than self-defence.

As he continued to wait in the shadows, he had time to finish his coffee. Due to the cold of the evening and the time he had taken to drink it, the last mouthful had cooled to the ambient temperature.

When the cup was empty, he placed it down on the ground beside his feet. Now, he had nothing more to do but wait.

As it turned out, he didn't have to wait long. Even though he had absolutely no idea what the time actually was. The last inkling was when he left his car at just after 7 o'clock, though that now that seemed eons ago.

Marshall heard a figure approaching from his left, from the direction of the grammar school. He listened intently. This was the only sound he could hear save from the dull hum of traffic beyond the churchyard.

As best as he could, given the minimal light available, Marshall scanned what he could see of the churchyard. He could no longer see the dog walker. Everything appeared to be as close to the conceived plan as it could ever be.

Marshall picked up the hammer that until then had been laying on the bench beside him. He rested it gently in his lap, holding it with two gloved hands. Despite his warm clothing, he still felt the cold metal against his thighs.

The footsteps drew ever closer. There appeared to be no echo to the footsteps, suggesting that it was only one person approaching.

Marshall had planned to wait until they had drawn level with the yew tree, then he would come out from the shadows of the tree behind them.

Marshall's hands gripped the handle of the hammer ever tighter. He did his best to control his breathing, and calm his racing heart.

For a moment, he again had doubts about what he was about to do. He knew he could still just walk away at this point. He had yet to cross the line into criminality himself, save for what he held in his hands. But he could dispose of that and no one would be any the wiser. Everything done thus far, if discovered and challenged, could be explained away.

It was then, as he pondered, that he had a momentary flashback, and images flashed across his mind; one was of his battered and bruised father laying in a hospital bed, and the other was of the bloodied faces of his children.

Although he no longer saw his children as merely being in a defaced photograph, now the image seemed prophesised, and seen as a certainty without his intervention. Then in that split second, all thoughts of what was right and what was wrong were drowned out under his overwhelming sense of righteousness.

It was then that he knew it was down to him to make this right. Not by relying on the police to get lucky in finding a suspect, or a jury in a court of law to reach a verdict, and for a judge dispense justice. At that moment, Marshall knew there was only one way to gain the justice he sought.

By now, the approaching footsteps had been joined by heavy breathing. That of someone too vain to dress appropriately for the conditions, breathing heavily in an effort to stave off the cold. Marshall was adamant that it was Fraser who was drawing level with the yew tree.

Marshall stood from where he was sat on the bench behind the tree. He turned to face towards the path. No one could be seen, as the tree obscured his vision. That also meant that he too couldn't be seen by anyone on the path.

Marshall stepped out from behind the tree. He stayed on the grass so to muffle his footsteps. He looked down at the hammer held in his right hand, and took one final deep breath.

"Payback's a bitch," he said softly, but with the intention of being heard.

Fraser stopped dead in his tracks. His drooped head raised as the hunched shoulders dropped. He then turned to face the source of the remark.

As he turned, Marshall stepped in closer to him and brought a single hammer blow down on him.

But Marshall did not strike him using the face of the hammer. Instead, having unintentionally allowed the tool to rotate in his grip, he brought the claw down, missing its intended target, and striking to Fraser's shoulder, with the claw penetrating the flesh behind his left collar bone.

The blow instantly caused Fraser to collapse to his knees. The shock of the attack, the excruciating pain he was suddenly feeling, and the cold air of the evening in his throat prevented him from shouting out.

Marshall then pulled at the handle of the hammer to retrieve his weapon. But unknown to him, the claw was caught behind the collarbone.

Marshall continued to pull, but this only resulted in stretching Fraser out on the ground with him only being able to cushion his collapse with his right hand.

Marshall found it problematic to remove the claw from Fraser's shoulder. After a moment of panic, he composed himself, and deduced that in order to remove the hammer, he had to push the head further into the wound before twisting it in order to release the grip it had on the collarbone.

By now, Fraser's eventual cries were muffled due to his constricted position, lying face down on the gravelled pathway.

With the hammer finally free, Marshall then delivered one final blow, the originally intended blow, to Fraser's head now as he lay beneath him on the ground.

With the deed done, Marshall briefly looked all around him.

His intention was to leave the churchyard using the same way he had come in, but not if this would put him in close proximity with anyone else. However, the coast was clear, and Marshall broke into a jog as he made his way from the churchyard.

Having left the churchyard through an alleyway, Marshall crossed over a surrounding residential road, and immediately ducked into yet another alleyway.

Once about mid-way along this one, he allowed himself to cease running. As he slowed to a walking pace, and as he struggled to control his breathing, he took a moment to look back the way he had come. No one was behind him.

On his way to the churchyard, Marshall had noticed a suitable location for what was now required. The idea occurred to him when he first found the hammer. Marshall then secreted the hammer in a tree, about eight feet off the ground.

With the hammer now secure, and not in his possession, Marshall made his way back to his car, appearing to anyone that might see him to be nothing more than a man out for an evening run.

Once back in his car, he drove a convoluted route home, ensuring that he only came out onto main roads having travelled several miles out of his way using back roads.

oOo

Once home, Marshall poured himself a drink. He looked at his makeshift working area on the dining room table. He then looked at his list that was sat prominently amongst his files.

He took out a pen, and clicked the end for the nib to appear. He was about the cross a line through Fraser's name, when he stopped himself before pen touched paper.

Marking the list was the wrong thing to do. The deed was done, *that* was all that mattered.

22

Friday was anticipated to be the last day of Garmin's trial. The prosecution had concluded their case against him the previous week, and they hadn't felt the need to recall any of their witness.

Marshall had also concluded the defence's case the previous morning, and the judge had adjourned the court for the day to allow for closing statements and the possibility of a verdict being reached the next day before the weekend.

As with the initial introductions and laying the evidence, it was the prosecution who first stood in order to summarise their case and highlight elements of their evidence to the jury in the form of a closing statement.

During this, they referred to the source material, the images that had incriminated Garmin, the severity of such an offence, and the likelihood that, if unpunished, of an escalation in his behaviour and consequently, the increased risk to society.

All was very concise, very eloquent, and most of all very factual. Then, after a short recess, if fell to James Marshall to address the court. He stood, and started to pace the area in front of the jury.

"Ladies and gentlemen," Marshall said as he began his closing statement. "As we have all seen and heard, I have responded to the prosecution's case against my client by delivering a somewhat complex defence... However, the prosecution's case was so meticulous in its preparation, that it covered every possible, and plausible angle that there appeared to be. As a result, there was very little I could do to undermine their evidence... It has been proven that the only illicit images found were on the defendant's *work* laptop. A laptop that was provided to him by his company to allow him to work away from their offices. A laptop that was password protected to prevent any unauthorised access... And, furthermore the prosecution has already stated that the item was issued to the defendant as its first *ever* user, fresh out of the box... They provided a dated invoice from the manufacturer, *and* a docket signed by the defendant showing the date he accepted sole responsibility for the computer… So, in order to challenge how these disgusting and abhorrent images got there, *and* give a plausible alternative explanation, am I supposed to convince you that a software technician either at the computer's manufacturer, or someone at the defendant's place of work somehow managed to download these obscene images *prior* to handing the device to the defendant? Who then continued to use the laptop *apparently* blissfully unaware of its sickening and repulsive contents…? After all, as the prosecution has *also* pointed out, the dates on which the images were downloaded were in fact *after* the device was handed over to the defendant for his *exclusive* use. And the abhorrent content was only found *after* the defendant had to take it to his IT department following a malware corruption warning…"

Marshall then turned to face the jury's box. He stood motionless for a moment, before plunging his hands into his trouser pockets and continuing. A look of disappointment was evident on his face.

"Now, ladies and gentlemen, I pride myself in always being able to cast doubt, and to also throw in some misdirection for good measure… But I fear *even* my limits have been tested by this case. I cannot offer you an alternative explanation as to how these abhorrent images ended up on the defendant's computer. Certainly not a plausible one anyway. One that is enough to cast reasonable doubt in your minds. It's days like this, ladies and gentleman, that I have to admit to failing in my sworn task… I thank you."

Marshall then walked despondently back to his seat, his head bowed in apparent shame.

A shocked silence fell over the courtroom as Marshall retook his seat. All eyes were on Garmin in the dock, and the look of pure hatred on his face, clearly directed at his counsel.

The silence then erupted into whispering and conjecture amongst those in the public gallery.

The judge, who knew he needed to remain impartial to the proceedings, had to do his best to salvage the situation that befell the court.

"Young man, would you please stand for me again?" he said, addressing Marshall. "I would like to say that in all my years on the bench

I have never heard such a closing argument from the defence… I see your point, but it is not *your* role to highlight that to the jury."

The judge paused to further reflect upon the spectacle that he had just witnessed.

"I have never seen a counsel for the defence go to such lengths to sabotage his own client's defence," he continued. "Let it be known and recorded here that on the conclusion of this trial I plan on submitting a report to the Bar Association to inform them of this, and Mister Marshall, I will be strongly advising your client that he do the same."

When Marshall was sure that the judge had finished with his summation, he offered his reply.

"Under the circumstances your honour, I would have to wholeheartedly agree with you," he said.

Again, silence fell across the courtroom. Marshall was effectively supporting the judge's campaign to have him disbarred.

"However," the judge continued, instantly grasping the attention of the whole room. "Despite your shocking summary, the cases for the prosecution and defence had already been laid…"

He then turned to face the jury, before continuing.

"Ladies and gentlemen of the jury, the spectacle you have just witnessed plays no part in undermining either the case for the prosecution *or* the case for the defence. I will therefore instruct you merely to disregard what you have just witnessed, and to reach a verdict based on the evidence alone… This court is now adjourned to allow the jury to reach a verdict."

The judge struck his gavel, and with that the hearing was over.

Marshall had remained on his feet throughout the judge's response. He then collected his briefs together and calmly walked out of the courtroom.

After a moment of hesitation at apparently becoming superfluous to the proceedings, Garmin stood up and followed on behind him.

In the corridor, he grabbed hold of Marshall's sleeve as before and spun him around.

"What the *fuck* was that?" he demanded of Marshall.

"Y'know what? The best thing you can do right now is to get the fuck away from me," came Marshall's reply.

He stared down at the hand that had spun him around. It was at that moment that Garmin realised that he had gone too far.

oOo

Despite what had happened during the recess, Marshall returned to court once it had been called back into session in order to hear the verdict. However, this time he sat in the public gallery, having been dismissed by Garmin as his legal representation.

Below him, Marshall could see that Garmin had been allowed to sit at the defence's table as opposed to the dock. He stood for the reading of his own verdict.

"Has the jury reached a verdict?" the judge asked.

"We have, your honour," madam foreperson responded.

"What say you?" the judge said.

"We the jury find the defendant not guilty," madam foreperson concluded.

The earlier sounds of gossip echoing off the walls resumed, as it appeared that Marshall was not the only person in the courtroom to be shocked by the inadequacy and ineptitude of the verdict.

Marshall knew full well that he himself had dotted some of the I's and crossed some of the T's that the prosecution's case had failed to substantiate. But even with his closing summary ordered to be discounted he felt confident that the verdict should have gone against Garmin.

Marshall left the building feeling somewhat despondent. A rare feeling for him, especially given that he had effectively won his case, and succeeded in keeping his unblemished record intact.

Marshall returned to his car, with his career effectively in tatters. But he did have one saving grace with which to console himself, and that was that Garmin was on the list, and with not guilty verdict, he was free to be included.

On his way home, Marshall had to take a short detour. He parked up in a residential road, and re-entered an alleyway to retrieve something that he had hidden away the previous evening: the blood-stained hammer. It was just how he had left it. Once it was retrieved, he then went home.

23

Marshall pulled up in front of the house occupied by his soon-to-be ex-wife Nicky and their two children. Finally, the other weekend, as in *every other weekend* had arrived.

Though as he waited anxiously, he half expected this time, the time that he was due to spend with his children to be cancelled at the last minute, much like the last time.

As he waited, Marshall looked over at the house. It was the house that he used to share with them, when they were a family.

As he looked, he saw curtains twitch. Moments later, the front door opened, and two children came running down the driveway towards him.

Their mother stood in the open doorway, and beyond her, Marshall was adamant that he could see another figure moving around in the kitchen at the end of the hall.

"Fucking hell," he muttered. "He's staying over already."

Marshall was referring to his wife's new partner. Apparently, he was halfway to moving in.

Suddenly, there were two small faces pressed up against his car window.

"It's my turn in the front," his son Nathaniel said.

"No, you sat up front last time, it's my turn," his daughter Evangeline argued.

They both pulled open the front passenger door, and then both struggled to be the first to sit down next to their father.

"It's my turn!"

"No, it's not!"

"It is Nat's turn," Marshall said, hoping to resolve the situation. "Remember Evie, you sat up front when I dropped you guys off last time. *If* you can remember that far back."

This last comment being meant as a dig at Nicky, as opposed to his daughter, referring the last visit being cancelled.

As this kind of squabble was a frequent occurrence, Marshall had to make a mental note as to whose turn it was to do certain things.

He had to be sure of any intervention should there be a disagreement, as they were of the age where if Marshall was incorrect then he might run the risk of being accused of unfairness, or worse still, favouritism.

Gleefully, Nathaniel took the seat next to his dad. He then turned to look back to where Evangeline had now got in behind him. He stuck his tongue out at her.

"I saw that," Marshall said. "So, what would you two like to do today?"

Marshall's divorce had yet to be finalised, so all access to his children was by discussion and agreement with his estranged wife.

Despite the insecure nature of this arrangement, it was far better than when he and Nicky first separated. However, as it was not regulated by a court order or any other official agreement, it did have the unexpected downside as was experienced when Nicky chose to cancel plans at the last minute.

Marshall was well aware that his wife had already reverted back to using her maiden name. This was evident with every email received from her work account.

Although both of his children were born within wedlock, and shared his surname, his son had chosen to also take his mother's maiden name, not in any official capacity, but his mother had spoken to his school to say that he would prefer to be referred to by this name.

Marshall felt that this was his son's way of reaffirming his bond with his mother, possibly after she had brought a new man into their lives, and given the most recent revelation, into their home.

But whatever reason spurred his son's decision, Marshall was happy to allow it to pass without making an issue about it. He felt his son was going through enough without making him aware of the upset it had caused his father. He was still his son, and nothing would ever change that, regardless of who else lived at home with him.

The weather had taken a turn for the worse. It had been cold all week, but it had been raining since Marshall had woken that morning. This would ultimately scupper any outdoor plans or suggestions he or his children might have.

"Well?" said Marshall, reaffirming his earlier question.

He looked at his daughter who had taken her enforced turn in the back seat.

He then looked over at his son who had adopted a very familiar pose, one that had his attention engrossed in a small rectangular screen of his newly acquired smart phone. This was the downside of him having his own phone, that Marshall was having to have a relationship with the top of his son's head.

However, it wasn't without its benefits. Since getting the phone, his son had come across, and was becoming quite adept at an online battle royale game. This rapidly became one of the things that he and his father shared an interest in, and as it was online, they frequently played together even though they were physically apart.

Unfortunately for them both, this had to be a secret pastime, as Nicky didn't share their enthusiasm for the game, and had deleted it from Nathaniel's phone on more than one occasion because of its age rating.

But, because it was one of the things that had brought Marshall and his son closer together since the split, he had no intention of enforcing his wife's ruling.

But, for all that benefits it had, it still prevented him from getting a response to the question at hand.

"Nat?" he asked of his son.

All Marshall got to even suggest that his words had made it as far as being heard, was a shrug of his son's shoulders.

When Nat realised that his father was still looking towards him, he reinforced his sentiment, verbally this time.

"I dunno," he replied. "Ask Evie."

Marshall knew that he had already spent too much time on this question, and looking back to where his daughter sat, he could see Nicky still stood in the open front door of the house they used to share with her arms folded.

He felt that any moment, she would begin to walk towards his car to enquire as to the reason behind the delay in their departure. To prevent this, he turned the key, started the engine, and started to pull away in lieu of any response from his daughter.

The conversation as forced and borderline uncomfortable as Marshall made attempt after attempt to drag answers from them.

"So how was school this week?"

"Do you have any homework with you?"

"Have you got your swimming gear for tomorrow?"

Each question, as before, had to be repeated before an unintelligible grunt, or inaudible shrug or fidget was meant to somehow signify an intelligible response.

Once back at Marshall's home, both of his children retreated to their respective bedrooms that they had there.

It had been agreed ahead of any division of assets as part of the divorce that Nicky would get the marital home in order to minimise any disruption to the children, as, to coin their expression, "you could hit a golf ball into their school playground from the driveway." So, it made sense for the children to stay put. Marshall had since rented a similar-sized house about five miles away.

"Close enough to be convenient, but far enough away *not* to be intrusive" was how he considered it.

Although the children's bedrooms were fully furnished, and even had a share of many of their favourite items, despite protests, Marshall had refused to allow them to have TVs or games consoles in their rooms. This was so they couldn't come over just to shut themselves away.

It might have been considered harsh, but he only saw them every other weekend, and ideally, he didn't want them to spend that time in their bedrooms, unless it was to do homework.

As Nat was still engrossed playing the battle royale game on his phone, Evie had exclusive use to the TV in the living room, with the online streaming services and Marshall's DVD/BD movie collection.

In typical fashion, as soon as she chose what she wanted to watch, the challenge went down from Nat, who had suddenly decided he no longer wanted to play his game, and wanted to watch TV himself.

oOo

The afternoon progressed into the evening with the same amount of disagreement and bickering over every decision that either of them made.

However, there was one thing that they did both agree on, and that was what they wanted for to eat for dinner.

On this occasion, like so many others beforehand, it was decided that it was pizza they wanted. But not anything that was available to be kept in the freezer for just such an occasion.

The pizza of choice would require either an online order for delivery, or for Marshall to go out and collect it himself.

"Okay, what do you guys want then?" he asked. "Lemme guess, pepperoni?"

This received an enthusiastically positive response from both.

"Wedges and garlic bread?" he added.

"Please daddy," Evie replied. "And ice cream?"

"I'll see what I can do," he replied.

Then knowing the answer, he asked a frivolous question. "Either of you want to come with me?"

He saw them both look towards the window to see that it was still crashing down with rain. He could then see them both shake their heads.

"Okay, I'll be as quick as I can," he said as he put his waterproof coat on.

oOo

The drive into town to where the pizza shop was, took hardly any time at all. But that's where things ground to a halt. Inside the pizza shop, there was a queue, with four or five people ahead of him.

Beyond the counter, Marshall could see a plethora of delivery boys, all dressed in waterproofs and crash helmets, waiting on their orders to take out for delivery.

Then it came to Marshall's turn to give his order.

"Can I get a large pepperoni, large meat feast, um, garlic bread, and some wedges, please," he asked.

After the cashier had typed in his order, he replied to Marshall.

"It's gonna be about a thirty-minute wait, is that okay?" he said.

Then having received a positive response from Marshall, he completed the transaction.

Seeing that there wasn't any provision available in which to sit and wait in the shop, Marshall again addressed the cashier.

"I'm gonna wait in my car, I'll be back in thirty," he said.

With that, he walked back out into the rain. He crossed over the road, and got back in his car.

What he had told the cashier was thus far correct, though he had no intention of waiting for the next half hour merely sat in a parked car opposite the shop.

Instead, Marshall started the engine and drove off. He had a quick errand to take care of in the time it would take to prepare his order.

oOo

Within minutes, Marshall parked up in the service road, lined with hoardings behind the derelict Iron Horse public house.

He turned off the engine, and for a moment sat motionless in the darkened interior of his car.

He then reached across to the glove compartment. He opened it and took a small container which resembled a canister of cigarette lighter fuel in size and shape.

He then got out of the car and tucked the canister away in an outer pocket of his coat.

It was still raining heavily, and as he stood beside his car, he was already getting drenched. Marshall turned up the collar up his coat, and walked towards the hoarding boards, specifically towards the dislodged panel where he had gained entry to the site only days earlier.

Between the car and the insecurity on the boundary, he hadn't seen anyone, so it was fair to assume that no one saw him. It was a cold and wet evening; as a result, it was darker than it normally would be at that hour. Also, being a Saturday, people were already busy doing whatever people chose to do at that time on a Saturday, *or* they were queuing to order pizza.

Marshall approached the derelict shell of the once-splendid pub. The rain and wind disguised his every footstep.

He reached the insecure door at the back of the pub. It had been left ajar from its last usage. It was open wide enough for him to enter without even having to touch it.

Inside turned out to be noisier than outside. The torrent of rain crashing down on the roof echoed within the voids that long since had been exposed to the elements.

Before venturing upstairs, Marshall needed to locate a few things in the area that was once the bar. He found what he needed in the form of a cardboard box that had once contained cheese & onion crisps, he also collected up a few old newspapers that had been left strewn around the place.

Lastly, Marshall took a couple of old bar towels from the shelves below the suspended optics to finish his shopping list. He then returned to the foot of the stairs carrying his acquisitions.

There was one last thing Marshall had to check before going upstairs. He approached the door to the cupboard under the stairs. It took a little persuasion, but eventually he managed to pull open the door without causing any discernible noise. He nodded and smiled with approval at what he saw inside the cupboard.

Marshall then returned to the foot of the stairs. He collected the cardboard box, which now contained the towels and newspapers, and tucked it just inside the open cupboard door. He stood up and listened. Beyond the sounds of nature around him, all was silent.

Marshall then ventured upstairs. He stayed near to the wall on every step to reduce any creaking on the swollen and partially rotten boards. As hoped, he reached the landing without making a sound.

He then proceeded to peer into each room in turn leaving the room he believed, from his previous visit to be the one that was occupied to last. No one was in any of the other rooms.

Marshall stood in the open doorway of the last room. He waited for his eyes to adjust to the light conditions. Although faint, in the far corner of the room, he saw a solitary figure in what appeared to either be either a drunken stupor, or a restless sleep, as they excessively fidgeted in a sleeping bag.

Next to the sleeping bag, draped over a beer keg, was the technicolour woollen coat that Marshall had seen McNeil wearing earlier in the week.

Marshall was convinced that there were no other signs of life within this room, or within the entire pub. Nothing with less than four legs, or without feathers anyway. Being satisfied with what he saw, he went back downstairs, exercising the same caution as before.

Having returned to the under-the-stairs cupboard, it was then that Marshall took the canister from his pocket. It did not contain liquid lighter fuel as the non-descript canister might suggest. Instead it contained linseed oil.

From Marshall's review of Charlie Maclean's file, she allegedly favoured the use of linseed oil as her ignition source.

The last fire that was attributed to Maclean, the one to which her trial was pending, was a church hall. This fire occurred after it was alleged that Maclean deliberately left a pile of linseed oil-soaked rags in a bin inside the cleaner's cupboard in the hall.

The fire was caused by an exothermic chemical reaction within the oil, which eventually led to flaming combustion.

Rags soaked with linseed oil, especially when stored in a restricted space where any heat produced could not dissipate are a fire hazard. This is because they provide a large surface area for the evaporation and oxidation of the oil.

Maclean had told Marshall in a privileged conversation that she preferred this method of ignition because it allowed her to get out of the property in good time, before the fire became apparent. She could then return to the scene, raise the alarm and be considered a hero. It was only when she had called in a significant number of fires did it become apparent that it was more than merely a coincidence.

However, no physical evidence existed against her. It was only similarities in the ignition source to her previous fires, and the fact that Maclean was found at the scene when the authorities arrived, which led to her being charged with arson.

The hero element of the incident was also documented within Maclean's file, as it lent itself to her defence as a possible symptom of Factitious Disorder Imposed on Another, more commonly known as

Munchausen Syndrome by Proxy, whereby a person creates a dangerous situation so as to become an object of attention or affection as a consequence of it.

Marshall spread the bar towels out on the floor inside the cupboard. He then emptied the contents of the linseed oil canister over the towels, discarding the empty canister towards the back of the cupboard.

The evaporating fumes in such a confined space caused Marshall to cough and splutter momentarily, which he had to stifle using his sleeve across his mouth.

He then gathered up the rags, and dumped them back into the cardboard box, before placing the newspapers on top of the towels. Finally, he tucked the box to the very back of the cupboard, underneath the stairs. He then crawled backwards out of the cupboard on his hands and knees, before finally closing the cupboard door.

Marshall stood up again, and walked back to the foot of the stairs. There was no sign of movement coming from upstairs. Evidently his coughs were sufficiently muffled within confines of the cupboard, and masked by the weather.

Marshall then left through the ajar back door, leaving it as he had found it. He jogged back to the gap in the boundary fence. Once again, he peered through the gap, out onto the street before committing himself. He gave a final glance back towards the pub. There were no external signs of the horror that now lurked within.

Marshall returned to his car. He checked the time. From there, he drove back to the pizza shop where he collected his order.

"Can I also have some cookie-dough ice cream please?" he asked.

Then having paid for that separately, he took his order and got back in his car.

oOo

A short while later, Marshall arrived back at home. He walked into the living room to find his two children exactly as he had left them.

"Okay, who wants pizza?" he asked.

"Meeeeee," they replied in unison.

It was as they enjoyed their dinner of pizza and ice cream, that the distant but distinct wail of emergency sirens could be heard.

Marshall concluded that this was most likely his doing.

24

The following day, after Marshall had dropped his children home to their mother following their swimming lesson, he had arranged to collect his own mother, in order for them both to attend the hospital to visit his father. They were hoping to see if they were any closer to taking him home.

As they made their way to the hospital, they heard a news bulletin come over the radio.

"Last night police and the fire brigade attended a large fire at a disused public house in Oakvale. It took firefighters over an hour to get the blaze under control... From early reports, it has been confirmed that one person, possibly someone sleeping rough, was inside and died in the fire. The fire is believed to have started around 8 o'clock in the evening, and the police are asking if anyone has any information that may help with their enquiries, to please call 101."

Marshall continued driving as if he had just heard the weather forecast. Much like the previous evening, he did not feel compelled to react in any way whatsoever.

His mother however, did respond to the bulletin.

"Oh, my Lord," she exclaimed. "That's awful."

Feeling that he couldn't allow his mother's comment to go unanswered, he fished for a response. One that reflected his own sentiments, but not *too* accurately.

"Well, whoever it was probably started it," he said. "Besides, they shouldn't have *even* been there in the first place."

"James," she said scornfully. "That's not the point, and you know it. I thought your father and I brought you up better than that?"

"Oh, you did, believe me," Marshall said, doing his best to appease the escalating disagreement. "I was just making a joke."

"Someone getting burned to death in a fire is *not* a joking matter," his mother reaffirmed.

"I very much doubt if they got a chance to be burned to death," Marshall said, correcting his mother. "Chances are the smoke got to them well before the fire ever did."

"Now, that's enough of that," she then said.

Marshall knew to quit whilst he was ahead. He was saved from any further awkwardness on the topic, as they pulled into the hospital car park, and his attention was diverted to finding a space to park in.

oOo

Marshall sat on the end of his father's bed, as his mother sat on the single chair afforded to his ward bed.

"I had a visit from a detective on Friday," his father began. "It appears they now have some sort of forensic evidence which may lead to them arresting someone."

This breakthrough didn't appear to have the reaction that his father was expecting from Marshall. Despite this he continued.

"It got me thinking, that maybe I should just drop all this... I never expected them to find anyone responsible... And I just don't want anyone holding a grudge and turning up again."

"I really wouldn't worry about that just yet," Marshall said, in an attempt to appease his father. "Just coz they've got a someone in mind for it doesn't meant they'll *ever* locate him, or that it'll ever go to trial... To be honest, I'm betting you won't hear anything about him again."

Seeing his father sigh, Marshall knew that his efforts had fallen short.

"I don't know, James," his father replied. "I just don't want the hassle of it all. Your mother and I are both still here, and a few bumps and bruises aside, it's like it never really happened, and that's all that really matters."

Marshall could see where his father was coming from, but nonetheless, he was somewhat disappointed by his stance.

"But wouldn't you want to be able to stop this from happening to someone else?" Marshall added.

"Son, sometimes it's not selfish to be selfish… I'm just looking to keep my family safe," his father added. "You're a father too, now wouldn't *you* do the same?"

It was to this remark that Marshall once again realised that the debated topic was over.

"Tell you what I'll do then," Marshall said. "I'll contact the detective and see if I can find out anything more for you, find out just how close they are to nicking someone for this. How's that?"

"If it makes you feel better about things, then go right ahead," his father replied. "But, certainly don't go to any efforts on my behalf."

With that subject exhausted, Marshall knew the conversation needed to move on to other more pressing matters.

"Any idea when they're gonna let you home?" he asked.

"Any day now," his father replied. "That certainly seems to be the buzz-phrase being used, *any day now*."

oOo

Having left the hospital, and whilst on his way to drop his mother off, Marshall phoned the local police station using the in-car hands-free set up.

Having previously been given the contact details of the officer in charge of his father's investigation, Marshall was able to use the automated option given over the phone to dial the extension for the detective he needed to speak to.

"Detective Constable Tappin, how can I help you?" the voice at the end of the phone said upon answering.

"Good afternoon, my name is James Marshall, I'm Leonard Marshall's son. I understand you're heading the investigation into his attack. I've just spoken to my father, and he's told me that you've had a development."

There was a short silence before a response came.

"Um, yes, Mister Marshall," Tappin replied, having been caught off-guard. "I'm not really in a position to discuss this matter with you over the phone. But if you and your father are able to come into the police station, I can then discuss the investigation with you?"

Although disappointed at the lack of progress that could be made over the phone, Marshall understood the need for confidentiality and date protection.

For all DC Tappin knew, Marshall could have been anyone, even someone linked to the suspect, or a member of the press seeking details for a story.

"That's going to be something of a problem," Marshall replied. "You see my father is *still* in hospital as a result of the attack, with no end as yet in sight."

"Ah, yes, sweet old guy, I popped in to see him late last week," Tappin replied. "Tell you what, if you're able to pop in, I'll see what I can do for you."

Given his immediate circumstances, an idea occurred to Marshall.

"How about I bring my mother along, as next of kin?" he added.

Marshall looked across at his mother sat beside him in the car. She nodded encouragingly so not having to verbalise her agreement.

"Better still," Tappin replied. "When can you come in?"

"We can be there in about half an hour," Marshall replied. "Is that any good?"

"Perfect," Tappin replied. "I'll see you shortly. When you arrive, have the front office call up for me."

oOo

Within the hour, and slightly longer than expected, both Marshall and his mother found themselves in an interview room adjoining the front office at the police station. They had been left there by the office staff in order to await the detective's arrival.

The room was sparsely furnished, with a single table situated centrally along the back wall, with chairs to both sides which were fixed to the floor.

On one side of the table was a touch-screen computer, and on the table was a microphone which were used to record interviews.

As they waited, Marshall past the time by pacing, whilst his mother had chosen to take a seat.

After a few minutes, the door opened, which startled them both. In stepped a man of a similar age to Marshall, who would have been immaculately dressed in a three-piece suit had not chosen to leave his jacket elsewhere.

Once having ensured that the door was closed behind him, he spoke.

"James Tappin," he said.

As he introduced himself, he extended a hand, first to Mrs Marshall, then to Marshall himself.

"So good to see you both… Please, take a seat," he continued, whilst gesturing for Marshall to sit down next to his mother.

Once everyone had taken a seat and had time to make themselves comfortable, Tappin continued.

"Sorry I took so long to come down, I was in the middle of something when they called up for me," Tappin said apologetically. "But, before we begin, I do know you, don't I?"

Tappin looked towards Marshall, having addressed his question specifically at him.

"Yes, you do," Marshall replied, not wanting to unnecessarily delay the update for the sake of playing guessing games. "I'm a solicitor… We have actually interviewed together."

"Ah, yes," Tappin regaled, once the penny had finally dropped. "Your father mentioned that his son was a solicitor. But even when he gave your name, though it sounded familiar, I just couldn't place it."

They both allowed a brief moment to enjoy the coincidence.

Tappin then reverted his attention to a manila folder that he had brought into the interview room with him, and had until then had discarded it on the table to allow for the formality of greetings.

"Well, as I mentioned to Mister Marshall in hospital when I visited him," Tappin said acknowledging the absent victim. "We have located an evidential sample from which we have been able to match to a DNA profile currently held on file. And from this, we have been able to identify a possible suspect in this investigation."

As a result of the earlier conversation in the hospital, it was evident that Mrs Marshall now had more interest in this development of this case than either her husband or her son.

From that moment, Marshall was confident that he knew every word that Tappin was about to utter, and his posture and demeanour reflected this.

"Now before I go into any detail with regards to the suspect, I need to make you aware that the sample we found was on the exterior of your home address... Now, as you may not be aware, Missus Marshall," Tappin said looking at Marshall's mother, before elaborated for her benefit. "That is what is considered circumstantial evidence in itself... Now, by that I mean it can potentially place someone at the scene of a crime, but it cannot prove their actions or any involvement beyond that."

Hearing these words caused Marshall to recall the numerous occasions and cases that he had fought, having had allegations dropped on the basis of such evidence being ruled as circumstantial.

He could almost hear the defence discrediting this evidence as he sat there listening to Tappin.

From his own experience, he knew that this was enough evidence to identify a suspect and to have grounds to arrest them. But, without anything more substantial, or an admission on the part of the suspect, then on its own, the police essentially had nothing.

Marshall's thoughts were brought back to the moment as he watched Tappin turn over a page in his file. He saw what he recognised to be a forensic profile. It had a name and a photographic image on it, but from the angle and the distance of which he viewed it, Marshall couldn't identify whose profile it was.

Tappin again started to speak, using the information provided by the forensic profile.

Here it comes, Marshall thought.

"Does the name Giles Quinn mean anything to *either* of you?" Tappin asked.

Mrs Marshall shrugged her shoulders, and shook her head.

"Never heard of him," she said.

Tappin's attention turned to Marshall.

"And you, sir?" Tappin asked.

Instead of offering anything by way of a reply, or even acknowledgement of being addressed, Marshall sat there in a momentary catatonic state of shock.

Seconds could easily have been minutes, and minutes could've been hours for all the relevance time had in that moment.

Tappin could see that the name had a reaction for Marshall, but even he could not deduce the rationale behind such a reaction.

"Mister Marshall?" Tappin asked in an attempt to re-establish contact. "Are you all right sir?"

This enquiry as to his wellbeing was enough to bring Marshall to his senses.

"I'm okay," he eventually replied.

Although in truth, he was far from it. He remained breathless, his lips dry, and his pupils were dilated.

"Mister Marshall," Tappin continued. "Do you know the name Giles Quinn?"

Had Tappin previously known who Leonard Marshall's son was, there was no doubt in Marshall's mind that Tappin would have already formed the connection between him and Quinn.

In lieu of being able to find it out for himself, Marshall decided there was no reason to withhold the information from Tappin.

"Yes," Marshall replied. "I represented him on one occasion."

His mother looked across at him in shock at this revelation.

Tappin sat back in his chair. It was in that instant that another penny dropped. Not in having established the link between Marshall and Quinn, but in other aspects of the investigation.

It had suddenly become apparent why nothing had been taken from the home of Marshall's parents when the attack had taken place. The motive was never that of a robbery.

With such a link now established between the victim and the alleged suspect, the motive was clear that this was a pre-meditated and targeted attack.

"And what can you tell me about the case in which you represented Quinn?" Tappin asked.

"I shouldn't really say anything, *not* with my mother here," Marshall said. He then looked over at her. "No offence."

"None taken," his mother said despondently.

Realising Marshall was right, Tappin chose not to mention this development any further.

However, there was nothing that Marshall could tell him that he couldn't find out through official channels.

"Okay, I'll look into that," Tappin said. "Is it okay if I call on you with regards to this?"

Marshall nodded, before verbalising his reply.

"Of course," he said.

He then took a business card from his wallet and placed it on top of the manila folder in front of Tappin.

With this, the meeting and the update were at an end. Marshall gave his mother some extra support as she eased herself out of the chair.

The entirety of the drive back to drop his mother off was in silence. Both of them had so much to contemplate.

His mother had to now consider that one of her son's former clients had such a grievance against him that he would infiltrate his parent's home in order to attack them in order to get back at him.

Whilst Marshall himself consumed with the same update, in addition to this, he needed to also come to terms with the fact that the attack on Robert Fraser was now possibly without motive.

25

After having dropped his mother off, Marshall then went home himself.

For the reminder of the evening he sat at his dining room table, and pondered what had happened, as well as what he considered still needed to happen.

But anything that still needed to happen couldn't happen *that* evening, so once again he had to play the waiting game.

It was this waiting game that tortured him, with his only solace and company being granted to him by a glass of whisky.

He went over and over the conversation he had with Detective Tappin in his mind.

He knew he hadn't disclosed anything to Tappin that couldn't be find out by other means. This was once again the game they played that was known as disclosure.

Marshall had been on the receiving end of disclosure more times than he cared to remember. Recently with Brett Cable following his arrest for the brutal hammer attack on Paul Greene.

The aim of the game was to be seen to be open and forthcoming with the information that was being handed across. But the trick was to ideally only disclose information that was already known, or that was readily available from other sources.

With that exchange in mind Marshall savoured his whisky in the assurance that he hadn't betrayed himself in any way with what he had told the detective.

With Giles Quinn once again at the front of his mind, Marshall revisited his case file that until then had been put to one side, having earlier excluded him using the criteria that had put others' names on his list.

The file Marshall had on Quinn was fairly historic, and as a result he expected the information he was looking to obtain from it to now be out of date.

It was one of Marshall's first major cases. Quinn had been arrested on the suspicion of murdering a man, having stabbed him at some point during an altercation in the street one evening.

Quinn maintained that he had been ambushed when he was attacked. He only admitted to disarming the victim, Marcus O'Connor, and using his own blade against him.

However, the prosecution had tried to prove that Quinn had engaged this O'Connor with the intent of killing him, which is why he was on trial for murder as opposed to manslaughter.

But the basis of Marshall's defence was that there had been no premeditation on Quinn's part, and that it was O'Connor who had entered into the altercation armed with the knife. This version of events was partially corroborated with the forensic evidence, having found fingerprints from both parties on handle of the knife.

From there, it was easy for Marshall to convince the jury that Quinn was merely acting in self-defence when he was attacked by a man wielding a knife.

This was something the prosecution could not disprove, though they did repudiate it. However, it was enough to cast reasonable doubt in the mind of the jury. Although it could not be disproved that O'Connor had died at the hands of Quinn.

Marshall was confident that he had done enough to secure an acquittal. But due to an oversight on the part of the fledgling attorney, the number of stab wounds on O'Connor's body went beyond what was reasonably considered to be an act of self-defence. Quinn was subsequently convicted of the lesser offence of manslaughter, and given a custodial sentence.

However, Marshall was looking through the case file, not because he was interested in the intricacies of the case, but because he was instead looking for the means by which locate Quinn himself.

Unfortunately, Quinn had been a frequent guest of Her Majesty, and as a result, he was never in one place for long enough in order to seek or need lodgings of his own.

He was known as a sofa surfer, one who had a tendency to sponge off acquaintances for a roof over his head for an odd day here and there.

Though, once again the term for him was *NFA*, or *no fixed abode*, as was the case with the recently deceased Patrick McNeil.

The file did however contain a correspondence address. An address where all communications intended for Quinn could be sent to, care of his mother, Mrs Margaret Quinn.

She was a widow back when this case came to court. Marshall hoped that her circumstances hadn't changed sufficiently in order for her to have moved on or changed her name.

But any enquiries in order to locate her, and in turn her son, would have to wait, as Marshall already had plans for the following evening.

26

Tuesday evening arrived, and with that Marshall had a fair assumption as to the whereabouts and commitments of acquitted, and as yet admitted paedophile Allan Garmin.

Marshall felt confident in describing Garmin as such, despite the fact that he had only been on trial for having illicit images of children on his laptop computer.

Garmin had earned his place on Marshall's list because, during a privileged conversation that had taken place in the time between him being charged and the subsequent trial, he had admitted to Marshall as having been actively involved in an online group that arranged the transportation of children around the country for the purpose of being abused by adults.

Garmin never actually confessed to any actions with a child himself, but he admitted that his actions facilitated putting a number of children in harm's way.

The reason Marshall knew Garmin's whereabouts and commitment that evening was because it had been suggested during the final week of his trial, that he should voluntarily seek a means of therapy to help with his compulsion. This had been suggested ahead of the verdict, with the intention to mitigate the damage should he have been found to be guilty as charged.

However, even despite Marshall's blatant attempt to offer his client on a plate to the jury, their ineptitude found him *not guilty* and acquitted him.

However, the suggestion for arranging therapy also had a secondary function, that of appeasing Garmin's wife.

Since he had been charged with the offences, she had taken it upon herself to ban him from the marital home where their children resided. She did not care if he had yet to be put on trial for the offences. She was erring on the side of caution, and understandably just wanted to keep their children safe.

It was a response to both of these factors that spurred the discussion between Marshall and Garmin at the beginning of the final week of his trial.

Marshall had also suggested that Garmin go through with the course of sessions that he had booked regardless of the verdict in order to further appease his wife.

This had been agreed to, and details of the sessions were given to Marshall before the spectacle that was his closing argument, as a result of which Garmin dismissed him as his legal representation, and the trial judge pledged to report him to the Bar Council.

Therefore, as a result of this prior agreement, Marshall now had a good idea as to where Garmin would be between 7 o'clock and 9 o'clock on a Tuesday evening for the next few weeks.

oOo

Earlier in the evening, Marshall had gone online, and used satellite imagery to determine where would be the best place to park for the evening's excursion.

He was also able to see what the best routes, both on foot and by car, would be between the various locations he would need to attend. He committed these to memory, as opposed to making any notes before heading out.

Before he left, he once again left as many of his personal possessions behind as possible. Though this time he kept his watch on, as accurate timekeeping would be crucial for what lay ahead.

Then, in addition to his own car and front door key, he only needed one other item, and that was Albert Foster's car key, that had been entrusted to him.

Once again, he ensured that he was going out dressed appropriately for the weather conditions. On this occasion, this included a pair of thin, black leather gloves.

oOo

Marshall parked up where he had earlier decided from the satellite imagery to be the best location.

From there, he walked through an alleyway, before walking to the end of the street it had come out on, paying particular attention to a couple of houses along the way.

He then walked back along another street that ran parallel to the first, paying particular attention to only one specific house on this occasion.

Marshall knew where he needed to eventually be, and roughly how long it would take to get there. He knew this because he had driven that part of the route before having earlier parked up.

The last house he had paid attention to was the home of Albert Foster, and in particular, where his car was parked. This was the same car that Foster had felt compelled to entrust Marshall with the key, because he didn't have the self-control not to drive it whilst on his ban. As a result, it had sat redundant on the road in front of the house since having been brought home, presumably by his wife, since his conviction.

Foster's house had a driveway, but it was only big enough for one car. Marshall concluded that they might have chosen to leave the driveway free for Foster's wife car to use to save her having to find a parking space in the street.

Marshall paused as he passed Foster's house on the opposite side of the street, hidden within shadows. He could see into the living room as the lights were on with the curtains open. He hoped that at any moment, someone would feel compelled to draw the curtains to stop any activity within from being a spectacle.

Marshall briefly glanced at his watch, he still had plenty of time before he needed to be elsewhere. As there was no immediate urgency, he continued on, walking past the house.

He walked as far as the end of the road, before turning around and walking back the same way he had just come.

When he got back to Foster's house, he found that the curtains had now been closed.

He crossed the road, and approached where Foster's car was parked. Marshall knew exactly which car it was from the information in the case file, which included the make, model, colour and registration number.

These details had been included as it was the vehicle that Foster was driving when he was arrested.

Not that this information was essential, it just made Marshall's job easier, as the key also had the manufacturer's logo embossed on it, confirming it was a Hyundai.

Marshall stood by the driver's door which was roadside, away from the house. He looked at the over the roof of the car towards Foster's house.

Given the height of their front wall and front garden shrubbery, he felt that the car's absence wouldn't be immediately apparent at a casual glance given out of a front window.

He pressed the button on the key fob remote to unlock the doors. The indicators flashed, and the doors unlocked. Marshall had a brief look around him to ensure he wasn't being watched before opening the door and getting in.

He then put the key into the ignition, and started the engine. Then having given another look round, he pulled out of the parking space, only turning the headlights on after he had driven a short distance down the road.

It didn't matter to him should the parking space he had left behind be taken prior to his return, not with what he had in mind.

Unlike the convoluted route he had taken home after the attack on Robert Fraser, Marshall was intent on driving Foster's car on main roads. Not only did he want to take the most direct and simple route on this occasion, but he also wanted the car to be picked up on the police's automatic number plate recognition (ANPR) cameras, as well as any CCTV along the route.

He knew from his experience of defending suspects of driving offences, as well as those charged with other offences where such camera evidence was used, that the images produced are very good at showing the occupants of a vehicle during the day, but in the evening, it was a completely different story. This was because within the darkened interior of a vehicle, especially with headlights adding to the glare and contrast, any facial features or characteristics of the vehicle's occupants were almost completely indistinguishable.

Marshall had planned and rehearsed this route, not only to include as many cameras as practicably possible, but also so he knew roughly how long it would take to reach where he needed to be, then adding a little extra time should anything unforeseen happen along the way.

The place he was driving to was the therapy centre where Allan Garmin was scheduled to be attending his regular Tuesday evening session.

Rather fortuitously, the therapy centre, which was set up in the hall of the local church, did not have a car park large enough for clients and visitors to park in. There was only a couple of bays, and a sign had been erected stating that they were for the use of staff only.

A recommendation published online was for the visitors to the church hall to park in the public car park on the opposite side of the road.

Prior to parking up, Marshall drove around the recommended car park. There he located Garmin's Audi, which he recognised from the law court's car park.

This confirmed that Garmin was attending his scheduled session, and from discussion on the subject during the trial, Marshall knew that the session would run from seven o'clock until nine o'clock.

Marshall drove back out of the car park, and pulled up in a bus stop lay-by on the same side of the road as the church hall. There he switched off the headlights, but kept the engine running.

Ahead of him, at a distance of about twenty yards was a zebra crossing, almost directly in front of the church hall. Marshall again felt confident that Garmin would most likely use this to cross over to the car park. It would also serve sufficiently well to illuminate him in front of the church hall, for Marshall to be able to positively identify him.

Marshall checked his watch. It was now ten minutes until nine o'clock. He compared it to the clock on the dashboard, one was accurate to the other.

As he waited, Marshall had a nosey look around the car. He looked in the glove compartment, but found that there was nothing of any interest in there. Then he looked in the back seat. There he saw something there that he considered might champion his cause even further.

On the backseat was a gentleman's flat cap. For those of a certain age, it was similar to the one that Grandpa Flump wore in the children's show from the late 1970s.

What Marshall knew about Foster, aside of his criminal past wasn't a great deal, but one thing he did know was that he had dogs. He drew the conclusion that the hat was probably kept in the car in case it was cold when he took them for a walk.

Realising the benefit this could have, Marshall reached back and grabbed the hat from the back seat, placing it on the front passenger seat beside him. He also wound down the window in the driver's door in preparation, shuddering momentarily as the cold of the night slapped him in the face through the window.

There was no longer any time to be nosey. Now his attention was on the door to the church hall. Marshall glanced down at the dashboard clock, 20:55, it read.

Any time now, he thought.

He ran through the impending scenario in his head. He debated whether in the crucial moment to come, should he have the headlights on, or leave them off?

His conclusions were reached having factored in that any persons in front of the car would have greater difficulty identifying the driver if he drove with his full beams on. So that immediately became part of the plan.

There was nothing more to contemplate, nothing more to decide upon, the only thing left to do was to wait and watch.

21:02.

In the distance, Marshall saw the doors to the church hall open. From what he knew about the particular therapy session that Garmin was attending, it took the form of one-to-one counselling. So, there was little likelihood of having droves of people coming out at the same time.

It was then that he saw a single person emerge from the open door. On first impressions, he was sure it was Garmin.

Marshall checked his mirrors, there was nothing coming up the road behind him, and nothing on the road ahead of him either.

Instead of choosing to walk back along the church hall's car park and come out of the vehicle entrance, Garmin chose to hop over a narrow flower bed that ran between the car park and the pavement.

This still brought him onto the pavement, but further up the road, beyond the zebra crossing.

Marshall then saw Garmin briefly glance in both directions as he prepared to cross the road back to his car.

Marshall quickly checked his mirrors again, still nothing was coming from behind him. He put the car into first gear.

Seeing the coast was clear, Garmin stepped out into the road, and began crossing it at a diagonal angle. This meant he would be in the road for much longer than had he chosen to cross it perpendicular to the pavement.

In the instant that Garmin had committed himself into the road, Marshall slowly pulled out of the lay-by into the carriageway, before accelerating as fast as the car would allow him.

Into second gear, gaining speed, and closing the distance. He kept it in second, over revving it, but accelerating hard.

Marshall closed the distance rapidly, and caught Garmin unaware. He only saw the Hyundai once the headlights were turned on. Until then it had been shrouded in darkness beyond the Belisha beacons of the zebra crossing. By then it was too late.

Garmin tried to break into a run to escape the path of the approaching vehicle. He had barely made it to the painted zig-zags that marked the mid-point of the zebra crossing when Foster's car ploughed into him.

The car hit Garmin squarely, launching him up into the air, and over the bonnet.

After the impact, as part of the plan, Marshall skidded the car to a halt. Whilst momentarily stationery, he threw the flat cap out of his window. It landed on the road next to the skid marks that he had just left behind.

Marshall then sped off into the distance leaving Garmin laying in the road, his condition unknown.

It was also part of the plan to drive as maniacally and erratically as he could whilst still ensuring he returned the car home in relatively one piece.

As a result, Marshall allowed himself to clip a couple of kerbs as he took corners, as well as knocking off a couple of wing-mirrors of parked cars along the way, just to add to the trail of destruction.

As he pulled into Foster's street, he slowed to a more civilised speed.

With Foster's house in sight, Marshall saw that the parking space that he had earlier vacated had become occupied in the Hyundai's absence.

This didn't matter to Marshall, as returning the car to where he had found it was never part of the plan.

Instead, Marshall lined up the Hyundai to drive directly at the corner of Foster's front wall. He undid his seatbelt, and again floored the accelerator. The economical family hatchback accelerated as best it could in third gear.

As it impacted the corner of the wall, Marshall threw himself across the passenger seat. The airbag deployed, missing him entirely.

Then once the car had come to a halt, he was out of the driver's door like a shot. He intentionally left the door wide open, and the key still in the ignition of the now-stalled car.

Marshall then ran up Foster's driveway, triggering a motion-activated security light as he did. He past Foster's wife's car and disappeared into the shadows beyond.

As he ran, lights were going on in windows of the houses all around the crashed Hyundai. But no one was looking at where Marshall was, or where he was running to; they were only looking at where he had been, at the devastation in front of Foster's house.

Marshall was relying on this misdirection to make good his escape, over the back fence of Foster's garden, and into the adjoining garden of the house that his backed onto.

Once there, Marshall slowed his pace, and casually exited the adjoining house onto the street.

This was the street that Marshall had earlier walked along, and had earlier given scrutiny to approximately where he felt he would be coming out.

From there, he walked towards the alleyway, before making his way back to his car, and heading home.

Marshall drove home with the car windows down. All the way home he heard the distant wail of emergency sirens responding to the carnage he had once again caused.

27

Police and paramedic units attended the scene of the hit-and-run road traffic incident in front of the church hall. Garmin had been declared dead at the scene.

It wasn't long after this that calls were made to the police reporting the collision in front of Foster's house, which police officers also attended.

Using the ANPR system, the police ran checks on Foster's car. It didn't take them long to determine it prior whereabouts, and draw conclusions that it was possibly his car that was involved in the collision that killed Garmin.

When asked what had happened, Albert Foster profusely denied any involvement, or even knowledge about what had taken place. His wife also protested his innocence.

The officers had to be careful not to ask too many questions having already established the offence what with Foster being their prime suspect.

This was because any further questioning would constitute an interview, and any impropriety or breach of his rights, to have legal representation whilst being questioned, could have a detrimental effect on the case, and any subsequent trial.

The attending officer also noted the smell of intoxicating liquor on Foster's breath. As a result, he was arrested on suspicion of dangerous driving, drink driving and failing to stop at the scene of a road traffic accident. At that time of Foster's arrest, the attending officer was unaware that the other incident had resulted in a fatality.

Whilst Foster was taken into custody, other officers called at his neighbours' houses to determined what, if anything they had seen or heard that could contribute to the investigation.

The police also had to make arrangements for Foster's Hyundai to be removed for forensic analysis in order to prove or disprove that Foster had been driving at the time of the collision, and to link the vehicle to the collision that killed Garmin.

In custody, Foster had to listen as the arresting officer as he gave the details of the arrest to the custody sergeant.

"The DP *[detained person]* is suspected of being the driver of a silver Hyundai, index Kilo-Victor-One-Zero-Hotel-Zulu-Quebec that was involved in a collision with a pedestrian on Church Road and failed to stop. Having attended the DP's home address, the car and DP were located, where the DP smelled of intoxicating liquor. He was arrested at twenty-one thirty-seven hours on suspicion of dangerous driving, driving whilst over the prescribed limit, and failing to stop at the scene of an accident," the officer said.

The custody sergeant reviewed the circumstances for which Foster had been arrested. He then addressed Foster himself.

"Do you understand why you have been arrested?" he asked him.

"I didn't do anything, I've been home all evening," he replied. "My wife said so."

The sergeant nodded to acknowledge Foster's response, however, he was not there to discuss the intricacies of it.

"Listen, Mister Foster, I don't care if you did or didn't do it," the sergeant replied, interrupting Foster. "I only asked if you understood *why* you're here... I'm not part of the investigation. That's down to my colleagues... Okay, I'm going to authorise your detention here for us to secure and preserve evidence by means of an evidential breath test and for questioning in an interview."

This was not a new experience for Foster, but on this occasion, he was truly unaware why he was there despite the explanation.

It was then that the custody sergeant handed the remainder of the booking-in process to that of a detention officer.

"Okay, Mister Foster," the detention officer began. "You have three rights whilst you're in custody, would you like to have anyone told that you're here?"

He shook his head, equally in despair and disgust.

"No, my wife was there when you morons arrested me," Foster exclaimed.

"There's no need for that, Mister Foster, my colleagues were only doing their jobs," the detention officer replied. "Secondly, you're entitled to free and independent legal advice whilst you're here, which includes the right to speak to a solicitor. Would you like to speak to a solicitor?"

"Yes, I would," replied Foster.

"Do you have your own one, or would you like the duty solicitor informed?" the officer asked.

"James Marsh…" Foster began, before cutting himself off mid-sentence.

"James Marsh?" the officer questioned seeking clarification.

Instead of offering a reply, Foster remained dumbstruck, contemplating Marshall's potential for involvement. In that instant, he remembered that he had entrusted his car key to him following his last conviction.

But he knew from his previous experiences of being in custody, of which there were many, and what the sergeant had so eloquently reminded him, was that there would be a time and a place to bring that fact up, and during the booking-in procedure was neither.

"Er, duty solicitor please," Foster confirmed.

This meant that Foster would be assigned whichever solicitor or legal representative was working on that rotation, and should the rotation allocate him Marshall, then it would be Foster right to decline him.

However, as Foster was arrested for a prescribed limit offence, drink or drug driving, the evidential procedure, with which to secure a sample breath, blood or in some cases, urine for use in court, did not have to be delayed in order to allow for a legal consultation as the evidence to be obtained was time critical.

This meant that the longer the wait until the sample was obtained, the greater the chance of the test result being reduced due to the passage of time, as any substance ingested would be naturally passed through the body.

As soon as the booking-in procedure was complete, Foster was taken to provide an evidential breath sample. This required him to give two specimens on a Home Office-approved device.

Foster was confident of his legal position, that he wasn't involved in any way in the offences for which he had been arrested. He therefore expeditiously provided the two specimens as required.

Previously, Foster had tried to outsmart the legal system by refusing to provide the specimens when requested to do so. At that time, he was unaware that failure to comply with the requirement carried as severe a penalty under law as if he had provided a specimen with a test result over the prescribed limit. A lesson that had resulted in his most recent conviction.

Foster provided an evidential breath test result of 97 micrograms of alcohol in 100 millilitres of breath, against a legal limit of 35μg/100ml.

But because Foster wasn't seen to be driving the car at the time of police involvement, and because there were other offences, he would need to be interviewed in order to establish his account and version of events. That was something that couldn't take place whilst he was still intoxicated.

As a result, Foster would have to spend the night in a police cell and be interviewed only after he had been given sufficient time to sober up. This ironically echoed his previous rant in court.

28

"Mister Foster, you were arrested last night when police officers attended your home address to find your car, a silver Hyundai index Kilo-Victor-One-Zero-Hotel-Zulu-Quebec crashed into your front wall... This was after it was believed to have been involved in a collision which resulted in the death of a pedestrian. You were also found to be intoxicated, having since given a positive breath test result. Please can you tell me what happened last night," the interviewing police officer asked.

Foster again found himself sat in the familiar surroundings of an interview room at the custody centre. He had the duty solicitor at his side, and across from him sat a police officer, and a sergeant from the roads policing unit.

Whilst Foster had been asleep, the police had been conducted enquiries through the night. In that time, they had viewed and downloaded footage from their ANPR and CCTV systems that covered the route between that of the fatal collision and Foster's home address. They had also completed their enquiries with Foster's neighbours.

Church Road, the scene of the fatal collision, had remained closed throughout the night as police officers conducted a thorough search of the area. This also included digitally mapping the crash scene to record the placement of all elements involved.

Having been in consultation with his solicitor prior to the interview, Foster had discussed the revelation that had dawned on him whilst he was being booked in.

Prior to responding to the officer's opening question, Foster leant across to ask his solicitor a question beyond their earshot, and inaudible to the recording being made of the interview. When he again sat upright, he saw his solicitor nod his agreement.

"Can you tell us how your car sustained damage?" the officer asked.

The officer felt compelled to re-ask and re-phrase his question in order to prompt a response.

"I don't know," replied Foster.

This questioned stunned the officer.

"You *don't* know how your car came to be crashed into the wall in front of your house late last night?" the officer reaffirmed.

"I think my client has already offered a sufficient answer to that question," Foster's solicitor interjected.

Feeling that this interview was about to turn into a "no comment" interview, the officer then went into a pre-planned list of question which were designed to address individual elements in order to allow for an inference to later be drawn should Foster decline to answer them.

"Who else could have driven your car?" the officer asked.

"Only me and my wife drive our cars," Foster replied.

"Who else has *access* to your car?" the officer asked, ensuring that the question was worded in such a way as to prohibit merely a *yes or no* reply.

"No one else," replied Foster.

"How many sets of keys do you have to this car, and where are they?" the officer asked.

"We have two keys for that car, my wife has hers," Foster began to explain, before pausing.

"And yours?" the officer asked.

"And I gave mine to my solicitor *James Marshall* after I was given my ban."

"And do you know where that key is now?" the officer asked after a moment of stunned contemplation of the disclosed revelation.

"I honestly couldn't tell you," answered Foster.

The sergeant then showed a number of photographs to Foster that until that moment had been laid face down on the table.

The first showed a close up of the Hyundai's interior around the driver's seat area. It showed a deployed airbag, and a key in the ignition.

"Is this your wife's key?" the sergeant asked.

"No, it isn't," Foster replied.

"That's right, no it isn't," the sergeant replied. "Her key is still with the rest of her keys. We know that because my colleagues have confirmed as much... Can you therefore explain how the *only* other key you have for this vehicle, *your* key ended up in the ignition when the car was found crashed in front of your house last night?"

Although he had his suspicions, Foster couldn't provide an explanation.

"No, I can't," Foster eventually replied.

The sergeant then showed a second image, this time it was of the front of Foster's car. It showed evidence of impact damage, including a cracked radiator grill, smashed headlight, dents to the bonnet and a cracked windscreen. There was also what appeared to be blood on the bonnet or the car.

"Please explain exactly how and when this damage occurred, Mister Foster?" the sergeant then went on to ask.

"I can't," Foster replied.

Both officers then looked at each other in disbelief.

The next photo to be shown was an image taken of Church Road. It showed a wide angle of the road. In the foreground and in the distance, police cars blocked the entire width of the road, closing it to the public. The focus of the image was of a zebra crossing, with skid marks extending beyond it.

It also showed an area of blood with medical wrappers strewn around it. There was also an apparently unrelated object on the ground beside this carnage.

The sergeant then laid another image on top of that one. It showed a close-up view of the previous scene. It included just the fading end of the skid marks, the edge of the blood pool, and only a few of the discarded medical wrappers. But the emphasis of the image was of the apparently unrelated item.

"Do you recognise the item in the picture?" the sergeant said, using his pen to point to the unrelated item that he was specifically referring to.

"It's a hat," Foster replied.

"And do you know whose hat it is?" the sergeant asked.

"I have absolutely no idea," Foster replied.

"Do you own a hat like this?" the officer when on to ask.

"Yes, I do," Foster replied.

168

"And, can you tell me where your hat is likely to be now?" the sergeant then asked.

"I keep it in my car," Foster resigned himself to admitting.

"Okay, moving on… Can you tell us why your neighbours reported seeing your security light coming on moments after they heard the crash in front of your house?" the sergeant went on to ask.

Foster shook his head.

"For the benefit of the audio recording, please can you verbalise all replies," the officer added.

"*No*," Foster replied, deliberately over emphasising his response.

From that moment on, all subsequent questions asked received a similarly vague and unconvincing response form Foster. As a result, the sergeant brought the interview to an unsatisfactory conclusion.

"Okay, Mister Foster," the sergeant began. "You're going to be released under investigation. In the meantime, we will have a chance to forensically examine amongst other things, your car, and follow up on other lines of enquiry… It will also allow us to speak to this James Marshall and see what he has to say in regard to your allegation. We will then be in touch when we're ready to speak to you further."

With that the interview was over.

Foster was then allowed time to be debriefed by his solicitor before being released from custody.

The officer and his sergeant remained unconvinced by any of the responses that Foster had to provide.

After they had left Foster with the custody centre staff, they conducted their own debrief of the interview.

"I don't believe a single fucking word he said," the sergeant said. "Trouble is, he's given us some hoops we've gotta jump through now."

"Yeah, me either," the police officer replied. "I admire his creativity about the bollocks with his solicitor doing it though. Never heard that one before."

29

Once again, having drawn on his experience, Marshall was fully conversant with the procedures surrounding drink drive arrests.

He had also fully expected Foster to put two and two together with regards to the car key.

As he had anticipated that, so he had factored it into his plan, and was able to remain several steps ahead of the police. Consequently, Marshall was able to solely focus on locating Giles Quinn.

As the information he had on him was limited, and potentially out of date, he only had one logical first port of call, and that was to speak to Quinn's mother, assuming that the address he had for her was still correct.

oOo

"Good morning, Missus Quinn?" Marshall asked as the front door was answered.

"Who are you?" came the surly reply from a short, stout elderly lady, who appeared to be wearing a long cardigan that had maybe started its life as one of a pair of curtains.

The reply didn't fit the question asked, but regardless, Marshall continued as he had been requested.

"My name is James Marshall, ma'am," he began. "I don't know if you may remember me... I'm a solicitor, I represented your son Giles a few years ago, when he last had to go to court."

"And?" Mrs Quinn interrupted. "He went away for that... Looks to me like you're not very good at your job Mister Marshall."

"Well, Missus Quinn, that aside, I need to get hold of Giles, as I understand he was released recently." Marshall replied.

His reply was intended to show a relatively up-to-date level of knowledge about Quinn, whilst deliberately testing the water to see how much she currently knew about her son, and consequently how much use she was likely to be to him.

"Yeah, so?" she replied, without the slightest hint of surprise in her voice.

Having confirmed her knowledge of his release, Marshall continued.

"There's a couple of things I need to discuss with him," Marshall said. "If I can come in for a couple of minutes, I can explain what it is, and how it may have benefits for him?"

He was hoping that a key word contained within his last statement, "benefits" would have the desired effect.

It evidently worked, as Mrs Quinn stepped to one side, opening the door fully as she did, subliminally authorising Marshall's entry.

Marshall stepped inside, meticulously wiping his feet on the doormat before taking a step further. These actions were met with approval from Mrs Quinn. Marshall had felt that it would, as it showed respect for one's property.

But he would even go a step further, to further seek favour from his host.

"Would you like me to take them off?" he added, referring to his shoes.

"No, that's fine, but thank you for asking," came the reply. "Take a seat in the living room... I was just about to make myself a cup of tea, would you like one?"

One thing Marshall had always remembered, as a small, almost insignificant titbit of information passed down to him from a mentor was, if ever offered a drink in someone's home, take it. It doesn't mean it has to be drunk, but never refuse.

Such a refusal of something so simple can be subconsciously deemed as an insult, and that can lead to negative thoughts, which in turn can be a hindrance should something be wanted from the person who had made the offer.

"Ooh, yes please, that would be lovely," Marshall replied. "White, without."

Marshall walked into the living room as directed, as Mrs Quinn continued down the hallway towards the kitchen at the far end.

171

But instead of taking a seat as suggested, instead he chose to have a good look around the living room.

There were countless framed pictures and photographs, some hung on walls, others placed on shelves or on the top of furniture.

Quite a few contained an ageing gentleman, but he seemed to have disappeared for the more recent, better-quality images.

Marshall then recalled from Quinn's file, that his mother, included only as his next-of-kin was documented as being a widow.

It would seem from the photographs that she lost her husband quite some time before Marshall had represented her son.

One of the earliest images to be seen showed her husband stood alone, dressed in army fatigues. Marshall guessed this was probably during his National Service. Marshall looked upon it with an eerie fascination. Quinn was a spitting image of his father when the photo was taken.

Then there was a younger woman seen with Mrs Quinn. Marshall concluded this to be Giles' sister. He also concluded that the children in the pictures, and most likely the senders of the obviously homemade greeting cards were Giles' niece and nephew, as his file stated that he had no children or dependants.

In amongst viewing Quinn's family history, he had a moment of nostalgia himself. From the direction of the kitchen, Marshall heard a sound that took him straight back to his childhood.

In order to make the tea, Mrs Quinn was using a kettle on the hob, and the sound he heard was the steam whistle letting her know that the water had boiled. This had caused his momentary distraction, and he smiled as he reminisced.

Looking back at the photographs, Marshall then saw that Giles himself appeared in a large number of photos with his mother. They covered a vast expanse of time, from when he was a schoolboy, right up until how he looked when Marshall had represented him in court.

This showed a strong bond between mother and son. Marshall knew that this could prove useful, should the need ever arise.

It was that that Marshall heard footsteps coming back down the hallway.

As he turned, he was expecting to see Mrs Quinn emerge from around the door frame carrying two steaming mugs of tea, much as his own mother would have presented to any guest. But instead, she returned carrying a small wooden tray, and on it were two empty cups on saucers, with a teaspoon on each, a teapot under a knitted cosy, a small jug of milk, and a pot of sugar. Everything appeared to be perfectly symmetrical, and with it, perfectly balanced. This meticulous preparation showed the traits of someone who was very house-proud.

"Can I help you with that?" Marshall asked.

"No, thank you, dear," Mrs Quinn replied.

Mrs Quinn then placed the tray on a small table between two very old-looking armchairs. They had exposed wooden arms, and the fabric was a once-deep, but now sun-bleached red floral pattern.

Before taking a seat herself, Mrs Quinn poured tea into the two cups.

"I'll let you do your own milk dear," she said. "I don't know how strong you like it."

In that instant, Marshall had realised the transition that Mrs Quinn had gone through since she had first opened the front door to him. She had been on the defensive from the outset, but due to lavish courtesy and respect on Marshall's part, he felt that he had successfully won her over.

Having added a dash of milk and a teaspoon of sugar to her own cup of tea, Mrs Quinn sat down, and prompted Marshall to do the same. She then picked up her cup of tea from the tray, and held it with both hands on her lap.

"What is it that you need to see my son about then?" she asked, restarting the conversation from where they had left it on the doorstep.

Marshall took a seat opposite her. He leaned in to add milk to his cup of tea.

"Well, despite his recent release, Giles' conviction has come up for review," Marshall began. "And, there appears to be some irregularities identified in the prosecution's case against him... Now, I have some forms that I need to have him sign so that I can proceed on his behalf as far as the review goes... Do you know how I can get hold of him to have him sign them?"

"I don't know where he's living, since he came out of prison," Mrs Quinn replied.

"Have you seen him since his release?" Marshall asked.

"Yes, I have," she replied.

"Did he come here?" Marshall asked.

Although he didn't want to appear to be putting her under any pressure, Marshall did still want his questions answered.

"Yes, he did," again came the reply.

"Do you expect him, or does he just turn up?" Marshall asked.

He was conscious that he was starting to sound too much like a cop. Which was the one thing he was hoping to have avoided. After all, this wasn't an interrogation, despite his need for answers.

"If I can represent him in this review, *and* if it goes his way, then there could potentially be a substantial amount of compensation due to him."

Marshall saw Mrs Quinn's reaction to the possibility of money coming their way. This appeared to indicate a lot about how their decisions, and loyalties were motivated.

"I've seen him maybe three or four times since he got out of prison," Mrs Quinn began to explain. "The first time was a surprise. Now he pretty much comes and goes as he pleases; he has his own key. And he's here more or less every week."

"Oh, that's lovely," Marshall replied, smiling. "So, when did you *last* see him?"

"Weekend just gone," Mrs Quinn replied.

Marshall nodded.

"And when do you next expect him to be here?" he asked.

"Well, I wouldn't be surprised if it was this weekend," she replied.

"Fantastic." Marshall exclaimed. "What I'll do, if it's okay with you, is I'll drop the paperwork around before then, that way he can go over it and sign it. I can then pick it up after the weekend… I don't s'pose you have a mobile phone number for him?"

"I don't I'm afraid, he tends to call me," she replied.

"When did he last call you?" Marshall asked.

"Hmmm, it was only a couple of days ago," Mrs Quinn replied.

Marshall knew what he needed to achieve, but in that instant, he wasn't sure how to go about it. Then it dawned on him.

"Do you have a pad of paper and a pen?" he asked. "I can leave you my number, so when he calls you, you can let him know that I popped round, and if he wants to then call me, he can."

"Oh yes," she replied.

Mrs Quinn then frenetically looked around the room. She was sure there was a pad of paper somewhere. Little did it occur to her that it was underneath the tea tray.

As she looked, Marshall took his mobile phone from his pocket, he unlocked it in readiness.

"I'll be right back," she said as she pushed herself out of the armchair. "Maybe I have one in the kitchen."

As soon as she was out of the living room, Marshall picked up the receiver of the telephone that sat towards the back of the table where the tea tray had been placed.

He placed the receiver to his ear, and dialled *1-4-7-1*. It was then he heard the number of the last call received.

As he listened, he typed the number into his own phone. The synthesised voice also said that the call had been received in the evening, two days earlier.

Marshall then replaced the handset in good time before Mrs Quinn returned to the room with a notepad and a marker pen that looked like it was used for bingo. She handed the pad and pen to Marshall.

"It's okay," he replied. "I've actually got a pen."

He then scribbled his name and mobile number down on the pad.

He then handed the pad back to Mrs Quinn.

"Sorry about that, I appear to have handed out my last business card," he said. "Well, I don't want to take up any more of your time, so I'll be off."

Marshall then stood up, having not touched a drop of his cup of tea.

Mrs Quinn then walked behind him to the front door. He unlocked the door, opened it, and stepped through.

From the doorstep, he turned to speak a few final words to Mrs Quinn.

"Well, if you do see him, or if he calls you," Marshall concluded. "Can you tell him that I'm hoping to speak to him? Like I say, it's certainly in his interest to get in touch."

"Of course," she replied.

30

"Sarge, y'know that fatal RTC we had on Church Road last night? Well, the owner of the car involved is insisting that it wasn't him driving, and that his solicitor s'posedly had his key for the car at the time," the constable said.

Following the interview of Albert Foster, one of the interviewing police officers attended the CID office. This was in order to obtain some advice following the revelation that had been disclosed during the interview.

"What's his version of events?" the detective sergeant said, without even having the courtesy to look up from his desk.

"He's saying that he wasn't driving at the time of the collision, and that he had given his keys to his brief having been given a three-month ban a short while back," the constable went on to explain.

"And do you believe him?" the DS replied, having finally looked up from his work.

"Well, what he's saying *does* fit," the constable replied. "However, it sounds highly unlikely, and this guy's got a shitload of previous for drink driving, even before the ban."

"And what do we know about this brief?" the DS asked. "Is he someone we know about?"

"You *could* say that, Sarge," the constable replied. "Unless it's a coincidence, he's one that we've seen in custody many times... A James Marshall of um, Reid, Salmon and Hounslow."

"James Marshall?" he repeated, and louder than expected.

The constable nodded confirmation.

Unbeknown to both of them, the conversation had attracted the attention of one of the sergeant's colleagues elsewhere in the office; Detective Constable James Tappin.

Hearing this name grabbed his full attention. As a result, he had stood up from his desk and slowly walked over towards the other two hoping to hear the conversation progress on his way.

"What's this about Marshall?" Tappin asked as he arrived next to the constable.

"Some guy we nicked last night for a fatal drink drive has stated it was this Marshall who was driving his car at the time of the collision, and *not* him," the constable said. "We've had to RUI our guy until we can get forensics back on his car."

"What's your interest in Marshall?" the DS then asked, wondering why Tappin had made an impromptu addition to their conversation.

"His parents were the target of a vicious in-home attack recently," Tappin replied. "Suspect is possibly by one of his previous clients."

There was silence as the DS took a moment to consider if these two occurrences could in some way be connected.

"Who's saying that this Marshall was involved in the RTC?" the DS eventually asked.

"The owner of the car involved, Albert Foster," the constable replied.

"You said *his* solicitor," the sergeant reiterated to the constable. "Has Marshall represented Foster as well then?"

"I haven't had a chance to look into that yet," the constable replied. "But, given the way he said it, it would certainly appear that way."

Realising the potential link between the two incidents, the DS turned to face Tappin.

"Are you able to see if you can shed any light on Marshall, and if he has ever represented Foster?" the sergeant asked.

"Off the top of my head, I couldn't tell you," Tappin replied. "I'll look into it, and get back to you Sarge."

Tappin then turned to address the constable.

"Can you let me know the results of the forensics on the crash as soon as you have them?" Tappin asked of him.

"Of course," replied the constable.

"Thanks," Tappin replied. "Cheers, Sarge."

Tappin then turned and returned to his desk. He sat down and looked at the computer screen.

Until then, he had been looking at Giles Quinn's criminal profile, with the possibility of forensics linking him to the attack on James Marshall's parents.

As he again stared at the screen, he rested his chin on the support his interlaced fingers had made for him. He then pondered the new direction his investigation might have just taken.

"Gotta be a coincidence," Tappin muttered at an inaudible volume. "Surely."

He would need to wait to be updated on the forensics report for Foster's seized Hyundai that had been involved in the fatal collision.

But in the meantime, there were plenty of other enquiries to keep Tappin busy.

31

The forensic reports had come back on Foster's seized Hyundai, the car key that had been left in the ignition, and the flat cap that was recovered from the road beside the deceased body of Allan Garmin.

The traffic officer who had interviewed Foster had requested the reports, and had upon receipt, had forwarded them on in their entirety to DC James Tappin.

It was a mixed bag of results from which Tappin had to draw conclusions.

There was no forensic evidence to suggest that anyone other than Foster had ever driven the Hyundai. There was nothing to even put his wife in the driver's seat, and certainly nothing to corroborate his allegation that it was James Marshall who was the driver of the vehicle at the time of the fatal collision which cost Garmin his life.

The flat cap found at the scene supported the same conclusion, that Foster was the offender. Sweat secretions isolated from the band of the cap were analysed. They returned a DNA match to the profile held in the name of Foster.

As this item was found at the scene of the collision, this would form the basis of further questioning when Foster himself was requested to return to be further interviewed.

The car key that had been seized from the ignition of the crashed car, having been abandoned outside of Foster's home address, did however tell a different story. This produced a partial fingerprint that was not a match when compared against Albert Foster's record.

In fact, this partial fingerprint did not match any record currently held on the nationwide database. All the forensic analysis could confirm was that this unidentified partial print was found on top of a fingerprint that was a match to Albert Foster.

Ahead of Foster being requested to return to be further interviewed, Tappin knew that identifying the originator of this unknown fingerprint was a top priority.

Had the road traffic collision been the extent of the incident, then it could have remained with the roads policing unit to investigate and prosecute.

However, as there now appeared to be elements that might link this incident to the attack on Leonard Marshall that Tappin was already investigating, the detective inspector in charge of his team insisted he take on the fuller investigation, drawing on the resources of other departments should the need arise.

Having now obtained the answer to a question previously asked by his sergeant, Tappin attended his office in order to provide him with an overview, and an update of what he had so far achieved.

"So, James, what have you got for me?" Detective Sergeant Staplehurst asked.

"It's hard to really say, Sarge," Tappin began to explain. "We got the forensics back on the car, and it was definitely the car the struck Garmin, as his DNA is all over the front of it… But it doesn't eliminate Foster's involvement, or prove Marshall's… Even the deployed airbag was clean, I mean you'd expect some blood or snot on it, at the very least. All forensics have confirmed is that an unknown fingerprint is on the car key that was found in the ignition… But, even if that turns out to be Marshall's, then so what? We knew that he's handled the key because Foster admits that he gave it to him after his trial."

Tappin knew very well the difference between direct evidence and circumstantial evidence. As a result, forensic evidence found on the key could potentially be considered as circumstantial, as the key could be handled by a person without ever having come near the car itself.

Conversely, had the airbag come back with a forensic result, then it would be difficult, if not impossible to convince a jury that someone was not in the car, *and* at the time when it was involved in an event which caused the airbag to deploy. In this case, the KSI RTC.

As with all evidence, the prosecution and defence teams would try to prove or disprove its relevance. But ultimately this would be for a jury to decide given the severity of the offences under investigation.

"Okay, so it's now looking like Foster was most likely bullshitting us after all then," Staplehurst replied. "What else do you have?

"I don't think he *is* lying, Sarge," Tappin continued. "Let me show you what else I've found out."

He then placed a single sheet of printed A4 paper on the desk in front of his sergeant, upside down to him, so that Staplehurst could read it.

Tappin then provided an explanation to accompany the paperwork.

"Well, given Foster's involvement in the RTC, and now the possibility of Giles Quinn's involvement in the burglary at Marshall's parent's house... I've taken a look at all the custody records that we have that show Marshall as being the representing solicitor," Tappin said. "Now, this is just going back a few months, but look what I've found."

He then pointed to lines of text that had been highlighted with a yellow marker.

"And?" the DS asked, having been unable to draw the same conclusions based on the information presented to him.

He could see that there were a number of highlighted references. But he still required Tappin to shed further light on them.

"We've got Foster marked here," Tappin said pointing to his corresponding entry on the paper. "And here is Allan Garmin."

"Who the fuck's Allan Garmin?" Staplehurst said abruptly interrupting Tappin mid-flow.

"Garmin is the one that Foster is alleged to have run over and killed... Coincidence...?" Tappin asked. "I'm thinking not!"

Staplehurst nodded as he started to see the picture that Tappin was painting for him

"Have you found any others?" Staplehurst asked.

"Well, there's a Robert Fraser," Tappin continued. "Marshall represented him a while back too... He also came to a rather grizzly end the other day. Bludgeoned to death in the churchyard of Saint Mary's."

"Fucking hell, this is *way* more than just a coincidence," Staplehurst exclaimed. "Did you find out if Marshall *ever* represented Quinn?"

"Yes, I did," Tappin replied. "Marshall did represent Quinn before he was sent down. That's not on here, coz it happened a few years ago."

They both took a moment to ponder the intricacies of what befell them.

"Okay, let's not get carried away here, we need to still look at this objectively," Staplehurst began. "Now, not having an identifiable fingerprint on the key doesn't leave us with a great deal on which to arrest Marshall, and it sure as hell isn't enough to get us a warrant... However, there is more than just a pattern forming here, and that *is* enough to suspect his involvement. But we're going to need something more than that, if we're going to make anything stick."

Although Tappin had an investigative strategy in mind, he was keen to hear his sergeant's thoughts.

"What do you suggest, sarge?" Tappin asked.

"Motive. At the moment, we just don't have one," Staplehurst replied. "The only thing I can think of, is that all of this must somehow originate from the attack on Marshall's parents... And somehow Quinn is the catalyst to everything else... If we focus on him then he may very well be the keystone in all of this."

Staplehurst pondered the situation momentarily, before continuing.

"We have the forensics linking Quinn to the Marshall crime scene. I suggest we bring him in, and see what he has to say from himself, see if he can shed any light on the rest of it for us."

"What are we going to do about Marshall though?" Tappin asked with concern.

"Until we have grounds to arrest him, we'll never find out if the fingerprint on the key is his, or not," Staplehurst explained. "You could always invite him in, see if he'd volunteer to give us an elimination set of prints... Certainly wouldn't hurt to ask?"

Tappin nodded enthusiastically.

"That way we could then compare it to all the crap *scenes of crime* collected from the Fraser job too. They went mad on that one, seized all sorts of rubbish... Seriously, they grabbed stuff from bins, and anything not nailed down," Tappin replied. "Any suggestions which we should attempt first?"

"That's a good question," Staplehurst pondered. "I think, if things go tits up and we haven't brought Quinn in, then we could be criticised for inaction... The way I see it, is there's no real justification to go after Marshall at this stage."

Tappin could understand the rationale behind the suggestion, but with that came a shortfall.

"The trouble we have with Quinn is that we don't know where he has been released to," Tappin explained. "He didn't give the prison a release address... All we have for him is his mother's address."

"Best start there then," Staplehurst replied.

"He's a nasty piece of work," Tapping revealed. "If he is there, he'll kick off, or scarper at the first sign of us."

"Better go mob-handed then," concluded flippantly. "Keep me updated."

"Yes, Sarge," Tappin said, as he stood up and collected his paperwork from the desk.

32

Mrs Quinn was awoken by a loud crashing noise coming from outside of her house.

When it eventually ceased, she thought that was to be the end of it, and as a result, she laid her head back down on her pillow, in the hope of falling asleep again.

Her respite was, however, unfortunately short-lived. As a second bout of crashing was soon heard, identical to the first, closely followed by a third, and then a fourth rendition.

Feeling there would be no end without her intervention, Mrs Quinn pushed herself upright in her bed. She swung her legs over the side, and inched forward until her feet finally made contact with the floor. There she paused, hoping to have heard the last of the unnerving disturbance.

Then came yet another crash, and another. They appeared to be getting louder, perhaps closer. For a seventy-something widow, this was an awful way to be drawn from a peaceful night of much-needed sleep.

With her feet on the floor, she braced herself as her weary joints took the weight of her body for the first time that day. She then eased herself into a balanced posture, and prepared herself to stand.

Then there was another crash, only this one was followed immediately with words being shouted. They sounded constrained and muffled. But only upon the second or third rendition, was Mrs Quinn finally able to decipher what was actually being said.

"Missus Quinn, this is the police," a voice bellowed. "Can you open the door please?"

These words echoed around her home, reaching Mrs Quinn as she left her bedroom into the hallway.

As she moved, she began slipping on a dressing gown to cover her modesty. However, her progress was hindered as the gown got caught on a key that protruded from the inside of the bedroom door lock. This was one of many tell-tale signs that the house was vastly out of date in terms of its décor and functionality.

She slowly, but surely made her way to the front door. The crashing and calling continued right up until the noise of bolts being retracted, and keys being turned in locks could be heard from outside.

Finally, she opened the door to behold a sight that resembled a 1950s Hollywood interpretation of an alien invasion.

On Mrs Quinn's doorstep stood a number of figures all dressed in black. They wore balaclavas under open faced crash helmets, leather gloves and protective equipment that would put American football players to shame.

Had someone not already announced themselves to be the police, this sight would have been equal to, if not even more terrifying, than being woken in such a traumatic manner.

Eventually, the same *someone* who had been knocking and calling out stepped forward from between two of the wannabe aliens.

He was dressed as normal as a human being should be dressed at whatever time of the morning this was. For Mrs Quinn surely didn't know the time herself. All she could deduce in the time it had taken to get from her sleep to the door, was that it was still dark outside, and cold, so very, *very* cold.

Then *someone* finally spoke again, initially to introduce himself, before giving some explanation as to why half of Mrs Quinn's neighbours had taken to curtain twitching as a pastime.

"Are you Missus Quinn?" the man asked.

This uncertainty made the rude awakening even worse given the vagueness of them *even* having the correct address.

Regardless of this, Mrs Quinn chose to respond without any of the flippant remarks that such a situation might demand. Instead, she simply nodded in response to the question asked and awaited an explanation.

"Missus Quinn, my name is James Tappin, I am a detective constable... My apologies for the intrusion... We are looking for your son, Giles... Is he home?"

Nothing in the way of a response emanated from Mrs Quinn.

"If I can come in, I'll explain to you why?" Tappin continued, in lieu of any reply.

Mrs Quinn felt that the last remark was not a question that she had any discretion over should she choose to offer any response.

Without saying a word, she stepped to one side, allowing enough space for Tappin to enter.

"Just you," she said.

Then once Tappin had cleared the threshold, she closed the door behind him.

Tappin knew that the house hadn't been checked to determine if her son was languishing upstairs, in the loft maybe, or in a cupboard somewhere.

But he knew he needed compliance from Mrs Quinn, and that any further intrusion or challenge could scupper his goal of obtaining much-needed information as to the whereabouts of her son.

With that to the fore of his mind, he allowed himself to be separated from the support team that had been positioned to the front and rear of the house. This had been in case Quinn had decided to try and flee through a back door or window, or to offer aggressive resistance.

Mrs Quinn followed on behind Tappin into the living room. He hadn't taken a seat, and she had no intention of extending such an invitation.

She stood there, in the living room doorway, her arms folded, looking as foreboding as she could, whilst standing five foot nothing in her nightwear.

"What do you want with my boy?" she asked. "He's only just got out, he's paid his dues... Why can't you just leave him alone?"

Seeing that Mrs Quinn was clearly on the defensive, Tappin knew he needed to reassess his approach in order to salvage as much as he could from the rapidly deteriorating situation.

He was planning to say that he needed to speak to Giles regarding an alleged offence, the incident involving Marshall's parents. Though he wouldn't be at liberty to disclose that level of detail to her. But given Mrs Quinn's defensive stance, he felt that he wouldn't get the desired response from such an approach.

"Missus Quinn," Tappin began. "We need to speak to your son because we feel that someone might also be looking for him, someone wanting to cause him harm."

Tappin knew this wasn't exactly the truth, but equally, it wasn't completely a lie either.

Regardless, he knew he had to balance his approach in order to stand the best chance of getting the information he needed from Mrs Quinn.

"Well, isn't that *your* job, to prevent that from happening?" she replied. "Not mine."

"Well, *you* can help him by telling us where he is... Then maybe we *can* do our jobs to protect him," Tappin replied.

Tappin realised that his response was maybe a touch flippant. But he was sick and tired of the parents of renowned and proven scumbags protesting their son or daughter's innocence, and then complaining about a biased police force.

Despite his chosen response, there was a moment of silence as Mrs Quinn considered the options available to her.

The foundation of her thought process was that she didn't trust Tappin. But she also knew her son wasn't an angel. She was also of the opinion that if her son was in any real danger, the police wouldn't go to such lengths to locate him.

For her, it didn't add up. Why they would prepare for a dawn raid just to let her son know that someone was after him?

She felt that this must have something to do with Marshall's visit the previous day. But she couldn't decide how.

On one hand she had James Marshall, a solicitor who had previously worked hard for Giles, and although the verdict went against him, he did have her son's best interests at heart. Added to which he was preparing to assist Giles further by attempting to secure compensation for him, too.

Then on the other hand, there was this copper, someone who was obviously concealing his true reason for being there, and lying about why he wanted to speak to her son. Mrs Quinn had made her decision.

"Yes, I have seen him, *since* he got out of prison," Mrs Quinn replied. "But I don't know where you'll find him, or even how to get hold of him... But, to be honest with you, after what happened last time, even *if* I did know, I wouldn't tell you."

Tappin sighed. Nothing he was hearing was breaking new ground for him. He had heard it all before.

"That's not a very helpful attitude to adopt, Missus Quinn," Tappin replied. "You don't want to get into any trouble yourself, now do you?"

"So, you *are* saying he's in trouble?" Mrs Quinn asked, having noticed Tappin's faux pas.

"I didn't say anything of the sort," Tappin reiterated. "Well, if you do see him, can you have him call me?"

Tappin then handed over a business card with his contact details on it.

Then realising he was fighting a lost cause, he said goodbye to Mrs Quinn and headed towards the living room door.

As she was still standing in the doorway, apparently refusing to grant him sufficient room to pass her, he had to resort to having to squeeze past her to leave the room.

He was then forced to let himself out of the front door as she had declined to follow him after he left the living room.

Once she heard the front door shut, Mrs Quinn took a seat in the living room. She picked up the receiver of the telephone, and dialled a number from memory.

"Hello," she said when it was finally answered.

33

Literally seconds after the police had left Mrs Quinn's address, she was on the phone, firstly to her son Giles, and then secondly to James Marshall. This was to tell them both what had just taken place.

"Mister Marshall," she began. "I'm sorry to call you so early, but I've just had the police here. They were looking for my boy. Oh, they gave such me an awful fright, banging on my door at such an ungodly hour."

Marshall pulled his phone from his ear. He checked the time on the illuminated display. It was 06:18hrs.

It was then he realised that what had just taken place was a planned raid, potentially with a search warrant to enter and search the address should Mrs Quinn have refused the police entry.

"I take it that Giles wasn't there?" Marshall asked. "What did you tell them, Missus Quinn?"

"No, no, he wasn't," she replied. "Oh well, the young man was *so* rude, and I'm sure he was lying to me. So much so that I chose not to help him at all."

"Lying?" Marshall questioned. "What made you think that he was lying to you?"

"Well, he said all he wanted to do was *talk* to Giles. In fact, he said he wanted to warn him that someone may be wanting to hurt him," she began to explain. "But I'm not silly, despite my years… I know that the police wouldn't come here at that time of the morning just to speak to him… I know that if they had found him here, they would have arrested him. I don't care what my boy is meant to have done, at least he never lies to me… So, when someone *does* lies to me, they'll get no help from me whatsoever."

"So, you don't think that someone is looking to harm Giles then?" Marshall asked.

"No, I don't," Mrs Quinn replied adamantly. "I think they only said that so I'd tell them where they could find him. I know they were only looking to arrest him for something."

Marshall then felt he could capitalise on this eventuality.

"To be honest with you, I wouldn't be at all surprised," Marshall began. "The police are always using underhanded tactics like that to knock you off guard... That way, you would arrange for Giles to meet with them, and probably never see him again... And, whilst we're on *that* subject, did you mention me to Giles at all, and the forms I need him to sign?"

"Oh, I'm frightfully sorry," Mrs Quinn confessed. "I was in all of a tizzy when I spoke to him, and it completely slipped my mind."

"Oh, it doesn't matter, there's no real urgency to it. Probably less so given what happened this morning... I tell you what I'll do, I'm in the area this afternoon, so how about I just drop the forms off, and then when he's had a chance to sign them, give me a call and I can pop back and pick them up... Are you in this afternoon?"

"Yes, I'm in all day," she replied. "I don't have any plans at all today."

"Perfect, I'll drop in later then," Marshall said as he ended the call.

He knew that this update, although dramatic, didn't hold any real significance for him. It certainly wouldn't change what he was planning to do.

The only real impact this would have on his plans was that he would need to bring his timetable forward in order to prevent any police intervention from interfering with what he wanted to do.

The way Marshall saw things, given that the police were now looking to speak to Giles Quinn, was that it was most likely in relation to the attack on his parents.

This in itself was inevitable given the forensic evidence that the police had revealed that they had on him, and as such, Marshall had already been taken into account.

Marshall also knew that it was also only a matter of time before the police noticed a pattern forming regarding recent events involving his past clientele.

As a result, it was again only a matter of time before the police would want to speak to him regarding these unfortunate events, as he was the only element that connected them.

Marshall knew that he would have needed to pay Mrs Quinn another visit. But by the way that things were progressing sooner than predicted, he should make this visit sooner rather than later. Which was why he had suggested that he pay her a second visit that afternoon.

34

Marshall parked up a few doors down the street from Mrs Quinn's address. This was despite having driven past her address, and having seen that there were in fact a number of available spaces in which to park that were considerably closer than the one he had eventually chosen.

As he walked back towards her house, he took out his mobile phone from his pocket. He then dialled a saved number.

Marshall slowed his walking pace as the call connected. However, it went unanswered. Instead it rang and rang, before connecting to an automated voicemail service.

Marshall terminated the call without leaving a message. He then continued on his way to see Mrs Quinn.

"Good afternoon, Missus Quinn, so good to see you again so soon," Marshall said as the front door was opened for him. "Here are the forms I promised you. I've marked where each one needs to be signed."

He held out a sealed brown A4 envelope for Mrs Quinn to take from him.

"Y'know, I've been thinking about what you told me this morning, and I think I can possibly help you and Giles out," Marshall said. "If you've got a few minutes for me again, I could go over a few things with you?"

Pleasantly surprised to hear that someone actually wanted to help her son instead of crucifying him, Mrs Quinn was only too happy to welcome Marshall inside.

He took the front door from her, and closed it behind him. He then followed her into the living room.

They both sat down across from each other, mimicking the positions they had each adopted on their previous encounter.

Given the warmth of the overly heated home, Marshall felt the need to remove his leather gloves, which he tucked into a trouser pocket, and undo his coat. Only once he was comfortable, did he begin to speak.

"*I* do suspect, as *you* do, that the police were in fact here to arrest Giles this morning," Marshall began to explain. "And as you probably know, he's been released on licence as he was released prior to the end of his actual sentence... This means that if he is convicted of *anything* during that time, then he'll be sent back to prison to serve the rest of that sentence *on top* of anything new that he's convicted of."

Marshall then paused, to allow what he had just said to sink in before he continued.

"Now, it's imperative that I speak to your son Missus Quinn, and *before* the police find him... *Do* you know where he is?" Marshall asked.

Marshall looked across at Mrs Quinn. He saw her head and shoulders visibly drop, as she conceded in a battle against herself. He then saw her subtly nod, whilst still looking down towards the floor.

"He's staying with a friend," she replied in a barely audible voice.

Again, Marshall paused. He accepted that disclosing this information wasn't an easy thing for a mother to do.

"Do you know the friend's name, or where he lives?" Marshall asked in a softer tone than before, in the hope that the information he sorely needed would be imminently forthcoming.

"I'm afraid I don't," she replied. "I think Giles mentioned his first name once or twice. It's Theo, I think?"

"Theo, I think," big help, Marshall thought.

"That's a shame, because with only a possible first name, I may not be able to find the rest out of Theo's name, and get to Giles in time to be able to help him," Marshall replied, intentionally labouring his point.

Mrs Quinn looked as disappointed as she probably felt. Then all of a sudden, she sat upright again.

"Oh, how rude of me... Can I get you a cup of tea?" she asked out of the blue.

Probably with the intention of momentarily changing the subject, relieving some of the pressure she was undoubtedly suffering.

"Yes, that would be lovely," Marshall replied, allowing the conversation to take this different direction.

He felt that he no longer needed to specify how he liked his tea, as he was expecting the bone china crockery set to once again make an appearance.

"I *could* call him to ask him if he's happy for me to give you Theo's address," Mrs Quinn went on to say.

"Or, how about you call him, then I can speak to him on the phone…? That way I won't need to know where he is, and he won't have to come here," Marshall said, suggesting a solution that should satisfy Mrs Quinn's angst and concerns at betraying her son's trust.

"Oh yes, that sounds like a good idea," she agreed. "Shall I give you his number?"

"Well, you could," Marshall replied. "But the battery on my phone has died… Would you be happy for me to speak to him on *your* phone."

"Oh, of course," she said. "Here, let me dial the number for you."

With that, Mrs Quinn handed the telephone receiver to Marshall. Then she dialled the number. Marshall watched intently as each key was pressed, committing the number to memory, in case of future need.

However, the process merely served to reaffirm that the number he had documented previously was Quinn's, having dialled 1471 from the same phone during his last visit and recorded the last number to call.

Marshall smiled with amusement, that the phone was of the keypad variety as opposed to a rotary dialler, as one would have been more in keeping with the overall superannuated décor of the house.

"He should answer it," she said, as she stood up to make the tea. "He'll think it's me calling, and he *always* answers when it's me."

The phone continued to ring, as Marshall watched Mrs Quinn leave the living room, leaving him all alone.

It was then answered.

"Hello mum," a male voice said. "Can I call you back in a bit, got something going on at the mo?"

Deducing that as a male voice was responding to a call from this number as "mum" it must be Giles Quinn himself, Marshall responded.

"Hello Quinn… Y'know, I would really appreciate it if you could find me some time right now," Marshall said. "And I certainly know your mum would feel better if you did, too."

"Who is this?" Quinn asked, his tone of voice going from jovial to stern in an instant.

"You really *should* know who it is," Marshall replied. "Go on, have a guess, take breaking into someone's parents' house as a clue."

"Marshall?" Quinn asked.

"Bingo," Marshall replied.

"Well, I see you got my message then," Quinn said, revealing himself as the culprit. "I wasn't sure if you'd remember me, but then again, I didn't want to leave a calling card with my name on it?"

The revelation of Quinn's blatant admission momentarily stunned Marshall.

"Well, if I'm to be completely honest with you," Marshall replied. "My first thought was that it was someone else… It did take a little while before the penny finally dropped."

"Not happy for bygones then? I mean, I considered us now even… What is it you want?" Quinn asked, now with a distinct sound of apprehension in his voice. "You think you can come after me…? You're just a piece of shit in a suit!"

It was then that Marshall heard the now familiar sound of the kettle's steam whistle coming from the kitchen. He knew this would signify Mrs Quinn's imminent return.

"Hmmm, what do I want?" Marshall pondered. "What was the expression you used when you attacked my father…? Oh yes, that's it, *payback's a bitch*! Isn't that what you said to him…? Well, now it's my turn *you* piece of shit! And you can bet that the reason I'm here is for some payback of my own… Now, the *only* choice you have, is whether it's you, *or* your mother that's *my* bitch… It's kinda similar to when you were in my parent's house. The only difference really is that I'm making my threats directly to you. Not acting like the spineless turd that you are, someone hoping to slip into the shadows after the deed is done… Now, listen carefully, if you're not here within the hour you'll be visiting your mother in hospital much like I had to… "How this turns out is up to you, you have one hour."

"You've got nothing to threaten me with," Quinn stated, trying desperately to assert his dominance on the conversation, despite the obvious disadvantage of being elsewhere.

"I wouldn't be so sure," Marshall replied. "You're forgetting where I am."

It was at that moment that Marshall heard the jingling of fine china on a tray coming down the hallway.

He hung up the call, he also disconnected the UTP cable from the back of the telephone base unit and allowed it to drop out of sight onto the floor behind the table. After all, he didn't want Quinn phoning his mother back.

He then wiped down the telephone receiver to remove any fingerprints, before finally doing his best to compose himself.

As Mrs Quinn re-entered the living room, she could see that Marshall still looked a little bit flustered.

"Oh, I know," she said. "It *is* a bit warm in here. It has to be I'm afraid, because of my rheumatism."

She then placed the tray down between them as before.

"Any luck?" she asked.

"Oh yes, we chatted about a few things, it was good to catch up," Marshall said. "He's gonna be popping over to sign the papers now. I said with that being the case that I would wait and take them with me when he's done. Y'know, save me having to pop back... Does he drive, your son?"

"Oh yes," she replied. "He's got this God-awful thing, it makes so much noise."

Marshall with nodded his understanding and amusement.

Mrs Quinn was keen to continue the conversation. But suddenly, Marshall wasn't as receptive, as he now had other matters on his mind.

As she continued to monologue, Marshall took the time to glance around the living room.

He was searching for a means to have Mrs Quinn kept out of the way by the time that her son arrived.

Marshall had given Quinn one hour, but that was a deadline. It was by no means an indication of how long it would actually for him to arrive.

It was then that the solution he sought presented itself. Due to the age and décor of the property, all of the internal doors still had handles with old-fashioned mortice locks, and Marshall saw that the living room door still had its key on the inside of the door. Although, over time it had been painted over by someone too lazy to remove it first. So now it matched the rest of the door.

It was then that Marshall heard a screech of tyres from somewhere outside in the street. He knew he didn't have much time.

"Is it okay to quickly use your toilet before Giles gets here?" Marshall said, already getting to his feet.

"Oh yes, of course," Mrs Quinn said. "top of the stairs, then it's the door facing you."

By this time, Marshall had already walked across to the living room door, and turned to have his back against it in order to receive his directions. He then withdrew the key from the inside of the lock.

"Would you excuse me for a moment?" he said.

Then before there was even the slightest reaction from Mrs Quinn, Marshall stepped out into the hallway pulling the door closed as he did. Marshall then stood in the hallway, and locked the closed door.

It was then that he heard another screech of tyres, this time, it was much louder and seemed closer than the first.

Marshall had drawn the right conclusion and had acted in good time. Having made preparations, he then waited beside the front door, so to be behind it when it was opened. After all, he already knew that Quinn had his own key with which to "come and go as he pleased."

Marshall put his leather gloves back on before reaching into the outer pocket of his coat. He had planned ahead for this eventuality, and he was ready.

After the second tyre screech, he heard a car door slam shut, and following that, there was the increasing sound of thunderous footsteps running ever closer.

Then there was a brief moment of silence, followed by a sound of metal on metal, as panicked hands tried to make a key fit in the door lock.

35

The front door eventually opened, and Quinn rushed in. But he was in so much of a hurry to get into the house, that he was oblivious to what was hiding in waiting for him behind the front door.

"Mum?" he called out frantically.

He then saw that the living room door was shut. This was something that he hadn't seen in a long time. As a result, it was the first thing that appeared out of place. He went to the door and turned the handle. Nothing happened. It was locked, which only added to his angst. He banged on the door, fearing what was on the other side.

"Mum, are you in there?" he says with a sense of panic in his voice.

"Yes," his mother replied. "The door's locked, I can't get out."

But before she had a chance to elaborate, or before Quinn could affect a rescue, Marshall slipped out from behind the still-open front door.

He silently came up behind Quinn, using the element of surprise, and the fact that Quinn was otherwise distracted to his advantage, and reached around in front of him with his left gloved hand.

The hand came across Quinn's chest, below his peripheral vision, before coming up and covering his mouth. The surprise attack confused and disorientated Quinn, as all of a sudden, he was staring up at the hallway ceiling.

Simultaneously, Marshall thrust the long slender shaft of a flat head screwdriver into Quinn's abdomen from behind.

It penetrated his body more or less where his right kidney was located. Marshall didn't need to know precisely where the screwdriver pierced Quinn's body, because he simply didn't care. It penetrated in an upwards trajectory, right up to the handle.

The hand over the mouth was to muffle his screams of pain, but also to pull Quinn's head back, arching his spine. This would not only close the puncture wound around the weapon, it also served to bring Quinn off balance, which weakened his stance should he have any fight left in him with which to retaliate. Having nothing left, Quinn fell to the ground at Marshall's feet.

Time was now of the essence, and Marshall knew that had to act quickly. He kicked the front door shut, before stepping over Quinn's prone body.

Having taken hold of both of Quinn's arms, Marshall dragged him down the hallway. The rug on which he lay slipped on the varnished floorboards, which made the task easier.

Marshall dragged him as far as the door behind the stairs. This door led to the integral garage, which he had taken the time to ensure was unlocked using the same generic key that he had used to lock the living room door, before hiding behind the front door.

Having left the door to the garage slightly ajar having unlocked it, Marshall was able to kick it open. He then dragged the limp body of Quinn through. The rug bunched up in the doorway, and got caught on the frame. It was eventually left behind as Marshall pulled Quinn down the single step into the slightly lower level that was the garage floor.

It was once there, on the concrete floor of the garage, that Marshall released his grip on Quinn. He took the briefest of moments to catch his breath, but also to compose himself.

Marshall took a roll of duct tape from his pocket, having previously turned the corner of the end under for easy location. He quickly bound Quinn's outstretched hands together around the wrists. He did the same around his ankles, then his knees, and finally his elbows.

This meant that his arms were restricted in any movements he might attempt, and that he could not strike out in any way. Lastly, Marshall placed a piece of tape over Quinn's mouth, which put an end to his whimpering.

Marshall had worked with ruthless efficiency. Quinn now lay bound, gagged and motionless before him. All this had been done with the intention of having him incapacitated before the shock and trauma of his surprise attack had worn off.

Marshall then went back to attend to the adjoining door to the house. He straightened out the hallway rug, so he could close the door, isolating them both from the rest of the house.

As he did, he could hear the faint calls of Mrs Quinn emanating from the living room become ever more muffled. He then locked the door using the living room key for good measure, leaving the key in the lock.

Now that Marshall had eliminated any distractions, he was able to focus his full attention on Quinn.

It was then that Quinn was starting the stir, and having become aware of his surroundings and predicament, he started to squirm. However, as Marshall was searching the garage and not paying particular attention to Quinn, he did not immediately notice this.

There was one thing that Marshall ideally needed to locate as he wasn't been able to bring it with him. Although he had something of a contingency in mind should he not have been able to find it.

Ideally, he was looking for a length of cord or rope. But, failing in that, he instead found an electrical extension cord on a reel, which he felt would sufficiently serve the same purpose.

Marshall took the reel, and went to the back of the garage, to be where Quinn could see him.

Marshall then leant up against the back wall, and as he watched Quinn, he unwound the reel, allowing the extension cable to unravel onto the floor.

It was then that he saw movement from Quinn. He first saw his head turn, trying to assimilate his environment and predicament. Marshall then crouched down so that Quinn could clearly see him.

"Good afternoon," Marshall said. "Or perhaps I should just say *afternoon*, as you're most certainly *not* going to be having a *good* one."

Marshall could see that Quinn was attempted to verbalise a response from beneath his duct tape gag. But whatever he had to say, Marshall was not the slightest bit interested.

Having prepared the extension cable, Marshall then coiled a small amount, much like a cowboy coiling a lasso. He then threw the plug end over an exposed roof beam, above where Quinn lay.

Then having retrieved the hanging end, Marshall then pulled the length he felt he needed over the beam.

Marshall then fed the plug through the gap between the wrist and elbow bindings on Quinn's arms. This caused Quinn some pain as the electrical plug had to be forced through the tight gap.

Again, Quinn tried to cry out in pain. But his attempts were once more muffled by his gag.

"Oh, stop moaning, for *fuck's* sake" Marshall demanded.

Having finally managed to feed the plug between Quinn's arms, Marshall then secured the cable by tying it in a double overhand knot, and wrapping the loose end around the wrists, before taping over it, in order to prevent the binding from slipping.

Marshall stood up. He looked upon his work, his gaze followed the path of the extension cable up and over the beam. He then retrieved the reel end of the cable from the floor, and began to wind up the slack.

Once the slack had been taken up, Marshall reached up as high as he could, and took hold of the cable.

He then collapsed his legs and allowed his body weight to drop. This firstly caused Quinn's arms to be pulled above his head, which resulted in him being turned from his front onto his side, then finally on to his back as he was hoisted higher.

As his body rotated, the screwdriver, which was still embedded in his back came into contact with the concrete floor, which drove it deeper into his body.

Quinn again tried to cry out in agony, but given the gag, his cries were barely audible.

Marshall repeated the process of reaching up and squatting down until Quinn had been elevated into almost a standing position. His feet still had contact with the floor, but his bent legs dangled limply beneath him, though not taking any of his bodyweight.

Marshall stopped as he knew he wouldn't be able to hoist Quinn any higher. This was due to their respective body weights and the friction of the extension cable over the wooden beam. So, any further attempts would be futile. Also, Marshall didn't want to risk compromising the integrity of the cable itself.

The friction played to Marshall's advantage as he kept the cable taut whilst he searched for something to tie it off on. This he found by securing the cable to the leg of a fixed work bench.

Once again, Marshall prevented any slippage of the knot by reinforcing the anchor with duct tape. He then took another moment to catch his breath following this exertion.

Marshall then stepped in close to where Quinn could again see him. He grabbed a mop of his hair, and lifted Quinn's head so that he was forced to look directly at him.

"If you had a grudge to bear, *why* didn't you just come after *me*?" Marshall calmly said to Quinn. "*Why* did you go after my parents?"

He knew that he wouldn't be getting much in the way of a response from Quinn in his current state. But seeing that he appeared to be wanting to say something, Marshall ripped off the duct tape gag.

"Something you want to say for yourself?" Marshall added. "And I don't wanna hear any of that *consider us even* bullshit. I know you'll never be content, and it'll *only* be a matter of time before you decide to go after my kids."

It took a few moments for Quinn to ready himself to make a response.

"Because..." Quinn stuttered. "Because of you, I did five years."

Quinn struggled to speak given his injury and the constriction of his body caused by his suspension.

"Because of me? Because of *me*?" Marshall exclaimed. "It's always someone else's fault, isn't it? Why can't you fuckers ever take responsibility for your own actions? It's no one's fault but your own... And if you bothered to remember, you piece of shit, I got it down to manslaughter... We *both* know you murdered that man. You could've got life... I did you a fucking favour, and this is how you repay me?"

Marshall then took a step back. For the first time, he was fuming. Until then he had been meticulous and calculating in his actions. But Quinn's revealed motives infuriated him.

It was then that Marshall took the last item he needed from his coat pocket. It was a small case, similar in size to that of a case for spectacles.

Having gloves on hindered Marshall in opening it. But he persevered and eventually managed it.

He didn't bother to specifically show the contents of the case to Quinn. He knew that he would find out what was inside soon enough.

Marshall removed the single item that was contained in the case, before replacing the case back in his pocket.

Marshall now held a syringe in his hand. The needle had a plastic cap over the tip, which he placed between his teeth before pulling the syringe away and removing the cap. He then primed the syringe by dispelling the minutest quantity of the contained liquid through the end of the needle.

He then approached Quinn again.

"What the fuck is that?" Quinn demanded to know, having seen the syringe.

But, this request for information had to go unanswered until the injection had been administered.

Marshall took hold of Quinn's left sleeve, and pulled it down to the elbow to expose the bare arm beneath it. He then took hold of the arm to steady it ready for the needle. Marshall then administered the full dose into Quinn's vein.

Marshall then stepped back, so that he could once again make eye contact with Quinn. He brought the syringe back to his mouth so that he could replace the safety cap.

Now being able to speak, he was able to reply to Quinn's question.

"What did you say?" Marshall said rhetorically. "Oh yes, *what the fuck is that...?* Well, I'll tell you *what the fuck that* is, even though it'll probably be wasted on a fuckwit like you. "

Marshall then took the case from his pocket, and replaced the syringe in it, before putting it away again.

"What I have injected you with is something called Warfarin," Marshall said. "I don't expect that means anything to you. So, as we've got a little bit of time on our hands, I'll explain a little something about it to you."

Marshall then went on to explain to Quinn what he had learned about Warfarin, which is an anticoagulant drug widely used to prevent and treat deep-vein thrombosis and pulmonary embolism, and to prevent stroke in patients who have atrial fibrillation, valvular heart disease, or a prosthetic heart valve.

"I expect you're wondering why I know so much about it? Marshall asked rhetorically. "Well, I'll tell you... I once represented someone, who like you, got away with murder because of me."

He got exactly the response he was expecting from Quinn, absolutely nothing.

"Now, that should just about do it." Marshall said referring to the passage of time during his anecdote about the origin of the drug. "Is there anything more you want to say to me before I leave you in peace?"

Quinn continued to remain silent. Either because he had nothing to say, or because he no longer had the physical ability to speak.

"Very well," Marshall replied. "I'll be off then."

Marshall replaced the duct tape gag over Quinn's mouth. He then reached around behind him and took a firm hold of the screwdriver that was still embedded in Quinn's body. Remaining in front of the now delirious Quinn, and using his body to shield him, Marshall pulled the screwdriver from Quinn's body in one fluid move.

But instead of pulling it straight out as it had entered, Marshall had to pull it out at an angle which caused the wound to tear both internally and externally. Then once it was free of the body, Marshall allowed the screwdriver to drop to the floor.

Now unplugged and ragged, blood flowed freely from the wound.

Marshall went towards the door that led back into the house. He unlocked the door and opened it.

From the open doorway, Marshall turned back to take one final look at Quinn.

The torrent of blood continued to flow freely from his body, thinned by the Warfarin. Marshall could already see how pale Quinn's face was becoming, as blood drained from his upper extremities first.

His complexion was a stark contrast to the blood that had run down his back and legs, rendered his clothing to appear almost black in colour, and forming a large pool around his feet.

"Oh, one last thing before I go," Marshall said, stopping himself in the open doorway. "Y'know, there's one thing you haven't mentioned the whole time that we've been here… You haven't once asked me about your mother. Just goes to show what a selfish fucker you really are!"

With that, Marshall walked through the door into the house, shutting it behind him, and locking it once again, taking the key with him.

Back in the hallway, Marshall took a moment to straighten the rug. He then headed back towards the front door.

Marshall opened the front door to give himself an apparent egress.

He then went back to the living room door, which he then used the key to unlock, before continuing down the hallway, into the kitchen and out of the back door.

From there, Marshall went across the rear garden and left through the shared communal area beyond.

36

After leaving Quinn's mother's address, Marshall eventually made his way back to his car. Once there, he drove to the hospital, as he wanted to see his father.

Having parked up at the hospital, but before leaving his car, Marshall tore off a small strip of duct tape, and stuck it to the back of his hand. He then tossed the rest of the roll of tape into the passenger side footwell.

Inside the hospital, Marshall discarded the torn-off piece of tape in a bin in the first toilet he came to.

Also, having entered his father's ward, but before reaching his bedside, Marshall disposed the now empty syringe into a biological waste bin which was marked for incineration that he found on a trolley near to the nurses' station.

With no other considerations, he continued on to see his father. Before he sat down besides his father's bed, Marshall took off his coat and placed it over the back of the chair. He then took a seat.

"I just happened to be passing," Marshall said. "So, I thought I'd pop in, see how things are…? Any news on when they'll let you home?"

"Nothing yet. I thought you'd be working at this time of day?" His father replied, having glanced at the clock on the wall.

"Normally, I would be," Marshall replied. "But I had some time off owed to me, so I thought I'd take it now and put it to good use… Y'know, tying up a few loose ends."

His father looked sceptical, as he hadn't known his son to voluntarily take any time off work. This had been part of the reason that his marriage had broken down.

"I don't believe that you just happened to be in the area," his father said. "Tell me, what's the *real* reason you're here?"

Marshall knew that there was no way he could circumvent his father's rationale.

"Well, it's *kinda* like I said," Marshall began. "I *have* been tying up a few loose ends... After the chat we had the other day, it got me thinking. As a result, I went through some of my old case files, to see where things maybe should have had a different outcome."

"And?" his father replied, prompting his son for more details.

"And," Marshall replied. "It's probably best I don't go into any more detail, at least not at the moment anyway... Look, if you're not allowed home in the next couple of days, I probably won't be available to drive you home. So, just in case take this, so you can get yourself a taxi, okay?"

Marshall said as he handed his father a twenty-pound note.

"And I promise, when the time is right, I'll tell you about all of this in as much detail as you like," Marshall continued. "Just not yet."

With that, Marshall stood up. He leant over his father, and placed the habitual kiss on the top of his head. He then left his father's bedside.

As Marshall left the ward, a nurse attended his father's bedside.

"Was that your son?" she asked.

"Yes, it was," he replied proudly.

"Is he coming back?" she continued.

"Probably not for a few days I'd expect," Leonard Marshall replied.

"Well, it looks like he's left his coat behind," she answered, indicating towards a coat that had been left draped over the back of the chair beside his bed.

"I tell you what I'll do, I'll put it in the bag with the rest of *your* clothes... That way it won't get forgotten when you go home," she went on to say.

The nurse then took the coat from the back of the chair. She folded it neatly, and placed it into the carrier bag that already contained what was left of the clothes that Mr Marshall's had been wearing when he first arrived in the hospital, along with what his wife had since brought for him to go home in.

She then put the bag back in the cupboard of the bedside cabinet.

oOo

Having left the hospital, Marshall drove directly to Oakvale police station.

He parked his car in one of the visitors' bays in front of the station. He then went into the front office.

He waited patiently as there was a queue of people waiting to be seen ahead of him.

When it was his turn to speak to the office clerk, he made his request.

"Please can I speak to Detective Tappin, or if he's unavailable, then someone else in his department please?"

Marshall saw the officer clerk scribble down Tappin's name, he was then asked for more details.

"Can I take your name please," the clerk asked.

"James Marshall," came the reply.

"And what is this regarding?" the clerk asked.

"I have some information regarding one of his cases," Marshall replied.

When the clerk had finished scribbling his notes, he stood up. But before he walked over to the telephone on the desk at the back of the office, he addressed Marshall.

"Okay, if you'd like to take a seat, Mister Marshall" the clerk replied. "I'll see if he's on-duty, and if he's free to see you."

Marshall did as was suggested.

He didn't have to wait long until an internal door opened, and Tappin stepped through in the front office.

Having seen Tappin enter, Marshall stood up and stepped forward to greet him.

"Good afternoon Mister Marshall," Tappin said. "How's your father doing?"

"Oh, he's doing well," Marshall replied. "Matter of fact, I've just come from seeing him… He's still in hospital, but we're hopeful that they'll let him home any day now."

"Oh, that's good," Tappin replied. "So, what can I do for you?"

Marshall smiled before he offered an explanation as to the reason behind his impromptu visit, as it appeared the office clerk had failed to do so.

"I have information regarding the recent incidents involving some of my previous clients," Marshall said.

"Are you able to be more specific?" Tappin replied, delicately requesting for the information without eluding to anything himself.

"*Specifically*, I have information regarding the deaths of Allan Garmin and Robert Fraser," Marshall replied. "And how Albert Foster and Brett Cable are implicated in the same."

Without trying to sound in anyway shocked or surprised by this revelation, Tappin did his best to offer a non-committal response.

"What are you saying?" Tappin asked.

"Oh, I'm sure you know *very* well what I'm saying?" Marshall replied.

There was a moment of silence, and an exchange of glances that allowed both men to ensure that the other was of the same understanding.

"Mister Marshall, are you somehow involved in the deaths of these people?" Tappin then asked.

Marshall did not verbalise a reply to this question. His only response was that of another wry smile.

Then without taking his eyes of Marshall, Tappin called across the front office to the office clerk.

"Can you put a call in to the response office," he said. "I need some uniform down here right now, at least two officers."

Tappin then returned his full attention to Marshall.

"Well, I'm sure you know how this bit goes," Tappin said. "Given what you're suggesting, I can't talk to you anymore about any of this, not just yet anyway."

Marshall remained silent. However, his smile got wider. His head bobbed slightly, to acknowledge his understanding of what Tappin had just said.

The front office remained silent for a few minutes, with both men stood across from each other. There was a tension in the air, almost as if they were wild west gunslingers in a stand-off before a gunfight. This was until three uniformed response officers came bursting through the front door of the office.

The request for assistance from the office clerk had evidently expressed a great deal more urgency than was actually required.

Tappin then asked two of the officers to take charge of Marshall, whilst he took the third out of earshot of the others, to be able to brief her on the situation without revealing anything to Marshall.

"There's an ongoing investigation into an attack on that man's father," Tappin said, nodding towards where the other officers stood with Marshall. "He's a criminal solicitor, and it would appear that some of his previous clients are now being targeted themselves. We've had two turn up dead so far for sure, with the likelihood of more. And somehow others are possibly being implicated in the killings."

Tappin paused long enough for the officer to understand the history of what had happened.

"Now, what I need from you is this," Tappin continued. "I need you to arrest Marshall on suspicion of the murders of an Allan Garmin and a Robert Fraser... I don't have the dates to hand. But get him down to custody, and by the time you get there, I'll have emailed the circs and a forensic strategy across... Get him booked in, then you'll need to seize his clothes and do hand swabs and all that, okay?"

The "circs" to which Tappin referred were the circumstances of arrest, or the rationale behind the arrest being made, which needed to be explained to the custody sergeant in order for them to decide if, firstly, that the arrest was lawful and necessary, and secondly, if keeping them in police detention was appropriate.

Also mentioned was a forensic strategy which forms part of the investigative plan. The strategy can vary depending on the severity and the nature of the offence to which the prisoner has been arrested.

In some cases, this can involve nothing more than photographing or seizing the prisoner's clothing for identification purposes. But on occasion it can be much more involved. For example, in the case of a serious sexual offence, then nail clippings, hair combings and swabs of the hands, and intimate and non-intimate areas may need to be taken.

Once Tappin saw that the officer had finished writing down the names of those involved and implicated, he led her back into the front office. There he let the officer take the lead.

"Mister Marshall, I am PC Adams. Based on information I have received, I am arresting you on suspicion of the murders of Allan Garmin and Robert Fraser," the officer said before cautioning Marshall.

One of the other officers then searched him, so that it was safe for them to transport him to custody. As Marshall was dressed in not much more than a shirt and trousers, the search didn't take long.

All that was found on him was a wallet, his phone and a bunch of keys. These were taken from him, not being seized as evidence, but for safekeeping, to prevent him using them as a weapon, or means of escaping.

Tappin took the keys from the officer that had performed the search. He held them up for Marshall to see.

"Where's your car parked?" he asked.

"Just out front," Marshall replied, nodding in the direction of the visitors' parking bays.

"Okay, I only need two of you to take him to custody," Tappin began. "I want the other one to take these keys and search his car… Then, once all of that's done, I want all of you to report back to me."

PC Adams then handcuffed Marshall before she and a colleague walked with him to their police car. It was as Marshall was being led back out of the police station, that he started to shiver, this was because for the first time in a long time, he wasn't dressed appropriately for the elements.

Adams got into the back of the police car with Marshall and her colleague drove.

It was standard procedure when transporting a prisoner in a car that the prisoner sat in the nearside rear seat, furthest from the driver. It was then the escorting officer's responsibility, in this case PC Adams, to protect the driver during the journey.

oOo

"Sarge, do you remember James Marshall, y'know the solicitor I told you about…?" Tappin asked of DS Staplehurst.

"Yeah, vaguely," Staplehurst replied. "What of it?"

Tappin wasn't in any fit state to offer an immediate response, as he had to take a moment to catch his breath. Having just rushed back up to the CID office, in order to update his skipper as he had been previously requested to do, although probably not with this degree of enthusiasm.

"Well… He's just walked into our front office saying he's got information about the deaths of two of his former clients," Tappin began, still in oxygen debt. "He didn't allude to anything more, and I didn't ask, but he did name them, and he's said that there are other of his clients who are also somehow involved… He's been nicked to prevent him from disappearing, and to get the eighteens authorised for his home address."

"Okay," replied DS Staplehurst. "You've got twenty-four hours to make something stick… If not, I doubt we'll get an extension, not if all we've got is a flimsy admission… I'd suggest that you get someone in to interview him as soon as you're able to… It may give us something more to go on… You'd better get to work, and let me know if you need anything?"

"Once I've got the warrant, I will need a team to go to his house," Tappin replied.

"You got it," Staplehurst replied.

Following an arrest, the Police and Criminal Evidence Act 1984 holds a legal power under *section 18* for police officers to enter a place of residence or other identified premises for the purpose of securing and preserving evidence. This is more commonly known as a *search warrant*.

It was this power that Tappin wanted to exercise in order to have officers enter and search Marshall's home address.

But as Staplehurst had already alluded to, Tappin only had twenty-four hours, and the clock was already ticking.

37

It wasn't long after his arrest that Marshall found himself in the familiar surroundings of the local custody centre.

He hadn't been there since that day, whilst in his role of representing a client, that their interview had been interrupted with news from his office, that his father had been taken to hospital following an attack at his parents' home. But this time, his reason for being there was not to represent anyone else, only himself.

As promised, when PC Adams came to book Marshall in, there was already an email from DC Tappin giving the information she required surrounding the circumstances of Marshall's arrest.

As per English law, this had to be read aloud for the prisoner to hear and understand, even though the same information was usually imparted at the time of arrest.

In some cases, where there was an inability to impart this information, due to intoxication or a language barrier, then it needed to be reiterated as soon as was reasonably possible.

"There's also a forensic strategy," the detention officer said, handing over a printed sheet of paper to Adams. "Once we're done here, you can use the dry cell for all that."

The dry cell was unique amongst cells in the custody centre, as it had no water dispenser or toilet. This was so a suspect could not compromise any forensic opportunities by rinsing his hands.

Under such circumstances, the suspect was usually accompanied by an officer to prevent any further loss of evidence. This was referred to as having the prisoner under *constant obs*, or observation.

With the booking-in process complete, PC Adams and her colleague accompanied Marshall to the dry cell.

Once there, both officers took photographs of Marshall in the clothing he was arrested in.

They then took swabs of Marshall's hands, before Adams stepped out to allow her male colleague to lastly witness Marshall changing out of his outer clothes into custody-issued, navy-blue sweatshirt and matching jogging trousers. All of Marshall's outer clothing was then seized as evidence for forensic analysis.

With this complete, the officers returned Marshall to the bridge, where a detention officer took him to have his fingerprints and DNA taken. They then left custody in order to report back to DC Tappin.

Gone were the days of using an ink roller and what was referred to as a *ten card*, where the suspect's prints were inked, and all ten digits were then rolled one at a time onto the card, hence the name.

The modern alternative was a device called Livescan, which scanned and stored the fingerprints digitally, and also conducted a live search for any matches against any stored records.

The method of obtaining a suspect's DNA was far less elaborate, merely utilising a serrated cotton bud to brush across the inside of the prisoner's cheek to remove sufficient cells for a profile to be extracted later.

After all that, Marshall was taken to a normal cell which contained a toilet, and a dispenser for drinking water. He was also asked if he wanted anything to eat or drink, which he declined. There Marshall was left to await interview.

In the meantime, Tappin was busy co-ordinating the efforts to progress the investigation in other directions.

He had seen the duty inspector and had gained the necessary authorisation, in the form of a section 18 search warrant to enter and search Marshall's home address for evidence of the offences.

It was fortunate that Marshall was in possession of his house keys when he was arrested, because the warrant to enter the premises also included the authority to force entry should the need arise.

But in this case, as the police had the keys, they would be able to enter and conduct the search, and secure the premises all without causing any damage.

By this time, the officer who had been assigned to search Marshall's car had completed the search, and had reported back to Tappin.

The boot space was immaculate, having appeared to have had nothing ever placed in there since the car had been bought.

The interior also looked like it had just come out of the showroom, or had been recently valeted.

As a result, all that was seized was the only item that appeared to be out of place in the whole car, and that was a roll of duct tape, which had been found in the front passenger's footwell.

38

Having deployed the uniformed officers to search Marshall's house, Tappin then set about preparing for his interview with Marshall.

The clock was ticking on Marshall's detention period as he languished in a cell in the custody centre.

Sergeant Staplehurst was right in the respect that at present they had very little evidence on which to charge him. They had no physical evidence to link him to the crimes, or even any of the crime scenes. They also had no witnesses to anything that had been reported.

All they had been given was a vague admission of knowledge of the crimes, as opposed to any actual involvement in them.

So, it was with his sergeant's suggestion in mind, that Tappin and a colleague went in to get an early first account from Marshall, in the hopes that it would give them new directions in which to investigate.

oOo

"I don't know about you, but I am getting a sense of déjà vu here," Tappin said, as he and Marshall sat across from each other. "Y'know I do remember us interviewing together… Seems all we're missing now is a suspect."

However, on this occasion, Marshall *was* the suspect.

On every previous occasion that Marshall had attended custody, he had been sat next to someone else. Someone whose future was in the balance. When there was no guarantee as to what would happen as a result of what took place within that room.

Only this time, Marshall sat by himself. He had been offered legal representation, as was his right, even though it was ironic given his circumstances. But regardless of that, he had chosen to decline it, as so many do, for whatever their reason may be.

For some, it's because they feel they don't need representation, as they know from previous experience how the game is played. For others, they have nothing to hide, and intend to tell all. But for Marshall, well, he was probably drawing on these reasons, as well as being more qualified to represent himself than anyone chosen to do the job for him.

Should the case go as far as a court hearing, then Marshall might have to declare himself as his own representation. But for now, this was just a conversation between opposing advocates of the law.

"Now, let me just recap, you came to us stating that you had knowledge regarding the deaths of Allan Garmin and Robert Fraser," Tappin said. "Can you please tell us everything what you know about the deaths of these two people?"

There was a long silence, which was made all the more uncomfortable as both protagonists stared at the other. Almost as if they were continuing their earlier stand-off, sizing the other up, and searching for a weakness to exploit.

Tappin was convinced that this would be another *no comment* interview, and was prepared as such.

So, when Marshall broke the silence, and replied with anything other than the expected response, this surprised Tappin. In that instant, he had underestimated his opponent, and as a consequence, the first point went to Marshall.

"Actually, if we're to be one hundred percent accurate here, I came to you saying that I had knowledge into the deaths of Allan Garmin and Robert Fraser, *and* how Albert Foster and Brett Cable are implicated in the same... So, should that be the question asked, I'll answer it... I have represented them *all* at one time or another. So in lieu of any other commonality linking these deaths, I do suppose you could very well have to look at me."

Having been initially caught off guard by Marshall's responses, Tappin had time to compose himself, and continued with his questioning.

"Are you saying that you are in any way implicit in their deaths?" Tappin added.

"No, I am not saying that," Marshall replied. "Although I do believe that *you* are implying that, otherwise I guess we wouldn't be here, now would we?"

Tappin knew that Marshall was possibly looking to deflect and evade every question put to him. But in order for a court to be able to draw an inference from his responses, each question had to be asked, and an opportunity given for it to be answered.

But as this interview was merely being used to find out what Marshall knew, and was prepared to divulge, Tappin didn't feel the need to labour each point, or delve any deeper at this initial stage. After all, time was still of the essence.

"Okay, moving on to these implications then... Did Albert Foster entrust you with the key to his car following his conviction and driving ban?" Tappin asked.

"Yes, he did," Marshall replied.

"And, where is that key now?" Tappin asked.

"Well, right now, I'm assuming it's with your forensics department, otherwise you wouldn't be asking me about it," Marshall began. "But I suppose what you really want to know is, what I did with it *after* I admitted that he gave it to me?"

"Well, yes," Tappin confirmed.

"Well, why didn't you just ask as such? I know I have all the time in the world, but you don't," Marshall replied. "Yes, Albert gave me the key as we left the court following his conviction. He said that he didn't trust himself not to drive the car during his ban... I took the key to avoid any unpleasantness at the time. But that evening, having realised that it's not *my* place to take that responsibility, after all I'm not on any retainer. He needs to have the willpower not to offend himself... So, the next day, I went to his house, and I put the key through the letterbox."

Marshall watched as Tappin and his colleague made notes as he spoke.

"Why didn't you knock on the door and hand the key to him personally?" Tappin asked.

"Like I said, the reason I didn't refuse at the time was because I didn't want a confrontation over it," Marshall replied. "So, I thought it best to just put the key through the door, and leave it at that."

Having noted Marshall's explanation, Tappin then probed somewhat to challenge this response.

"Obviously we've spoken to Foster and his wife, and neither of them have any knowledge of you returning the key," Tappin stated. "Can you explain that?"

"Detective, really?" Marshall replied. "His car has been involved in a fatal hit and run collision... So, of course he's going to look for a way out, and me having had the key in the recent past, potentially gives him just that... Added to which, his wife is just being loyal, so of course she'll say whatever he wants her to... Have you looked at any history of domestic violence, or coercive behaviour in their relationship?"

Tappin had already realised that, although he had managed to obtain signed accounts from both Foster and his wife, they were of absolutely no evidential value. Now Marshall had also given him nothing.

This realisation caused yet another silence. Although this one only caused Tappin to feel distinctly uncomfortable.

He knew that Marshall had the upper hand. He was offering responses to every question put to him, and his responses were shutting down every line of enquiry, and every challenge that he could think of raising.

This silence was mercifully interrupted by a knock at the door to the interview room.

For Marshall, this was eerily reminiscent of the interruption that advised him of his father's attack. An irony that wasn't wasted on him as being the event that began all of this.

"Pausing interview," Tappin said, as he tapped on a touch screen computer next to him, in order to pause the audio recording.

He then stood and went to open the door. He had been expecting an interruption, and was grateful for its timing.

In the corridor, and out of earshot of Marshall, Tappin spoke to a detective colleague from CID.

"We've had a call from a Ruth Quinn, mother of a Miles Quinn," the detective began. "She's just found her son dead at their home, Sarge said you'd want to know."

This was not the interruption that Tappin was expecting, as what he had been waiting for was the result of the search warrant at Marshall's home address.

"Fuck me!" exclaimed Tappin. "He's another former client of the guy I've got in here on suspicion of another two killings... I was only at his house this morning looking to arrest him, and now he's dead... Have we got officers there yet? What has the mum said?"

"No update from the scene yet," the detective replied. "Officers are on their way."

Tapping nodded, as the escalating situation appeared to be in hand.

"Okay," he replied. "What else have you got?"

This was the update that Tappin was expecting.

"Oh, you're gonna love this, we've had an update from the section eighteen at your guy's home address," the detective continued. "Get this, he's got case files for all his past clients are spread out on a table, and there's a list of names including those who have died."

Tappin's eye's opened wide in disbelief.

"Is Quinn's name on it?" he asked.

"No, he wasn't," the detective replied. "But, you're not gonna believe this... There was a hammer, just lying there next to the files, with blood on it, just there, on the *same* table in plain sight... They're all done there, and everything's on its way back to the nick... Is he coughing to anything?"

"Not yet, he's given us fuck all to work with," Tappin said. "I'd better get back in there and finish this off. I'll catch up with you in the office."

Tappin then went back into the interview room where his colleague had been waiting with Marshall.

Having retaken his seat, Tappin resumed the audio recording.

"Continuing interview with James Marshall, only persons previously introduced present," he said before continuing. "Well... That was an enlightening interruption."

If Tappin was expecting a response from Marshall, he was sorely disappointed.

"What would be the relevance of me mentioning the name Giles Quinn to you right now?" Tappin asked.

"Well, he's a former client of mine. And he is *also* the person you recently stated that left his DNA profile at or near the recent attack on my father."

"That's right," Tappin confirmed. "But, also in the last half hour, his mother has found him dead at her home address."

"Oh, that is a shame," Marshall replied.

"What's a shame?" Tappin asked, leaping on the remark.

"A mother finding the dead body of her son," Marshall replied. "That's awful."

"Yes, it is," Tappin replied. "Okay, this isn't getting us anywhere, so I'm going to end this interview there… Get yourself some rest, James, I'll be back to speak to you a little bit later on."

Tappin then announced the time for the benefit of the audio recording, before pressing the stop button on his touchscreen.

"Can I leave you to do all the necessary here?" Tappin said to his colleague. "I need to get back to the office."

Having received an acknowledgement from his colleague, Tappin left the interview room.

39

Having ended the first account interview, Tappin went straight back to the CID office in order to be able to view everything that had been seized as a result of the searches of Marshall's car and his home address.

The photographs that PC Adams had taken of Marshall before being stripped of the clothes he was wearing at the time of his arrest were also waiting for him.

Tappin's first question was to the detective that had given him the news about Quinn's death.

"Have we had any update from the Quinn job yet?" he asked.

"Sarge Staplehurst and the DI have gone to the scene," he replied. "They've been gone a while, hopefully they won't be too much longer."

That came as welcome news to Tappin. As the update on Quinn was still pending, he was able to immerse himself in what had been retrieved from the searches.

The CID office was a cacophony of activity. It was unusually crowded as all the response officers involved with the searches had commandeered CID workstations in order to write their statements evidencing what that had seized and to place updates on the arrest record and crime report.

Tappin started off by looking at the hammer that had been seized. It had been placed in a plastic tube, which was then sealed into an evidence bag. The reason for the tube was to eliminate any abrasion to the tool, which could compromise any latent fingerprints.

There was nothing remarkable about the hammer as far as having any uniquely identifying characteristics. The description on the exhibit label on the evidence bag in which it had been placed in said it all;

Claw hammer w/black handle
w/apparent blood on head

Police officers were not able to determine if something that appeared to be blood was in fact blood, only that it was *apparently* blood. Only after a forensic analysis could this be determined, and then documented as such.

Next Tappin looked at the list of names which had been seized from Marshall's home address.

This had been placed in an evidence bag. Through the back of the bag he was able to clearly view the names written on it:

Robert Fraser
Allan Gormin
Charlie Maclean
Albert Foster
Bradley Simons
Akbar Jumal
Patrick McNeil

Tappin's colleague had been right that Quinn's name did not feature on the list, and this puzzled him.

But what shocked him the most was how many names did appear that had yet to feature in any reported incidents.

He couldn't help but consider that this was a list of intended targets.

But if it was, and it showed a work in progress, he wondered why Marshall would hand himself in before he had completed his work?

Tappin could understand it if they had found Marshall and arrested him, effectively interrupting his work. But Marshall having giving himself up as he did didn't make any sense to him.

Tappin took the list to the photocopier and ran himself off a working copy that he could write on and refer to.

Once he had this copy, he amended it to show a distinction between those whose involvement was known, and those who were still unaccounted for, and potentially at risk;

Robert Fraser
Allan Garmin
* Charlie Maclean
Albert Foster
* Bradley Simons
* Akbar Jumal
* Patrick McNeil

The names that had been struck through denoted their known involvement in whatever capacity, and those marked with an asterisk had yet to have their relevance determined.

The reason that Tappin couldn't cross through McNeil's name was because his relevance and inclusion on the list was unknown. As although a body had been found within the debris of the Iron Horse public house fire, it had yet to be formally identified.

"What do we know about Maclean, Simons, Jumal or McNeil, anyone?" Tappin called out, intending for the entire CID office to hear, and hopefully respond.

When no response came, Tappin knew that he had to conduct any to research the names himself.

None of the names readily leapt to Tappin's mind as having any dealings with them personally. It was then that he realised that the answer may lay within the files that had been seized from Marshall's home.

They had been photographed in situ on Marshall's dining table before being collected up. They had then made it to the CID office in a collapsible storage box with a lid.

As the files themselves weren't evidence of anything other than an underpinning knowledge and commonality of those involved, Tappin didn't need to exercise the precaution of donning examination gloves prior to sifting through the box.

It didn't take Tappin that long to find the files for MacLean, Simons, Jumal and McNeil. From there he was able to determine Marshall's professional relationship and involvement with each of them.

But none of the files gave any indication as to why these people, drawn from Marshall's entire case history would be singled out to make it to such a list. As a result, the purpose and intention of creating a list in itself perplexed him.

As he still had to wait upon the return of his sergeant and the DI, Tappin spent this time casting an eye over some of the other files from Marshall's previous cases.

oOo

It was as Tappin was taking a break, and made himself a coffee, that he saw his sergeant, DS Staplehurst, and the detective inspector enter the office.

Tappin was anxious to know what the Quinn incident had so far turned up.

He quickly turned one mug of coffee into three, and approached Staplehurst's office where he and the DI had congregated.

Tappin stood in the open doorway of his sergeant's office, waiting to be noticed.

Then when that failed to achieve the desired result, Tappin felt the need to try another approach.

"Coffee?" he said, as he held up a tray with three steaming mugs on it.

"Ah, fab," Staplehurst said seeing that refreshment was imminent. "How did the interview go with Marshall; did he give us anything new to work with?"

"Absolutely nothing, Sarge," Tappin replied. "I was expecting him to go *no comment*, but it was just the opposite. But nothing he said implicated him in any way… I paused the interview when I got news of the Quinn job, but even mention of that didn't seem to faze him."

"Did he avoid any questions?" Staplehurst asked.

"Not at all… If anything, he elaborated on the questions asked. He just kept himself on solid ground. We've got nothing new to work with," Tappin replied. "What about Quinn?"

"Take a seat, and I'll fill you in," Staplehurst said. "We've still got uniform, photographers and scenes of crime there. But the gist of the job is that allegedly Marshall went to visit his old dear this morning, feeding her some cock and bull story about needing forms to be signed by Quinn for a compensation claim or something... He then supposedly speaks to Quinn on the phone, and Quinn's again supposedly meant to come over... She then gets herself locked in the living room. She's sure she then hears her son in the house. Then, after about half an hour, all of a sudden, she tries the door again only to find that it's now unlocked. Then when she comes out, she finds the front door wide open."

"When was all this?" Tappin asked.

"This afternoon," Staplehurst replied.

"Why did it take till now to report the body?" Tappin asked.

"She's saying that she called it in as soon as she found it," Staplehurst answered. "She thought that Quinn and Marshall had maybe left together, forgetting to close the front door properly... It was only when she had need to go into the garage that she found him."

"And what had happened to him?" Tappin anxiously asked.

"He was bound and strung up from the ceiling of the garage. There was blood all over the floor, no spray, just a huge puddle around him... From a prelim of him in situ, it looked like there was a single puncture wound to the abdomen, possibly from the screwdriver that was found in the puddle at his feet... We're not sure if that was the cause of death yet, it's still too early to say. But, given the size of the wound, there must have been something else involved to cause such immense blood loss. He also had a fresh needle mark on his arm, but as he's got previous for being a user, it may just be that he's back on the gear since being released."

The circumstances described instantly struck a chord with Tappin.

"I'll be right back," Tappin exclaimed as he launched himself out of his chair.

The outburst and excursion surprised both Staplehurst and the DI.

"After that, I hope this is worth it," the DI jested.

Moments later, Tappin was back in the sergeant's office flicking through a case file. It was the case file for a man named Victor Bergstrom.

"It's Warfarin," Tappin said with an inappropriate amount of excitement in his voice.

He then spread a case file out in front of his audience, and pointed a finger to the exact reference before continuing.

"That's the exact MO that this guy, Victor Bergstrom, used to kill his old man a few years back... He's since died of old age himself. But guess who his brief was?"

"Marshall," both Staplehurst and the DI said in unison.

After taking a moment to glance at the information put before them, Staplehurst was the first to reply.

"Well that would certainly explain the massive blood loss through such a small puncture wound," he said.

Tappin could also see the DI nod his agreement.

"But all of this, as compelling as it sounds, still doesn't prove a damned thing," the DI interjected. "And unless the hammer or the screwdriver are shown to be directly involved somehow, and more importantly specifically implicate Marshall, then we'll still have nothing... The way I see it is this: we certainly can't bail him to see what else we can dig up, or for the DNA results to come back, not if there's potential targets still on the list... And even if James here is right about the Warfarin, and given what we do have, which I have to say isn't much, I very much doubt you'll get the Superintendent to authorise a custody extension. I would say our only safe option will be to charge him."

"Sounds good to me," Staplehurst added. "That way, at least he'll be remanded."

Staplehurst was referring to the severity of the offence. Choosing to charge Marshall with murder, would result in him being held in custody to await a first trial hearing, as opposed to being released with an appointment to attend court at a future date.

"I've still got a fair amount of time on his detention clock," Tappin said. "I'll see what I can get done before that starts running low."

Although Tappin said he had a fair amount of time, so much of what needed to be achieved was beyond his control.

The forensic analysis of the clothing, weapons, and scenes would take days if not weeks as opposed to hours to produce a result, and the toxicology report, as well as the post-mortem investigation into the cause of Quinn's death, would take an equally long time.

As a consequence, the decision to charge Marshall would be based on what the police already had in hand.

oOo

It wasn't long before Tappin found himself back in an interview room with Marshall.

Tappin was alone on this occasion as most of his team had gone home, having terminated their duty. This would be the last thing that Tappin would be doing himself, as anything further could be passed on to the next team on-duty.

"Why did you go to see Ruth Quinn yesterday morning?" Tappin asked.

This question was technically accurate in the fact that it was now yesterday morning, as this second interview had commenced after midnight.

"I'm afraid I can't discuss that with you," Marshall replied. "That is a confidential matter."

"Are you refusing to answer the question, James?" Tappin asked.

"No, I'm not refusing to answer the question Detective Tappin," Marshall replied. "You know as well as I do, that I cannot discuss the intricacies of any clients with you or anyone else."

Resigning himself to the fact that the question would remain unanswered, Tappin moved on.

"Can you tell me what happened to Giles Quinn?" Tappin then asked.

"I don't know what happened to him," Marshall replied.

"Did you kill him?" Tappin asked.

It was becoming evident that as he grew ever more tired, that Tappin's level of patience and tolerance was rapidly diminishing.

"No, I did not," Marshall replied adamantly.

"How did he die then?" Tappin asked.

"That's really not my area of expertise. I'm not a pathologist," Marshall flippantly responded.

"Do you know what this is?" Tappin said as he placed a photograph of the apparently bloodied hammer on the table.

"You mean beyond the obvious?" Marshall replied.

"Yes, of course I mean beyond the *fucking* obvious," Tappin said, his decorum now in tatters.

"Well, it's a hammer… And if it's the hammer you found on my table, and you want to know how I came to be in possession of it… Well, I found it whilst I was out walking one evening," Marshall answered.

"Where did you find it?" Tappin asked.

"It was in the graveyard of Saint Mary's church," Marshall replied. "I found it in amongst the graves, and I didn't want it to fall into the hands of children, so I thought I would take it home… It was then that I saw what could be blood on it. I then decided I'd best hand it over to you. After all, you don't know if it's been used to do something unsavoury."

Tappin sighed at Marshall's arrogance.

"Will we find your fingerprints on it?" Tappin went on to ask.

"Oh, that's highly unlikely," Marshall replied. "If I recall correctly, it was a cold evening that night, and I'm pretty sure I was wearing gloves."

"And I suppose we won't find your fingerprints on this either then?" Tappin said.

He then placed a photograph of a screwdriver that was even more bloodied than the hammer.

"Or this?"

Tappin placed a third photograph on top of the other two. This showed a small painted mortice-lock key.

"Or this?"

He finally placed a fourth photograph, that of the telephone in Ruth Quinn's living room, on top of the others.

"It looks like you've covered your tracks well," Tappin concluded. "But it's not going to do you the slightest bit of good… You're going to be charged with the murders of Garmin, Fraser *and* Quinn… But before we're done here, tell me one thing, are Charlie Maclean, Bradley Simons, Akbar Jumal and Patrick McNeil in any danger from you?"

"Absolutely not," Marshall exclaimed.

"And why's that?" Tappin asked.

"Because, unless I'm mistaken, given that I'm about to be charged with three murders, you're not going to be releasing me anytime soon now, are you?"

Tappin muttered an expletive under his breath.

"Very well, you just carry on playing your games," Tappin said. "We're done here."

With that, the second interview was at an end, having achieved nothing, but leaving Tappin infuriated and frustrated.

40

James Marshall was charged with three counts of murder, and as Detective Sergeant Staplehurst had also eluded to, Marshall was also remanded. As a result, he was kept in the custody of the police until he was able to be transported to the local magistrate's court later that morning, the day following his arrest.

Yet again, James Marshall found himself in a new role in a once familiar situation. He was now the accused. He was the defendant. In addition, he was also his own legal representation. Consequently, he stood alone at the defence's bench within the courtroom, having been granted permission to present his plea from there as opposed to the dock.

"You stand charged with three counts of murder, that of Allan Garmin, a human being, Robert Fraser, a human being, and Giles Quinn, a human being," the magistrate read out. "How do you plead?"

"I plead not guilty on all counts your honour," Marshall said vehemently.

"Very well, let the record show your plea," the magistrate continued. "The trial date will be set for the first Monday in September at ten o'clock in the morning, and you are to remain in custody until then. Do you have anything else you wish to say?"

"No, your honour," Marshall replied.

"Very well," the magistrate replied, as he struck his gavel.

That signified the end of the hearing, and the court security staff then stepped into handcuff Marshall and escorted him back down to the court's holding cells.

From there he was transported to a convenient prison in which to await his trial.

41

James Marshall had been transferred from the relative tranquillity of the holding cells at the courthouse to the assigned prison in order to serve his remand as he awaited his trial date.

During this time, as he was representing himself at the upcoming trial, he was offered access to a legal library in order to prepare his defence.

But despite the offer being repeatedly made, Marshall chose to decline it on every occasion. Instead, all he requested was a supply of writing materials.

oOo

During the same interim, DC James Tappin was busy ensuring that all the evidence was ready for the prosecution. These included statements being obtained Ruth Quinn, and from Albert and Mrs Foster, even though he was still the subject of a police investigation himself.

The exhibits requiring forensic analysis had now been dealt with, and results had been produced.

One item came back with very perplexing results. The hammer that had been seized from Marshall's home address was found to have DNA from two different sources, and from three different people, none of which matched the samples obtained from Marshall when he was arrested.

When the results were made known to Tappin, he immediately felt the need to consult with his sergeant.

"Sarge, a bizarre thing has turned up with the hammer in the Marshall case," Tappin began. "The forensic report shows three forensic matches: two blood samples and one from fingerprints."

"That's good, isn't it?" Staplehurst replied. "Helps bolster the case against him."

"Not exactly," Tappin replied. "None of the matches are from Marshall."

"How can that be?" Staplehurst exclaimed.

"No idea," Tappin replied. "But this is where it gets weirder... One blood sample comes back to Robert Fraser, now that much we were expecting, as he's one of Marshall's alleged victims... But the other blood sample is for a Paul Greene. Now Greene was attacked some time back, and is not linked to Marshall in any way. He was attacked by a Brett Cable. Cable got found nearby and nicked for it, and is currently RUI... Now, guess whose prints are on the hammer, and who his brief was when he was brought in?"

"You're shitting me?" Staplehurst remarked.

Tappin shook his head as he smiled broadly.

"Do you think I should exclude this from the Marshall case, and save it for when Cable comes back in?" Tappin asked.

"Hmmm, that's a tricky one," Staplehurst replied. "No, leave it in for the time being; it doesn't prove Marshall's involvement in anything, but at least have the court hear how he came to have it in his house when it was searched... Apart from that, how's things coming together?"

It was then that Tappin lost his smile.

"To be quite honest, I really don't think we've got much of a case here," he remarked. "I think we may've jumped the gun, and put too much hope on the forensics. We've got nothing with Marshall's DNA on it, no fingerprints anywhere. Also, we've got no witnesses to anything untoward that he's supposed to have done."

Staplehurst pondered the situation that befell them.

"Well, it was a lawful arrest, and it was the courts that chose to remand him until the trial," Staplehurst rationalised. "We just collect the evidence. After that, it's down to the courts to make sense of it, and decide what needs to be done... I wouldn't lose any sleep over it if I were you. I certainly won't."

42

The first day of the trial arrived soon enough. Marshall was transported to the crown courts by a secure prison transport.

Whilst still in prison, Marshall had received and reviewed the vetting list for potential jurors. Once again, as with the repeated offers of privileged access to a legal library, this was dismissed with minimal regard.

He simply returned the still sealed envelope, with a handwritten message on the front, that read:

No Challenges

As he was considered to be a *litigant in person,* Marshall was exempt from having to wear the gown and wig that was part of the crown court tradition. Instead, he wore a three-piece suit that was clearly bespoke. It was one of his own, something that he hadn't had the chance to wear for some time. Something that was a far cry from the inmate uniform he had had to wear whilst being a guest of Her Majesty.

However, as a result of him losing some weight whilst in prison, the suit was slightly looser than he remembered it being, from when he had last worn it.

Once the court was assembled, the usher brought everyone to their feet before announcing the entrance of the presiding judge.

Then following an acknowledgement from the judge to begin, it fell to the barrister for the prosecution to open the proceedings.

"Ladies and gentlemen, my name is George Massey. I am the barrister for the prosecution. I represent Her Majesty the Queen and the crown of the United Kingdom in this case... It is my job, and my responsibility to present the crown's evidence to you against the defendant who is sat before you."

Massey then turned to face where Marshall sat.

"The reason he sits at his desk alone and not in the dock is because he is himself a very successful and well-respected criminal solicitor... He has therefore chosen to represent himself in this matter. I must add that this is a right to which a defendant is entitled to, regardless of their occupation or prior legal experience."

Massey then turned back to face the jury, resting his hands on the rail at the front of the jury box.

"He stands before you charged with a number of heinous offences. These offences do not solely involve the terrible deaths of some of his former clients, but also with him perverting the course of justice. Throughout this trial, you will hear just how deceptive and manipulative the defendant has been, and as a result of that, you may choose *not* to like him. However, your judgement should not be based upon your opinion of this man, but solely upon the evidence as it is laid before you."

With that, Massey stepped back from the jury box. He then turned to face the judge, giving the minutest of bows, before returning to the prosecution's bench, where he retook his seat.

"Mister Marshall," the judge began. "Would you like to give the court an opening statement?"

"Yes, I would, your worship," Marshall said as he rose to his feet.

He then walked around his bench, buttoning a single button on his suit jacket as he did, before standing proudly, and immaculately presented before the jury.

"Good morning to you all," he began. "As the prosecution has so eloquently mentioned, I am in fact a solicitor myself, I have been for many years, and as a result I will be representing myself throughout this trial... Though, I didn't feel he needed to labour the point as he did... Personally, I think he's just jealous, because although we essentially do the *same* job, although on opposing sides of the law, although I do get paid *considerably* more, take nicer holidays and drive a swankier car, and today, I don't have to wear one of those daft wigs."

Marshall smiled a broad smile, as if expecting the jury to share his joke. Without wanting any response, he continued.

"And what's all this about a jury of my peers? Ha, that's a joke in itself... All I see is twelve people too stupid to get themselves out of jury duty… I mean, you can't convince me that you actually *want* to be here. Wouldn't you rather be at home watching Jeremy Kyle or Phil and Holly?"

Once again, Marshall was the only person to enjoy his joke, as no one else in the courtroom appeared to find amusement in it.

"Anyway, back to the matter at hand. I will reiterate what my esteemed colleague has said. And that is you must base your verdict on the evidence brought before you, and *not* in any way on your opinion of me."

Marshall then started to pace back and forth in front of the jury box.

To see the jury's reaction alone, it would appear that they were watching tennis, as they glanced left and right, aiming to keep Marshall central in their vision.

"It is on the balance of this evidence that you will need to reach your decision," he continued. "*However*, what my esteemed colleague has failed to mention is that evidence in *any* situation can fall under one of two headings… And you will have to decide under which heading each piece of evidence ultimately falls."

Marshall then stopped midway, and again turned to face the jury, resting his hands on the rail, almost mimicking what the prosecutor had done only minutes earlier.

"Evidence can be either direct or it can be circumstantial," Marshall explained. "It can either prove someone's involvement, or simply provide a tenuous link between two elements. And again, it is for you to decide which is which. But, for now, I thank you for your attention… We shall speak again as the trial continues."

With that, Marshall returned to his bench. There he unbuttoned his jacket, before taking his seat.

Once seated, he looked up towards the bench to see the judge throwing a cold stare in his direction, no doubt in response to his impertinent comment about the jury's level if intelligence.

This he responded to with an inward smile. He felt he had achieved everything he needed to.

43

The trial had been scheduled to last upwards of three weeks. But by the Wednesday of the second week, both the cases for the prosecution *and* the defence had been presented.

This was largely due to Marshall offering a minimal cross-examination of the prosecution's witnesses and evidence, and only a meagre and brief defence by himself, having called no witnesses at all.

All that remained was for both the prosecution and the defence to summarise their cases before the jury retired to deliberate the evidence and to hopefully reach a verdict.

oOo

During the trial, Albert Foster and his wife were both called to give their evidence. They both confirmed their accounts exactly as they had previously given to the police, and provided in the form of a statement.

The only other non-expert witness to be called was Ruth Quinn, whose attendance was solely to testify that Marshall had attended her home address on two consecutive days, the second occasion being the day that she had later found her son dead in the garage.

The judge had to repeatedly warn Marshall for badgering the Fosters during their testimonies. Though nothing of the sort needed to be said when it came to his cross-examination of Ruth Quinn.

Beyond that, the only testimony given for the prosecution was from expert witnesses, substantiating the physical evidence as it was presented.

As Marshall was on trial for multiple charges, the jury would have to reach a verdict for each charge independently of all the others.

They could very well find Marshall guilty of all the charges, or equally of none. Similarly, should they find him guilty of some, this should not lead to the presumption of guilt for them all.

oOo

When it came to given their closing summaries, as before, it fell to the prosecution to go first.

Massey QC rose to his feet and walked around to be in front of his bench. There he stood in the middle of the courtroom.

"Ladies and gentlemen of the jury. At the beginning of this trial, I said that the crown would overwhelmingly prove their case against the defendant before you… You've now had a chance to see the evidence, and you've heard from the witnesses, all of which have confirmed the defendant's involvement in the most appalling acts, which have resulted in the death of three people."

Once again, Massey gave himself the cue to turn from the jury to lead their looks of disdain towards the defendant.

"There he sits, before you, having portrayed himself as the archetypal professional. Yet beneath that calm and immaculate exterior is a callous and calculating killer… He was once entrusted to represent those who sought his help, and he has abused that trust to his own end."

Massey then again approached the jury box to deliver his final message.

"It is now that the crown and I must entrust *you* to do *your* duty, to go and deliberate what you have absorbed throughout this trial, and to reach the only verdict you can, and that is that the defendant is guilty as charged… Thank you."

Massey then solemnly stepped back from the jury box, before walking back to his seat with his head bowed as if in mourning.

The judge then beckoned to Marshall to offer his response in the form of his summary.

This time Marshall didn't make any effort to stand. He began addressing the jury from his seat across the courtroom. He merely rotated himself sufficiently in his chair, in order to face them.

"Hello again… You may recall in my opening statement to yourselves, when I mentioned about the two different kinds of evidence. Some of which has since been exhibited before you?" Marshall asked as he began his summation. "You *should* do really, and after all it *was* only last week."

It was then that he stood, and approached the jury box.

"Well, let's do a quick recap, shall we? Because having looked around the room during the trial, I'm sure some of you weren't paying enough attention, and I fear that there are others of you who are just too gormless to know what was being said, and too *ignorant* to ask anyone about it."

Marshall then turned side on to the jury, so they could still hear him, but allowing his attention to include Massey.

"Added to which, I think even the prosecution could do with listening in for this bit? Because having witnessed their performance thus far, I think that they could certainly do with a refresher course"

"Are you having fun there, Mister Marshall?" the judge said, interrupting Marshall's speech.

"Immensely, your worship," Marshall replied. "May I continue?"

This disrespectful reply gained the added disruption of sniggers heard from elsewhere in the courtroom, although the acoustics meant their directionality couldn't be determined.

"Enough of that young man," the judge demanded, taking obvious displeasure in the approach that Marshall appeared to be taking. "Need I remind you that you are on trial for multiple murders? And I would appreciate it if you could take the matter at hand a bit more seriously, and give the petty insults a rest"

"Yes, your worship," Marshall replied, as if responding to a regimental sergeant major.

Once again, Marshall knew when to draw a line, having made his point.

"Where was I?" Marshall questioned himself following the interruption. "Ah yes... During this trial, the prosecution has brought you a number of items of *so-called* evidence to your attention. *Evidence* in respect that it was introduced with the sole intention of implicating me in the crimes for which I stand accused, and *so-called*, because it had little or no bearing on the actual case... And as a consequence, nothing which the prosecution has presented has in any way connected me to any of the crimes for which I stand accused."

Marshall then went back to his bench. He turned and perched himself on the corner of it.

"However, as each exhibit was shown and explained to you, it was said to have specifically incriminated me in the events as they unfolded... I would again suggest that there is nothing, absolutely *nothing* presented in the prosecution's case that implicates me... Or at the very least eliminates reasonable doubt to suggest I have played a part in any of this."

Marshall threw his hands up in apparent disgust.

"Now, let's look at the extent of their evidence. A number of case files that include the names of the deceased, whoop-dee-doo... Is it a crime that I choose to keep my files at home as opposed to an office...? Then the prosecution would have you believe that names on a piece of paper somehow show premeditation to what has happened to some, but only *some,* of those on that list."

Marshall then stood up again, and sighed.

"Nothing on this piece of paper suggests any intention whatsoever. There are names on that piece of paper of persons that are still alive... Ohmigod! So, should we place them under police protection, as they must surely be in mortal danger from me?"

Marshall was clearly getting fed up by this, and his speech was being improvised to account for that.

"Look, I'm nearly done, I promise you that much. But then again, apparently, I can't be trusted... Then, there was this roll of duct tape which was seized from my car that was parked in front of the police station at the time of my arrest. This is supposedly evidence because one of my alleged victims was bound with tape... Now, I'm sure there's more than one of you that has a similar roll of tape at home... So, the prosecution would have us believe that you are all equally culpable."

Marshall again turned to face Massey.

"The prosecution has again failed to prove that this roll of tape is a specific match as, although the tape is likely to be the same brand, the torn ends do not match in any way whatsoever."

Marshall then paused to catch his breath.

"Then, we have the hammer that was found at my home address. And as you may recall, when I took the stand and was questioned myself,

I stated that I merely found it whilst I was out walking one evening, having been discarded in a churchyard... And being the community-spirited person that I am, I didn't want some child to get their hands on it, so what did I do? I took it home... Now you may not believe my account of this, but at the very least, it *is* plausible... And whilst we're in the churchyard, metaphorically speaking of course, the prosecution brought up the evidence of a discarded coffee cup found in the same churchyard as one of my alleged victims. I've already said I was in the churchyard, as that's where I found the hammer. So, as I don't see littering down amongst the charges against me, I really don't see its relevance."

Marshall then chose to return to his seat and sat down, before continuing. This was either a result of his having grown weary of the sound of his own voice, or that he had just become bored with the situation.

"Anyway, I'm digressing, back to the hammer... The prosecution told us that a forensic sample isolated on the hitty end of the hammer matches two separate DNA profiles. And that fingerprints found on the holdy end matches that of a third profile. Well, guess what? None of them were said to be mine. So once again, the hammer proves nothing."

It was then that Marshall allowed for a moment of silence. As there was no discernible end to his speech, the court was unaware how to react to it. So, it then fell to the judge to clarify the situation.

"Have you finished Mister Marshall?" he asked.

"Not yet, nearly there... Just catching my breath," Marshall replied. "Then... We have a convicted criminal, a prolific drink driver. Someone who takes to the stand, swearing blind that I took his car, used it to run over someone else one evening, *only* to return it by then crashing it into his front wall... He states that he gave me the key following his previous conviction. Now, that bit *did* actually happen... However, I felt that it was not down to me as his *former* legal representation, and let's be clear about it, it *was* because I was no longer getting paid, to prevent him from having to adhere to this recent drink/drive conviction which resulted in a driving ban. So, after having taken the key from him just to shut him up, I put it through his letterbox the very next day."

Marshall then turned in his seat to look towards the public gallery to where Foster was now sat with his wife. Marshall smiled and winked at him before turning to the face the jury again.

"Now, to ensure a conviction, the evidence presented needs to eliminate coincidence, conjecture and circumstance. I'm sure I've read that somewhere… And if I'm not mistaken, the crown has failed on *all* three counts."

Marshall then again rose to his feet again, in order to show a final gesture of respect to the court.

"Now, a number of people have had their lives ruined as a result of the decisions I have made as a solicitor… Sometimes the decisions I have made may not have been morally correct. But I believe I can say beyond any shadow of a doubt that what happened to my *alleged* victims was as a result of the choices that *they* made… So, ladies and gentlemen, when you do retire to deliberate your verdict, I do hope you remember at least *some* of the things that we have discussed. As I would rather *not* have to go over them *again*."

Marshall then retook his seat, and although his posture suggested that he was speaking to himself, the volume by which he spoke had clearly intended that it was for the whole courtroom to hear him.

"To think my future *and* reputation is now in the hands of twelve people too stupid to get out of jury duty," he said.

The courtroom was draped in a shocked silence. Even the judge was dumbstruck, before realising his place and giving final words of direction to the jury.

44

"I'm sure we both know which way this is going to go," Tappin said.

"Oh, of that I have no doubt," Marshall replied.

In the recess created when the jury had retired to consider a verdict, DC Tappin had taken it upon himself to visit Marshall as he waited in the court's holding cells for the court to be called back in.

"It's a question that has yet to be asked, and the way things are going, probably won't *ever* be. But it's something *I* need to understand," Tappin began. "Why did you do it? You can tell me, it's just the two of us here, and besides, it's not going to make any difference now,"

Marshall sat across from Tappin, with only steel bars separating them. He glanced down the hallway to ensure no one else was within earshot, before replying.

"To be honest with you, I thought it would have been perfectly obvious," Marshall began. "We've all made bad choices in our lives. Sometimes we realise them, sometimes we don't. Sometimes we realise them in time, and we choose to do something about it, and *that* was the case here... Now, whatever the outcome is here, I can leave this courtroom knowing that for once, I've done the right thing."

Tappin realised that Marshall had answered his question, even if his words hadn't said as much.

"Y'know, there's no way I could have discussed any of this with you, what they had admitted to me, without being disbarred... Even if I had broken privilege and told you what they had done, for *you* to act upon it, the end result for me would've been the same."

Again, Marshall's answer made perfect sense.

"One last thing," Tappin asked as he stood up. "Tell me, why are you insulting everybody in the courtroom, the prosecutor, the judge, the jury, and yeah, I saw you wink at the Fosters? Surely you need the jury to reach their verdict in your favour. At this rate they despise you."

"And that is precisely *why* I am doing it," Marshall explained. "I need them to despise me. I need their judgement to be clouded with their resentment of me. All the time they are despising me, they are not focusing on the evidence in front of them. If they despise me, then they'll want to find me guilty."

Tappin could again see the logic.

"Well, as we are laying our cards on the table, I have a little confession I want you to hear," Tappin began. "I've never understood why anybody would want to do your job. I've always thought that your profession is, well, essentially scum. Taking money and success over morality... It's just a shame that it's taken all of this for you to realise it too. Had you taken the role of prosecutor, who knows? We may have well been friends."

Without warning, Tappin extended his hand between the bars of the cell hoping that Marshall would take it as a gesture of respect, if not friendship.

Marshall took the hand, and shook it. There was certainly a mutual respect between the two of them.

Tappin then left Marshall alone to contemplate the inevitable.

45

Following a lengthy period of deliberation, the court was called back into session.

Tappin had again taken his seat in the public gallery in time to see Marshall brought up from the holding cells beneath the courtroom.

Since he had last sat there, and as a result of their last conversation, a mutual respect and sympathy was now felt between the two of them.

The judge was the last to enter the courtroom, and after the everyone had taken their seats, the court was again in session.

"Has the jury reached a verdict?" the judge asked.

The foreperson, a person from the jury who had been nominated to speak on their behalf rose to his feet.

"We have your worship," the foreperson replied.

With that, the usher, who had previously been calling the proceedings, approached the jury box. There he took a piece of folded paper that the foreperson was holding ready for him.

Without opening the folded paper, the usher walked towards the judge and handed it across to him. There he then waited.

The judge opened the paper for his private viewing. He remained silent and dispassionate to what was written within it. He then folded the paper again, and handed it back to the usher. The usher in turn returned the paper to the foreperson.

"What say you?" the judge asked.

"We, the jury, find the defendant guilty on all charges," the foreperson said.

There was a silence that fell across the courtroom. This was only disturbed by whispered remarks coming from the public gallery.

Foster and his wife were evidently enjoying this.

"Thank you for your verdict, and thank you for your service," said the judge. "However, I cannot rule on the verdict as you have decided it."

The judge then turned to face the courtroom, and shuffled slightly in his chair before commencing his address.

"Throughout this trial I have heard the same evidence as the court has. And, as the defendant has repeatedly made us aware, there *are* in fact two kinds of evidence... And, I do believe that the prosecution has failed to present a single iota of direct evidence to eradicate reasonable doubt."

The judge paused, sighed, and continued.

"Now, despite the prosecution's warning to the jury to rule solely on the evidence, I fear they have reached their verdict based upon their loathing of the defendant... Now, just because they detest him, doesn't make him guilty. Believe you me, I do not like him any more than you probably do. But as this is a court of law and *not* a popularity contest, we have to remain objective and dispassionate despite all influences... So, it falls to me to adjudicate on the verdict. And I cannot allow the guilty verdict to stand. I am therefore overturning the verdict as reached by the jury. The defendant is to be found *not* guilty, and is free to go."

The judge then brought his gavel down, signifying that the court session, and the trial was at an end.

oOo

As on many previous occasions, James Marshall had walked out of the courthouse accompanying a free man. But, on this occasion he walked out of the courthouse by himself, *as* a free man.

Free of conviction, free of obligation. He felt vindicated, not by the courts, but by himself.

Outside, of the courthouse, James Tappin approached Marshall from behind.

He was the only one who had waited for Marshall to go through the necessary formalities prior to being released from detention, and being able to leave the courthouse.

As he got closer, he placed his left hand on Marshall's right shoulder. He felt Marshall shudder with surprise under the contact. Tappin then circled around to stand face to face with Marshall.

There, they shared a second handshake, this time with no words spoken. Their only exchange was a mutually respectful smile. Then once that was at an end, Tappin took a step back.

"So, have you given any consideration as to how you're going to get yourself home?" Tappin asked.

Marshall smiled, before shaking his head.

"To be quite honest with you, I didn't even know if I was going to be going home today," Marshall replied. "I certainly haven't made any provision for it."

"Come on then," Tappin replied, bobbing his head in the direction of the courthouse car park. "Let me give you lift, it's the least I can do… And, I'll even let you sit up front this time."

This was a little joke onto Tappin's part, alluding to the last time that Marshall was a passenger in a police car, having had to sit in the back as a prisoner.

The gesture came despite the fact that until that day they had been playing on opposing sides. But it was now very much a case of game over, a game where neither man felt that they had won. But conversely, neither man felt as if they had been defeated.

As they walked off, side by side, both men shared a common conundrum, which was to ask themselves if justice had been truly served on this day?

Epilogue

After James Marshall was found not guilty of all charges, he walked from court a free man.

However, given his reportedly unacceptable defence of Allan Garmin during his earlier drink-drive trial, Marshall was disbarred as a practicing solicitor. As a result, he lost his job with his law firm.

Following the section 18 search of Marshall's home address, when the hammer, files and list were found, the hammer was sent away for forensic analysis.

For Marshall's trial all that could be determined was that the hammer was found to be in his constructive possession at the time it was seized. There was nothing to forensically link him to the attack on Robert Fraser.

However, given the forensic results, the same hammer soon became a key piece of evidence in the investigation of Brett Cable for the attacks on both Robert Fraser and his earlier victim Paul Greene.

This newly introduced evidence against Cable was incontrovertible, and he was charged with one count of causing grievous bodily harm against Greene, and one count of murder against Fraser.

Although Cable only pleaded guilty to the charge of causing grievous bodily harm to Paul Greene, he was subsequently convicted of both attacks, and was sentenced to a total of twelve years in prison.

Allan Garman died as a result of the injuries he sustained when Albert Foster's Hyundai struck him as he crossed the road following his counselling session.

Foster continued to deny any involvement in this incident. He was however charged with causing death by dangerous driving. He was subsequently convicted as charged and received a five-year prison sentence, reduced to two years, to be followed by a three-year driving ban. The reduced sentence was on the condition that he attended and completed an alcohol rehabilitation program.

Marshall knew that, following his disbarment, along with everything else, he would never be in a position to represent Charlie Maclean when her trial date finally arrived.

But instead of abandoning her for his own benefit, he took it upon himself to prepare a full and comprehensive defence for her. This included prewarning all the expert witnesses that would be required for her case. As a result, Maclean was expeditiously found to be not guilty by the jury.

During her trial, reasonable doubt had been raised following the inclusion of a strikingly similar offence that had taken place when Maclean was able to prove that she was out of the country on holiday in Kefalonia.

The cause of this similar offence at the Iron Horse public house was determined after firefighters had painstakingly sifted through tonnes of debris to find the seat of the fire. The cause was found to be linseed oil. This was concluded after trace amounts were located in the closed under-stairs cupboard that had protected the evidence from firefighting efforts.

After the case against Maclean was dismissed, a fresh investigation was opened into the fire at the Iron Horse. This is still an open case, which is being treated as murder. The victim being an as-yet unidentified male.

Marshall was also indirectly responsible for feeding information about an ideal house to burgle to Bradley Simons, the prolific burglar whose name had made the list. This was done via a reliable third party.

A woman, not entirely dissimilar in appearance to Charlie Maclean, stated to Simons that this particular address was known to frequently contain vast quantities of cash on certain days due to the fact that the owner was a street market trader.

The address in fact belonged to Akbar Jumal, the fraudster with a penchant for targeting the elderly and vulnerable, who had also made Marshall's list.

During the commission of the burglary, the police received an anonymous tip-off from a female caller, to which they expeditiously attended.

They arrived to catch Simons in the act. But what they weren't expecting was to find a cache of evidence of Jumal's criminal activity at the same time.

As a result, both were now serving lengthy custodial sentences for their respective offences.

Leonard Marshall, James' father, made a full recovery from his injuries. He looked forward to seeing his son following his acquittal, as he didn't feel up to visiting him in prison.

He never mentioned the conversation he had with his son to his wife, as she remained steadfast as to her son's innocence, and she never mentioned finding blood on her son's coat when it was found amongst her husband's possessions following his return home from hospital. Instead she just arranged for it to be laundered.

Finally, sometime later, James Marshall received a box of personal items from his former employer. Amongst the items were some dress items for court, ties and a fresh shirt, as well as some stationery items, including a Mont Blanc pen set.

Also included were some photos of his children he had framed on his desk, and lastly, there was a postcard from Kefalonia from Charlie Maclean.

After all, she had assured him that she would send him one, and she was good to her word.

The End

Glossary of terms

Disclosure refers to a step in the legal process in which the police have an obligation to inform the defence of the nature of the suspected offence as well as a summary of the evidence that led them to the decision to arrest and detain the suspect. They have to share the identities of all those suspected of being involved, along with the place and time where the alleged offence was committed. Also, to be included is a summary of the evidence against the suspect from whatever source. However, this is where a grey area can open up. For example, the police could say they have CCTV footage, but unless specifically asked, it might very well not show anything relevant to the incident. Lastly, the police have a responsibility to make the defence aware of evidence that could undermine the prosecution's case, or assist the defence in exonerating their client.

Entrapment is when someone causes another person to commit a crime they would not otherwise have committed. It is also referred to as an "agent provocateur." As the latter name suggests, it is from the French legal system, although it is regularly referred to as such by English Courts.

RUI or *released under investigation* is a relatively new disposal from the arrest process which is less invasive than imposing bail conditions. But being released under investigation is issued with a reservation to the suspect that they were still being investigated, and that the police could recall them to be spoken again should the investigation warrant it.

Mens rea, Latin for *guilty mind*, is the intention or knowledge of wrongdoing that constitutes part of a crime, as opposed to the action or conduct of the accused, referred to as *actus reus. Actus non facit reum nisi mens sit rea* literally means *an act does not make a person guilty unless the mind is also guilty.* It's been taken that a person is guilty only if they are proved to be culpable or blameworthy in both thought and action. This essentially translates to someone needing to know that what they are doing is wrong in order for them to be found guilty of the offence that their actions have committed.

Modus operandi is a Latin phrase, with the approximate translation of "mode of operating." It reflects someone's habits of working, particularly in the context of business, but also and more generally it is used within criminal investigations.

Rigmarole means complicated, bothersome nonsense, so it might seem that, like gobbledygook or kerfuffle. The word's origin is apparently an alteration of *ragman roll*, originally denoting a legal document recording a list of offences.

Linseed oil evaporates very rapidly, causing an exothermic reaction which accelerates as the temperature of the rags increases. When the accumulated heat exceeds the rate of heat dissipation, the temperature increases and may eventually become hot enough to cause the rags to spontaneously combust.

Factitious Disorder Imposed on Another (FDIA) previously called *Munchausen Syndrome by Proxy* (MDP) is a psychological disorder when someone falsely claims that another person has physical or psychological signs or symptoms of illness, or causes injury or disease in another person with the intention of deceiving, or to gain attention. MDP is a rare condition, and its exact cause is unknown. However, researchers theorize that both psychological and biological factors are involved, with abuse during childhood being a common factor amongst those diagnosed with MDP.

Driving Whilst Over the *Prescribed Limit*. If the proportion of alcohol in a person's breath, blood or urine exceeds the prescribed limit and they drive a motor vehicle on a road or other public place they are guilty of an offence. If found guilty of this offence it is likely that they will be disqualified from driving, and could face imprisonment.

RTC is an acronym for a *road traffic collision*, which replaced the previously used term of RTA (road traffic accident). This was changed as the term 'accident' suggest no one is to blame. There is an addition police term for any incident for which there is a fatality *(Killed)*, or someone has sustained life-changing injuries *(Seriously Injured)*.

The discovery of *Warfarin* originated in the 1920s on the prairies of Canada and North America when it was discovered that previously healthy cattle began dying from internal bleeding with no obvious cause. It was only when a Wisconsin farmer drove a dead cow 200 miles to an agricultural experimental station where he presented a biochemist with a milk can of unclotted blood that they were able to identify the active compound that caused the haemorrhagic disease. The work was funded by the Wisconsin Alumni Research Foundation (WARF), hence the name Warfarin. It was following this, that, despite its slow acting properties it was reconsidered as a poison. However, in 1948 is was marketed as a rodenticide, a poison to kill rodents, rat poison. In 1951, a US Army inductee attempted suicide with multiple doses of Warfarin in rodenticide, but fully recovered after being treated with vitamin K in hospital. Studies then began on the use of Warfarin as a therapeutic anticoagulant.

Under the *Police and Criminal Evidence Act 1984 (PACE),* a person under arrest is only allowed to be detained for a nominal period of up to 24 hours, after which an officer of Superintendent rank or higher has to authorise any extension.

Constructive possession is a legal term to describe a situation in which an individual has actual control over property without it actually being in their physical possession. In law, a person with constructive possession stands to be in the same legal position as a person with actual possession.

CPSIA information can be obtained
at www.ICGtesting.com
Printed in the USA
BVHW032210190520
579993BV00002B/36